Shesl

Two Bullets

To Joanna

I hope you like it!!

XOXO

Shannon
Smith

two bullets

Two Bullets
Second Edition
September 2016
All right reserved

Cover Design: Sheshanah Smith

To:

Jay and Karen Smith
Thank you for allowing me the freedom to do what I do

4

two bullets

Two Bullets

"I writhe in pain unable to locate its origin in my body,
I cry only to feel no relief in my soul
Bitter at the thought, I realize the ailment of unforgiveness
Betrayal is a disease to my bones,
Relentless, lingering and unchecked it will be my demise."
--Anonymous

two bullets

Prologue

I heard someone say once that the worst pain one will experience goes beyond physical agony. Even further, it plunges deeper than any emotional turmoil. People try to sugar coat it, tie it up in a nice little bow and use a hundred different words to explain the feeling, but the outcome is always the same; betrayal hurts. It causes you to rethink everything, it makes you wonder what's so awful about you to make someone mistreat you so badly.

There is even a grieving process. Denial, anger, bargaining, depression and acceptance, although I think acceptance looks different for every individual.

I guess for me I'm still working on getting through the first four steps-all at once like a tornado of fire. Caught in the eye of the storm like a rag doll, I'm helplessly whipped around as blurred images spin around me, memories engulfed in white hot flames.

Who am I? What have I become? How did I end up here? I know at one time I was confident, and maybe just a bit naive about the world, hungry for love, and ready for any adventure that I could find. I used to be brave. I used to laugh. I used to be happy.

But everything changed the day I was shot. My understanding of friendship. My reputation. My confidence. My sense of self worth.

Everything.

I was accused of being a dirty cop. Of being involved in a drug deal that had gone bad. Word got around quickly about where I had been found shot; a

8

neighborhood where drug deals and prostitution were the normal. All the people that I thought were my friends assumed the worst and turned their backs on me. Everyone seemed to be of the opinion that I was a troubled cop with secret vices, even though I told the detectives who came to talk to me in my hospital room the truth; my own partner had shot me after I found him in the middle of buying drugs.

There should have been an investigation into Danson. The department should have had my back. Danson should have been arrested. But for one reason or another, the truth just wasn't pursued and I was left out in the cold.

Even though there was no proof that I had done anything wrong other than be in the wrong place at the wrong time, my fellow officers still weren't convinced of my innocence and gave me the cold shoulder. I was abandoned by those closest to me, and Danson got away scot-free. My heart and resolve broken into pieces, I made the difficult decision to turn in my badge and gun. I went through all the proper procedures and filed the paperwork, and I felt something inside me die. All I knew was being a cop. And for years I had depended on the bond that comes so naturally when facing death alongside fellow officers on a daily bases. But in the end, none of that mattered.

I'd never felt so broken and alone as I did in the days that followed. Were it not for the reassuring support of my parents there at my side, I know I could have easily succumbed to the desire to give up and pull my own cord. They would take me for walks, pushing my wheelchair down the sidewalks outside in the courtyard. We'd play card games, read books, talk, and watch old movies on my dad's laptop. Their love and attentiveness was a balm to my butchered soul.

A few things happened in the weeks that I spent recovering in the hospital that made me think I was still in danger, but the most vital and chilling instance was when I awoke one morning to see the very distraught and concerned faces of my parents. Mom stood next to my bed and handed me a crisp white piece of paper. My world spun as I read the lines of scrawled handwriting;

"Next time, you won't be so lucky. See you at your funeral, kid."

Someone wanted me dead. Again, I was reminded just how alone I was.

The next twenty-four hours became a blur of activity. My mom made some calls, my suitcase was packed, and then under the cover of darkness, I was slipped out of the back door of the hospital and driven to the airport.

I went along with everything without much arguing. I was so numb, so lost in my own head, that I didn't even have the wherewithal to cry. I just hugged mom and dad at the gate and boarded the small plane bound for Washington State and took my seat. In gray sweats and a hoodie that hid my face, I watched the Cincinnati skyline disappear into the black abyss of night.

Something had taken me from a passionate, driven, female cop with a bright future to this sullen, broken and deathly pale image in the window. Something had pulled the rug out from under me and stolen the very air from my lungs.

Betrayal.

Betrayal, and two bullets.

Chapter One

Wednesday

It was five-thirty in the blessed AM. The sun was slowly beginning to make its appearance over the top of Harkin Mountain, one of the tallest peaks cutting through northern Washington. Dark rain clouds were rolling across the dawn sky, bringing trails of rain from the horizon out into the country side in gentle, constant sheets. Thick gray mist clung to the tree tops and folded its way through the low valleys, floating quietly like a ghost. The rainy season had arrived, and it made quite the dramatic entrance.

Safely tucked away in a cozy bed somewhere in the Chelan mountains, only a messy mane of blonde curls and two green eyes were visible from under the folds of a soft, puffy comforter. Elizabeth Locksley lay staring up at the chain hanging from the ceiling fan above her, the thing wobbling lazily as the blades stirred up the air in the vaulted ceiling. Though tired, those green eyes continued staring upward, sleep having not come easy in the previous hours and the spinning fan had been about as helpful as counting sheep.

The room she had been sleeping in for the past few days was at the back of the two bedroom ranch house, the ceiling above her so high she couldn't have touched the chain of the fan even if she stood up on the bed. All of the rooms in the house were like this one she occupied; large and open under high ceilings. Cream colored walls flowed from one room to the other, decorated with surprisingly good taste for being the home of a bachelor. The large windows opened up to the picturesque forest hills surrounding the property, budding trees and green underbrush announcing the arrival of spring and new life.

The somewhat newly constructed house sat at the end of narrow valley, tucked up against the ascending slope of a hill that stretched out on either side in a low ridge and made a natural barricade for the country home. Outside of the valley, more coulees, gorges, and the rising and falling of majestic mountains stretched out in all directions for miles, split and scarred by rushing rivers and man made switchback roads that became treacherous in the winter time. The location of the home gave the illusion of isolation from the outside world, but was really only about a fifteen minute drive down the mountain into town.

It was a safe place for Lock to recover, and for now, it was home.

It had been four days since her flight from Ohio had touched down on the small tarmac just outside of Barrier Ridge. The entire flight, Lock had been nervous about her impending reunion with her uncle, Sly Malone, but the moment she deboarded the plane and stepped foot on to the runway, all her worry melted away at the sight of his familiar smile. She had practically fallen into the young man's arms when she had reached him, drawing strength from his body into her mentally exhausted one as she tightly held on.

So far, her stay at the single pastor's bachelor pad had consisted of quiet mornings with hot cups of coffee out on the deck, games of scrabble at night, and minimal conversation the rest of the time. The past year or so had seen their once iron-clad bond begin to rust and break apart. But now, Lock was in need of sanctuary. And Sly, having wanted to reconnect with his beloved niece and fix their damaged relationship, had opened his arms and home to her and welcomed her in.

She needed space, time to heal, and protection. Sly was able to provide that.

Sly was twelve years Lock's senior, and had always been more of an older brother to her rather than an uncle. They had grown up together, Sly having lived with Lock's family from the time she was six. He had been right there for all of the major milestones in Lock's life, and had always been her confidant and best friend. They shared the family green eyes and dark blonde hair, though Lock's had changed shades over the years. They both had been high school athletes, and had coached summer softball together for a couple of years. And they both had shared a faith in God. Only recently, Lock seemed to have lost hers.

Around seven o'clock, the door of Lock's room suddenly burst open and in came Sly like he owned the place. Thirty-six years old and not even close to looking like a preacher, he wore baggy sweat pants and a green zip-up hoodie, the baseball cap on his head was flipped to the back.

"Come on, Lizzy," he called, walking up to the bed, "time to get up."

She tugged the edge of the comforter the rest of the way over her head, groaning as she hid her face and sank deeper into the mattress. Sly reached down and ripped the blanket away in dramatic fashion, leaving Lock protesting and instantly shivering as her heat was taken away.

"It's a beautiful day outside, and we are going to enjoy it."

"It's raining," Lock countered as she draped her good arm over her face.

"You love rain!"

"I love watching the rain, Sly. Not being out in it."

"Oh, please. You were the one who used to drag me out in the middle of thunderstorms to go running, remember? It's your thing." He bent over her and slipped his hands under her back and hoisted her up, bringing her to sit on the edge of the bed. Lock couldn't help but gasp in pain as her body protested, her hand quickly cradling her right side.

"The doctor said you need to get up and moving if you want to regain all your physical strength." Sly reminded her.

"But it hurts," she said, still cringing.

"Oh, it doesn't hurt that bad. Just bite the bullet and get up."

Sly knew she needed a change of scenery. She'd been hiding in the house since arriving, uninterested in going outside, much less changing her clothes, and he knew a rainy day was just what she needed. They had always been her favorite.

While Lock rubbed her sleepy eyes and clutched the warm comforter close to her body like a two year old, Sly slipped a pair of tennis-shoes on her feet and a sweatshirt over her head. Then he stood and said, "Alright, let's go, Dracula; a whole new world awaits outside!"

Begrudgingly, Lock rose and followed him through the house to the front porch. Once outside, she grimaced at the distorted daylight and haughtily flipped up the hood of her sweatshirt, looking like someone with a bad hangover. She purposely ignored the smell of fresh air and patter of rain that at one time had brought her happiness. She didn't feel like enjoying herself.

"It's so cold!" She complained with a pout.

Sly sighed, beginning to feel a little annoyed. "Quit your whining, sour puss."

He turned away then and lumbered on down the porch

without her, his tennis shoes squishing in the wet grass as he headed across to the driveway. Judy, his gray Timberwolf trotted at his side, trained to stick with him until dismissed.

Lock watched after the pair for a minute, realizing that the wolf was a better sport than she was about this whole morning walk in the rain thing. With remorse for being such a punk, she gave in with a sigh and started moving down the porch steps.

Sly looked back from the road and saw her limping down the steps and he slowed, his irritation softening at the sight. She wasn't the same girl she'd been a few years ago. She'd changed, and not just because of the shooting. Sly knew depression and four walls make for a toxic cocktail, and he knew eventually she'd thank him for pulling her out of her funk. It would just take one step at a time.

When Lock finally got to where he stood in the road, Sly offered her his arm for support and she took it, linking it with her own. They started moving again, Sly taking it nice and slow, looking out around them as he took a deep breath. "Do you smell that, Lock?"

He wanted her to see it all of this; the colorful world around them thriving in the rain, to hear the birds calling in flight over head, to feel that charge of energy that was in the wild around them. The beauty of the countryside was doing its very best to get her attention and show off. She just had to give it a chance.

"Mm." Lock replied absently.

After a few more steps in silence, Sly tried again to engage her. "So I talked to your mom this morning."

Lock's mom was Sly's older sister, and the oldest of four kids. Sly was the only boy, and the youngest. He wasn't close with most of his family, but he was close with his sister.

"Oh? How is she?"

He told her that her parents hadn't wanted to return to their home right away, just in case whoever had left the threatening note got the notion to go after them when it was discovered Lock had skipped town. They'd headed south to New Mexico to visit the Malone side of the family. Lock's dad was spending most of his time fishing with grandpa and the Malone cousins, while her mom Kerri was catching up with her mother and sisters over numerous games of Scrabble.

"That's good," Lock replied with a sigh. "I'm glad they're safe and having fun."

She squeezed Sly's arm tighter as she realized just how much she missed her parents.

"Did the rest of the family ask about me?" She asked, but Sly just bit his lip and slowly shook his head. He lifted a hand and turned his baseball cap around, placing the bill in front. Lock hadn't really thought her extended family would ask about her, but it still stung knowing they hadn't.

Sly nudged her with his elbow, "Don't worry about it; they didn't ask about me either."

For the first time since arriving, Sly saw a genuine smile light up her eyes and wrinkle her cheeks. "Hey," she said, "we have something in common again!"

Sly laughed in agreement.

Years ago, he'd been the first one in the family to start going to church. When he started bringing home talk of Jesus and the Bible, his mama and pops wanted nothing to do with it. When he refused to stop going or stop sharing with them his new beliefs, his parents had quickly kicked him out of the house. That was when he had moved in with his sister's young family.

To most of the Malone family, religion was a cult and

only for the crazy and mentally disturbed. Lock's mom on the other hand had been open to Sly's invites to his new church. Later when she herself became a born-again Christian, she too was excommunicated from the rest of the family. Although eventually Kerri had been able to get back into her parent's good graces, Sly was still the "black sheep," especially now that he was a full blown pastor with his own church.

Unlike her mom and uncle, Lock had grown up knowing nothing else but church and faith. Up through her teen years, she had loved Jesus, loved talking about Him, and wanted to live a life pleasing to Him. She'd always found it totally weird and ironic that in the Malone family, to be a Christian meant you weren't to be trusted and were labeled "troubled."

Things began to change in Lock when she moved out at nineteen and started a new chapter in her life. She began doubting what she had been raised in, and started questioning if having a little fun was really such a bad thing. Her shift in convictions and morals had caused her to start smoking and drinking and hanging out with people who wanted nothing to do with God or Christianity.

This had worried Sly, seeing his little niece slipping into that world, especially after everything he had gone through to bring faith in Jesus to his family. She'd stomped all over it, and once in an anger-filled moment, he had told her this over the phone.

That had been the last time they had talked, nearly five months ago.

Arm still draped through Sly's, Lock's smile faded as she remembered why her and Sly's relationship had become strained. She'd hurt him, and the guilt made her stomach queasy. All at once then the weight of her past, along with the pain of her partner's betrayal, came down on her in full force like a heavy blanket, smothering her back down into depression.

Sly saw the shadow cross over her face. He instantly turned around mid-stride and said quickly, "No, no, no. What just happened? Where'd you go?"

They came to a stop in the road. Lock shrugged. "What do you mean?"

"I mean, I almost had you laughing a second ago. What happened?"

Lock refused to look him in the face. She shrugged. "I have good days, and I have bad days. Comes with the territory."

"Bad days, nothing; you got lost in your head thinking about something. What was it?"

"Sly, don't..." a rogue tear escaped and dribbled down her cheek and she quickly wiped it away.

Sly was walking a thin line emotionally between impatience and desperation. He wanted Lock to talk to him. He needed to know what was going through her head. He needed it for his own understanding, but he also knew her well enough to know she needed to talk things out. She'd been abandoned and betrayed by her partner and left for dead, but she didn't want to talk about it. If he had to listen to her cry through the night one more time he was going to drive to Ohio himself and find Danson.

Aware of her fragile state, Sly tried to figure out what he should do. He felt something tell him he needed to back off for now, so he didn't pressure her with any more questions today. Instead, he dropped his chin towards his chest and nodded, letting out a sigh.

"Okay," he whispered as he stepped up to her and

wrapped his arms around her and quickly kissing her forehead. She laid her head on his shoulder and returned the embrace, squeezing her eyes closed as more tears tried to push their way out.

"I'm okay, Sly. I promise," she lied into his sweatshirt.

Rain fell gently down onto them as they stood there in the middle of the road, neither even bothered by the dampness seeping through their clothes. Then Sly's cell phone rang from his pocket, breaking the moment and they pulled apart. Lock wiped at her face and turned her attention onto Judy who had been sitting nearby waiting patiently while Sly answered his phone.

"Hey, Cass."

He listened, nodded, then his lips bunched up together. "Oh man. Yeah, I can be there. Wait for me to get there before you talk to the parents. Ok, see ya then."

"Work?" Lock asked, crouched low, hand rubbing Judy's head. Sly nodded, putting the phone back in his pocket.

"There was a fatal crash up on the ridge. I need to get to the hospital to be with the families."

Lock nodded and took the help he offered to stand back up, then they turned and headed back to the house.

"Can I come with?" Lock asked honestly.

Surprised, Sly glanced over at her. "You want to come?"

She nodded.

"You'll just be sitting around waiting for me. Could take awhile."

"I know. I just want out of the house."

"Alright," he agreed, taking this as a good sign. Hurrying on up the stairs to the house he said back to her, "but you've only got ten minutes to get ready."

two bullets

"Deal."

They split up and Lock went to her room for dry clothes, then slipped into the bathroom to get changed. Judy lay on the tiled floor near the closed door, head on her paws, eyes following every move that Lock made as she tried to hurry and get ready. First she washed her face with a damp towel, then quickly applied a layer of make-up over her pale skin. Her wet curls fell in waves around her face, and she worked in some hair product before leaving the curls to air dry on their own.

Then she moved on to getting dressed, knowing this would take her the most amount of time. She pulled on a pair of clean jeans, then slipped into a tank top with a plaid button-up shirt on top. She didn't bother to button the shirt closed, leaving it to hang open over the gray undershirt. The bulk of the bandage covering the right side of her stomach was visible through the thin fabric. The bandage on her collarbone was even more obvious, but there wasn't much she could do about it.

Suddenly her head began to swim and her breathing became haggard. She bent over the sink, pausing to let the nausea pass, concentrating on her breathing so as to not pass out. Irritated at her body's lack of strength for such simple tasks, she groaned angrily and slapped the counter a couple of times before being able to move on. She washed down two natural pain relievers with a cup of water, tossing the paper cup into the trash.

She paused on her way out of the bathroom to give herself a lookover in the mirror. From her pale skin to her dull eyes, she looked exhausted and ill. The heavy bags under her eyes revealed her lack of sleep and the nightmares that were the cause.

She sighed. Oh well. She'd been shot a little less than a month ago; she had a right to look like death warmed over. She collected her phone from its charger on the kitchen counter, slipped back on her tennis-shoes and coat, then hurried back outside.

Thunder rumbled loudly overhead as she closed up the house behind her. The temperature had dropped significantly since she'd gone inside, and the sky had grown darker and looked more menacing.

With a steadying hand on the railing, she quickly made her way from the porch and out into the steady fall of rain. Sly was in the process of backing the red pickup out of the garage, the engine rumbling loudly as it crawled backwards out into the wet weather. Lock shuffled around the front to the passenger door and let herself in, feeling ridiculously small in size next to such a beast of a machine. She was an ant trying to climb up onto a dog's collar.

"You need to buy me a step stool for this thing," she panted when she was finally up and in her seat.

Sly grinned, hand moving to rest on the gear shift in the steering column. "It's a good excuse for me to help a lady in when I find one."

Lock held her arms open at him, "Oh, but you leave me, your injured and pathetic niece to make the hike on her own?!"

"Yeah, well..." Sly cleared his throat, then changed the subject by exclaiming happily, "Ladies and gentlemen, this is your captain speaking; please return your trays to the upright position and fasten your seat-belts..."

Lock was laughing at him as they began to pull back out of the driveway, reaching over for her seat-belt.

Chapter Two

It was only about a mile down the descending driveway out onto a narrow, gravel road. They followed the rough road around the curves of the mountains like a bad roller-coaster; up and down, over and around and down. Finally coming to a T in the road, they caught the four-lane highway and headed east.

Hidden deep in the folds of the Crimson and Chelan mountain ranges, the town of Barrier Ridge sat nestled in a natural round valley, unpretentious and quiet with nothing to prove. From above, the curve of the mountain barrier looked like something like a bowl's rim, the south end stretched out in a oval with the blue/green water of Gibson Lake.

Barrier Ridge was hidden and far away from the pressure and tension of Seattle, some three hours away to the west. Five hundred and three people called this place home, and did so knowing that there was no other place like it for miles. Small town morals and ideals flourished here on the banks of Gibson Lake, and everyone, save for the contrary few, worked hard to keep their sweet town that way. While Lock had grown up in small towns most of her life, her adult years had found her living in cities of no less than a million people. Over the last few years, she had grown accustomed to the metropolitan world, with its chain coffee shops and rush hour traffic.

But here in Barrier Ridge, everything moved at a much slower pace, and with much more emphasis on family and tradition. Monday through Friday was meant for hard work, while the weekends were used for hiking, hunting, skiing, swimming in the lake and moments of complete boredom and bliss. Everyone knew everyone, and kids were allowed to play outside without fear of abduction. Melted snow rose the waters of the lake in the spring, bringing the water's edge up to its highest point, and made for the best fishing in three counties. There was one stop light in the center of town, two if you counted the broken one that hung in front of the Department of Transportation building.

To Lock, visiting her uncle's town felt like coming home, even though she had only ever seen it by pictures. She gazed dreamily out the window as they passed by small homes with smoke curling out of chimneys, dogs sleeping on porches, and green shrubbery everywhere.

Through downtown, she noticed that the popular coffee shop chains that sit on every street corner in the city were replaced in Barrier Ridge by locally owned cafes and ice cream parlors patronized by the young and old. Main street was lined with brick and wood buildings with names like "Mary's Fine Clothing," and "Rick's Feed Store." Influence from German culture was evident in the Bavarian architecture, mixed with a '90's feeling that some would call outdated, but Lock thought it refreshing.

She found herself never wanting to leave this picturesque town with dated architecture and poor cellphone service.

As the main road through town began to curve and take them south, she caught sight of a church down a passing street. It was a plain white church with a tall steeple and functioning bells in the tower, sitting on a lot flourishing with tall cottonwood trees and beautiful flower beds. On a rainy day like today, the lonely building looked a little haunting, but on a warm summer day in delicate sunlight, Lock imagined it to be serendipitous and charming. Every girl would dream of wearing her white wedding dress and having her first kiss in such a place.

Sly gave a short lived honk and waved out the window at two elderly men sitting on a bench in front of the barber shop, and they smiled and waved back.

"Do you know them?" Lock asked.

"Oh yeah, they're always the first to church on Sunday morning. But the rest of the time you'll find them right there."

Sly had been after Lock to move to Barrier Ridge since long before she'd graduated from high school. But after choosing to move from Missouri to Ohio for college, and then joining the police department there, she had all but forgotten Sly's tempting offer. She couldn't help but wonder as they drove along what her life would look like if she had taken him up on his offer back then.

Just up ahead, at the farthest south end of town, appeared the Carlyle Medical Center. The newly constructed hospital sat overlooking the blueish-green glacier waters of Gibson Lake and the towering mountain beyond it. The structure of the modern building looked a little out of place in such a historically rich town with its modern finishes and walls of windows that reflected the world around it.

Sly found a parking space near the building's main entrance and pulled in. They hunkered down in their coats against the continuing storm and stuck close together as they took off for the ER entrance on the far left side of the building.

Lock followed Sly inside through automatic doors to a quiet guest desk, empty at the moment. Taking an immediate left, they walked down the long hallway with floor to ceiling windows facing the parking lot, chairs lining either side of the space. At the end of the hall, there was a small cove that housed four elevators, and a hallway that branched off to the right, down deep into the belly of the hospital. Sly turned to go down the hall, leading Lock directly to the main treatment area of the ER.

Once they stepped through the swinging doors, they were hit with the loud noise of commotion and busyness. Voices of all tones and pitches spoke at the same time all across the room. Machines beeped, beds and wheelchairs squeaked, and an unanswered phone continued to ring until someone came over the PA system with a page for a Dr. Hyde. Everyone was busy with the teens that had been brought in with the car accident.

For Lock, this was all a familiar sight. Before getting shot, hospitals had never bothered her. She had actually liked getting nominated to stay with a patient or family until they could give a statement, or were finally released. She'd known all of the nurses and doctors by name. ERs and waiting rooms had become like a second home.

But then she had spent three weeks laying in a crummy bed, eating crummy food with nothing to do, and her affection for the medical world had been quickly ruined.

The room before her wasn't massive by any means, but it was large enough to be adequate. Four small beds were lined up perpendicular along the wall to the right with monitors and other medical equipment at each station. There were a half dozen nurses and doctors rushing in and out of the aisles between the beds, then hurrying away across the room. A number of doors and hallways led to other areas of the hospital, creating a circle around the main trauma area.

There was a reception desk just inside the swinging doors to the left where medical staff seemed to freely come and go. Banners and posters hung on the walls behind the desk bearing smiling faces of doctors with perfect hair and teeth, inviting those who were interested to get involved in the medical field.

Standing in front of the reception desk was a group of three men. Two of them wore black coats with the word 'Sheriff' stitched in bold white lettering. The third man in the group wore a white lab coat and a stethoscope around his neck. They all stood in a small circle talking to each other, and when the doctor saw Sly over the heads of his friends, he waved him over.

Lock let Sly get a little ahead of her, caught up staring at the trauma room, overwhelmed by everything going on around her. As Sly approached his friends, the two men in the black jackets turned to look and dropped back in line with the doctor.

"Cassidy," Sly said, greeting the first man in line with a smile as they shook hands.

Once the captain of Seattle SWAT, Sheriff Cassidy still carried an in-charge air about him, his stocky build and wide shoulders adding an intimidation factor. But despite the man's physicality, he had a charming smile that over took his face and gave a much softer first impression.

"It's been a whole twelve hours, Cass," Sly said, "did you miss me that much?"

"Well it was either you or Hobson on call..."

"And let me guess; Hobson didn't answer?" Sly said with a playful grin.

"I'm still holding out."

Sly chuckled at the good-natured jab, then stepped back to motion to Lock, bringing her forward to the group. She tore her eyes away from the ER and turned her head just in time as Sly said, "This is my niece, Lock; Lock, this is everyone."

The sheriff's dark green eyes flashed as his face lit up with a fresh smile and reached for her hand. "It's a pleasure to finally meet you. I've heard a lot of good things."

Lock returned the smile as she gripped the man's hand, "Same here."

Cassidy then gestured to the younger man standing behind him, "This is my favorite deputy; Bastion Jones. But we just call him Bass."

"He says that about all of us," the man said with a wink as he stepped forward to shake Lock's hand. There was a faint hint of an accent when he spoke; a slow and purposeful drawl with an air of breaking out into laughter at any minute.

As she met his gaze, Lock suddenly realized how striking his blue eyes were. Dark and bright all at the same time, with soft flecks of light that seemed to shimmer when he smiled. They pulled her in like a cold pool of water on a hot day.

He was still smiling at her, and she was staring, their hands still touching. The moment lasted much longer than a normal introduction. The last place Lock had expected to see such a handsome face was in the middle of Barrier Ridge at eight in the morning at the ER.

"Where's Jimmie?" Cassidy asked, his voice bringing Lock back to reality. She quickly drew her hand back with a nervous smile as the middle aged doctor to her right answered, "I think he's still back helping Rachael."

"Oh, okay," Cassidy said, nodding. Then he gestured to the doctor and said, "Lock, this is Dr. Martin."

The gray haired doctor had close-cropped hair that gave him a sophisticated charm. His hand was warm and soft as he shook Lock's hand and said, "It's nice to finally put a name to the face, Elizabeth. I know your surgeon in Cincinnati well; it'll be my honor to look after you while you're here."

She smiled. "I appreciate that, thank you."

As the topic of conversation turned to the reason for Sly being called in, Lock tried to ignore Deputy Jones and his hypnotizing blue eyes. She guessed him to be quite a bit older than her. He was very tall, easily six foot three, with shaggy blonde hair and a freshly shaved jaw. He was undeniably handsome, and she felt embarrassed with her rain-soaked hair and chapped lips. Sly could have warned her that his friends were attractive.

Sheriff Cassidy and Dr. Martin went on to tell Sly that three of the four teens involved in the morning's accident were in critical condition. The fourth had been declared dead at the scene. They had held off speaking to the family of the fourth teenager, wanting Sly to be there when they delivered the tragic news.

Lock didn't envy Sly or the others for what lay ahead of them; giving a worried family the worst news of their life never got any easier. It was one of the few things she wouldn't miss about being a cop.

"Bass," Cassidy said now to his deputy, "go on and check on Jimmie. He's been back there awhile, make sure he didn't get himself into trouble with Collin."

Deputy Jones nodded and started to step away, tipping his hat specifically to Lock as he left. She tried not to blush, instead turning to face Sly.

"I'll try not to be long," Sly assured her. "If you need anything I'll just be in that room over there." He pointed to a window in the wall on the other side of the ER.

"It's okay. I'll be fine," She said, offering him a smile.

two bullets

"Bass will be around too," Sheriff Cassidy said, and she nodded gratefully to him.

The words "have fun" almost left her mouth as the men left, but she bit them back. Sometimes inappropriate humor helped alleviate a stressful situation; but now didn't feel like the best time for satire with what awaited them.

The three men disappeared through a door that led to a hallway where the waiting room was located. Lock found a seat in a row of chairs behind her up against the wall in front of the reception desk. She slowly lowered herself down and settled in, having a front row seat to everything going on in the ER. Nurses in pale blue scrubs hurried frantically across the floor, practically running at certain times as someone yelled out an order. It seemed that most of the chaos was now contained in one particular room off the main ER to the left.

Lock watched the staff members go about their job around her and she couldn't help but feel a little bit jealous. All of these people had a purpose, knew exactly where they belonged in the world and what to do. At one time, back in Cincinnati, she too had been a part of the solution amidst the problem. But now, she was just another civilian left to wait on the sidelines. She tried not to feel sorry for herself, but her pride was still very much active.

She sighed, attempting to relax and get comfortable in her own little world, but soon her mind became fuzzy. One second she was watching a dark haired woman in floral scrubs hurrying for the elevator in the back corner, the next minute everything around her became a blur. The colors and sounds blurred together like cans of paint being poured out all at one time. All the voices around her seemed to be moving far away down a narrow tunnel, like someone had turned down the volume on a stereo. Instantly the small town ER was replaced with sights and smells taken from a memory she knew all too well. Her heart started beating wildly inside her chest as the panic attack began.

Like a time warp, she was back to that day when she had been one of those people lying on a gurney, her life in the hands of strangers in scrubs. She remembered seeing the blinding lights overhead rush past while stranger's voices blended together as they tried to assure her that she was still alive and safe. She could smell it, see it clearly like she was back at Cincinnati General, hear the snip of scissors as her clothes were cut off and discarded into a bloody heap on the floor. It had been so loud as countless people gathered around her, poking and prodding, asking questions, telling her to stay with them. She'd been unable to remember her name, feeling something pulling her away from the voices, smothering her like a blanket of black tar.

Someone had told her later that at one point she had flown out of control, not realizing the people around her were trying to save her life, and had taken out two orderlies before getting pinned down and given a sedative.

Somewhere across the Barrier Ridge ER, a tray was accidentally dropped to the floor, sending the contents clattering to the floor. Lock jumped in her seat, quickly bringing her hands up to her face in fists as she squeezed her eyes shut, fighting off the lapse in reality.

"Oh God," she pleaded desperately, *"help me. Please help me."*

Chapter Three

Deputy Bass Jones walked down the hallway far from the crowded ER towards Exam Room One. He slipped past familiar faces and smiled, but his mind was somewhere else. He couldn't shake the feeling that his world had just been turned on its head by a woman in a blue jacket. He knew about Lock only by reputation; Sly was always talking about his niece, letting everyone know how proud he was of her. Bass had seen a couple pictures here and there of the woman, but they didn't do the real thing justice.

He purposefully shook his head to clear his mind. He was being ridiculous of course; he didn't even know the woman. She was beautiful, there was no denying that. But she was his best friend's niece, and she was going through a pretty rough time. He couldn't be so selfish as to think that he had any shot with Elizabeth Locksley from Cincinnati.

But man, Sly could have given him some sort of warning.

He came to the room he was looking for and gave the closed door a tap with his knuckles. The door opened inward and Nurse Rachael greeted him with tired eyes and a pensive look on her face. Standing behind her just inside the door was a tall, dark haired man wearing a uniform shirt identical to Bass's. Lieutenant Jimmie Reeves stood with his arms crossed, eyes narrowed, fixated on the opposite side of the room.

"Everything good?" Bass asked as he stepped in.

"I don't know," Jimmie said curtly, watching the other man gather his wife and daughter's coats. "Are we good,

Collin?"

"This is crap!" Collin spat, his jaw clenched tight, eyes glaring as he shoved a coat at the tentative, pale woman next to him. Bass knew Collin and Sadie from the numerous domestic calls he'd responded to at their home.

"Please, Collin," Sadie whispered, "you're embarrassing me." Her dirty blonde hair hung in ratty tangles over her shoulders. Her face, strained from years of abuse, made her look ten years older than her young twenty-seven years.

Collin, a forty-something lumber mill worker, scoffed sharply. "I'm embarrassing you?! How is this my fault?"

Sadie just shook her head, zipping up her coat before bending down to help her daughter with hers.

Bass stepped out of the way for Collin to pass, the large man stomping as he went, his face dark with anger. Sadie hurried to keep up, her daughter in her arms, quickly flashing an apologetic smile at the deputies before entering the hall.

"Making friends, I see," Bass said, grinning at Jimmie. The lieutenant, just a few years older then Bass, stood a head taller then six feet. He was the sheriff's right hand man and was being groomed for someday taking over as the sheriff. He kept his black hair buzzed short on the sides, and still carried the confidence of a former military man.

"It's just Collin being himself." Jimmie said as he and Bass stepped out of the room. "His insurance hasn't kicked in yet, so the x-rays on the little girl's arm aren't covered."

"Is her arm broken?"

"Probably. She fell off the arm of the couch."

"Or so Collin says."

Jimmie just nodded, scratching at the five-o'clock shadow climbing his sharp jaw.

two bullets

They took a turn down the hallway that led back to the ER, stepping out of the way of a janitor's cart.

"Cassidy in with the families?" Jimmie asked

"Yeah, Sly came in and Martin took them back."

"Guess I got off easy."

"Me too." Then Bass said, "Sly brought his niece with him."

Jimmie looked at him in surprise. "Oh yeah? She's here?"

"Yeah, she's waiting around for Sly in the ER."

"She nice?"

"She's quiet, but seems nice."

"Is she pretty?" Jimmie asked with a suspicious look at his single friend.

"Yep," was all Bass said.

They came to a stop in front of the doors that led into the ER and Jimmie turned to face Bass. "Well I'd love to meet her, but I need to head back to the station. Try to not scare her off, huh?"

Bass just smirked at his friend's coy smile. "I'll call you if we need you."

Jimmie nodded and turned, heading down to exit for the side parking lot.

Bass stayed where he was for a second, glancing through the window on the ER door, into the bustling room. He had a couple of options of what to do next. He could go to the break room and get a cup of coffee, or he could go find his friend Jack who headed up hospital security. He could also go outside and make a few work phone calls that he'd been putting off. But there was really only thing that he actually wanted to do.

He pushed open the doors and stepped into the ER.

✱   ✱   ✱   ✱

"Mind if I sit?"

Lock's eyes popped open at the voice, drawn out of the world her mind had convinced her was real, to see someone standing in front of her, blocking her view of the ER. She looked up to see a brown uniform shirt and black jacket, then let her eyes travel up to see the face of Deputy Jones. He was looking down at her with a gentle, curious look on his face, then quickly flashed her a smile when he saw that she recognized him.

She tried to cover up her emotional turmoil, feeling embarrassed to be found in such a state. She fidgeted in her seat.

"Sorry. What?"

"Mind if I sit down?" Bass motioned over to the empty chair next to her. She quickly straightened and nodded as she looked down at the chair.

"Oh! Of course, be my guest."

"Thank you." He pulled his hands out of his jacket pockets and turned, sighing as he lowered himself down into the chair. "My partner headed back to the station so I'm all yours."

Lock tried to smile, rubbing her palms together awkwardly. Bass leaned forward a little, eyes on the room in front of them. "Hospitals, huh?"

A nervous laugh, louder than she had intended, left her mouth. "Yeah."

"I reckon you've spent your share of time in them, aye?"

Lock cleared her throat, eyes down on her hands in

two bullets

her lap. "Uh, yeah, a little bit."

"You're a cop, right?" Bass asked, his elbows resting on his knees as he glanced back over his shoulder at her. Lock had to keep her eyes down for fear of turning into a puddle of mush. Just the way the man looked at her made her nervous. She nodded at his question.

"Once upon a time." Not that anyone would guess that from the way she was acting right now. Her nerves were still on fire from the flashback, and she couldn't seem to stop shivering.

The room around her had returned to normal, the small town hospital replacing the memories of Cincinnati General and the day she had almost died.

"I'm not a fan of them myself," Bass went on, pretending he didn't notice anything out of the ordinary. He held out his left hand to her so she could see. "I was in a work related accident a couple of years back and nearly lost my hand. Spent a lot of hours learning how to grip a pacer again."

Lock looked down at his rough hand, seeing the scar running down from his knuckles to his wrist. It wasn't much different from the healing scar on her collarbone. But her mind was stuck on the word "pacer."

"What's a pacer?" She asked.

"You know, one of those pencil's that you refill with lead?"

"Oh! Like a mechanical pencil?"

He nodded, taking his hand back.

"What happened?"

Bass sucked on his teeth, leaning his body towards her a little as he said in a much lower voice, "I thought I was being smooth and instead, took a harpoon straight through."

She gasped and pulled away as she winced. Bass

laughed and nodded, "It wasn't pretty. Took fifty-four stitches to close it up, and they told me that I might never get feeling back in my hand for it. The muscles and tendons took a major hit."

"Well I would guess so. A harpoon? How does one get stabbed by a harpoon as a sheriff's deputy?"

"Oh, I wasn't a deputy back then. I was a helmsmen on a fishing boat. This big storm came in and we were all running around trying to get everything battened down. One thing led to another and I came up with the brilliant idea to use the harpoon to secure a line that was coming undone. But when my buddy shot the hand-held thing, I didn't get my hand out of the way in time."

Lock recoiled, "Oh my gosh!"

"Yeah. There may have been some alcohol involved...Anyway, needless to say my days on the sea ended then."

"Cause you couldn't work anymore?"

"More like I realized I was a terrible fisherman." Bass said with a humorous wrinkling of his nose. Lock choked on a laugh, immediately feeling her tension begin to ease with this stranger talking to her. He was strong and sure of himself, but had no problem laughing at his own misfortune. She loved the way his accent faded in and out as he talked. It was obvious he had a great sense of humor. She soon realized her nerves had settled down and her hands were no longer shaking. She was still chuckling as she sat up a little straighter in her chair.

"You've got a great laugh, you know." Bass said quietly, and she realized he was being serious. She thanked him because she didn't know what else to say. The reddening of her face was doing most of the talking for her today. She looked away in hopes he wouldn't notice. A janitor was mopping the small floor space between two beds, clearing away the blood and trash in just a few easy swipes.

"How long have you lived in the U.S.?" Lock asked, moving the focus of conversation back to the deputy.

"About ten years. Barrier Ridge for half of that."

"Where were you before?"

"All over. My pops was a Navy Colonel and he moved us to Louisiana when I was eighteen."

Just then an employee of the hospital, who was passing by in front of them, commented saying, "There are no Colonels in the navy, moron."

Bass cleared his throat at the interuption from his friend, and shot the man's back a dirty look.

"Thanks Jack... I meant 'commander.'"

Turning his attention back to Lock, Bass continued as if nothing had happened, "Anyhow, my brother and I took to traveling, getting to know our father's homeland. I was living in Alaska when Cassidy found me."

"He found you?"

"I was living in a rented room on the beach, babying my hand and feeling sorry for myself, because I thought my good years were behind me. The only thing I ever did that got me out of the house in those day was to go down to the marina and watch the boats come in. So, I was out there one day when Cassidy and a friend of his came in after a week long hunting trip out in the Bitter-Root Forest across the way. Cassidy's never met a stranger and we ended up talking for awhile. He found out that I was in the market for a new job, and told me that when I got my hand healed up to give him a call."

Lock smiled. "I'm assuming you made the call..."

"Took another six months, but it's a good thing I did. The idea of becoming a deputy gave me something to work towards. I started going to my therapy, I started getting healthy again and-" he held out both arms in front of him as he leaned back into the chair, "-here I am."

Lock smiled over at him as he crossed his arms over his chest. "And just think; if you hadn't gotten harpooned, your life may have taken a different path."

"That's right. And I would have never met you," Bass grinned. "That's something to thank God for, I think."

Lock just shook her head, hiding a grin behind her hair falling freely around her face. "You need to stop doing that."

"Do what?"

"Making me feel special."

"Someone's got to do it. It's obvious you can use more of it."

"It's obvious huh?"

He gave a curt nod, eyes on the floor. Then he tilted his head back as he looked at her sideways through slitted eyes, "That and your uncle already spilled the beans on ya."

"Ah," Lock grunted and looked back at her hands, feeling rather exposed. Her personal woes apparently made for casual conversation between Sly and his friends.

"Do you want to talk about it?"

Lock gave a slow shake of her head, "Nope."

"Fair enough."

It was then a woman's sudden scream echoed across the ER.

$$\ast \quad \ast \quad \ast \quad \ast$$

Two men, one white and one black, had burst in

two bullets

through the Ambulance entrance, a trail of bloody footprints left in their wake. At first no one had seen them, but then the young nurse screamed and then everyone saw them.

"We need a doctor over here!" The man called, practically carrying the teenager.

The teen was slipping in and out of consciousness, unable to hold up his own head as blood seemed to be pouring out of every inch of him. Ezra Crane's right arm hung limply at his side, the blood gushing from his shoulder, dripping from the tips of his fingers. His bottom lip was split, his left eye swollen shut.

Medical personnel sprang into action, rushing from all directions across the room towards the Ambulance entrance and the two men.

"I need a bed, now!" A woman doctor yelled as she sprinted towards Ezra's side and helped support his weight. Two orderlies were already halfway to them with a rolling bed.

"What happened?" Dr. Avery asked, her voice verging on panic as she helped lay Ezra on the bed and began cutting off his shirt.

"He was attacked by a motorcycle gang over in the Gorge," the first man said, stepping out of the way as a second doctor wiggled through.

"Ezra, can you hear me?" Dr. Avery asked, but Ezra wasn't hearing her.

Bass pressed his way in through the mass of people, peering over heads down at the young man he knew only slightly. Blood was everywhere, getting on everything. Ezra groaned in pain while hands moved over his broken body. Bass moved on to where the good Samaritan stood and urged him to step back so they could talk. The man had blond hair, a little longer than Bass's, but his was pulled back into a pony-tail. His eyes were gray, almost appearing silver, with flecks of blue, and the wrinkle in his brow was more out of compassion than worry as he kept his eyes on Ezra.

"What did you see?" Bass asked.

"It happened at the campground up in the Gorge. He was walking to the bathrooms with his girlfriend."

"You saw it happen?"

Seeming a little irritated by the question, the man shook his head no.

"Wait a second," Bass said, lifting a hand, "I heard you say it was a group of bikers."

"That's true."

"So how do you know that if you didn't see it?"

Now openly impatient, the man took a deep breath and looked Bass right in the eye as he said in a low voice, "Deputy Jones, you should be more concerned about protecting the people of this hospital than arguing details with me."

Bass cocked his eyebrow, surprised at the man's frankness. "Protect them from what?"

"A storm is coming. I'd suggest locking this place down."

"You're going to have to give me more than that."

Despite the chaos going on behind him, Bass could hear the man say, "Hatred turns a man's soul black. Not even locked doors can keep him from finishing his mission."

The dull roar of talking suddenly rose in intensity and made it nearly impossible for anyone to speak or be heard, stealing everyone's attention.

"Get him in to trauma one!" the head doctor was shouting.

"Trauma one is already taken, Ma'am."

"Well UN-take it! We need to find the source of this

two bullets

bleeding!"

"Trauma two is open!" Someone else called.

The woman nodded. "Fine. Let's move!"

The bed carrying Ezra Crane was then pushed forward towards the room surrounded by a sea of doctors. When the chaos dissipated behind closed doors, Bass turned back around to pony-tail guy, only to find that the man was nowhere to be found.

"Okay, that's weird," Bass growled, spinning himself in a circle in search of a glimpse of the Good Samaritan.

But he was gone.

Chapter Four

When Bass had gone running towards the developing crisis on the other side of the emergency room, Lock had watched him go with a twinge of jealously. There was excitement brewing, but she wasn't needed. She considered hurrying to join him to find out what had happened to the young man being carried in, but she stayed in her seat, watching Bass leave her to do his job. Her job, once upon a time. Instead, she decided that it was a good time to slip outside and have a cigarette.

Her habit of smoking had only started as a social thing. She had no intention of ruining her health and shortening her life span, but having a way to relieve stress while sitting in a dark corner of a bar while shooting the breeze with her friends had become almost a necessity after long, heart wrenching shifts. And now, after her life had blown up in her face, she sought the comfort and the feeling of normalcy of the old days more than anything.

She stepped outside to find it still dark and cloudy with rain pouring over the eves. She walked down the sidewalk a ways and took out the pack from her coat that she'd been nursing for the last week. She pulled free one of the last remaining sticks and slipped it between her lips. Then she retrieved her lighter, and cupping her hand over the end of the cigarette to protect it from the wind, she flicked the cheap lighter and slowly edged the flame close. The rolled tobacco and paper caught fire and she took in a deep breath, immediately releasing her thumb from the button that kept the fire lit. As she slipped the lighter back into her coat pocket, she lifted her other hand and slipped her fingers around the cigarette, pulling it from her mouth. She gave a relaxing sigh as she breathed out the bitter stream of smoke. The white smoke drifted out from under the overhang out into the falling rain and held on as long as it could before dissipating into nothing.

Everything is a process when it comes to smoking. A ritual that many people require to enjoy the experience. Some have to light their cigarette with the same hand holding the lighter every time. Others pinch the cigarette between two fingers when they take it out of their mouth, while others merely hold it between the knuckles of two fingers. Some have to start every new pack with smoking the same cigarette from the same row every time.

For Lock, all that mattered to her was the smell. She could care less about the nicotine that would almost immediately be running through her system; she just wanted to smell the burning tobacco and relax. There was just something about the smell of cigarettes that helped calm her down and remind her that even if everything else around her changed, this smell wouldn't. A momentary safety blanket if you will.

Her eyes were closed and her head rested back against the rough exterior of the building behind her, thinking about the friendly deputy who had sat with her and his brilliant eyes. The sound of light footsteps approaching her on the sidewalk caused her to open her eyes. Flicking away the ash on the end of her cigarette with a practiced flick of her finger, she rolled her head over to the right to see who was there.

Approaching her from the direction ambulance bay was the man who had called for help as he'd carried in the young black man. The man with a blond pony-tail and leather airman's jacket nodded to her when their eyes met and came to a stop a few feet away, pulling his own pack of cigarettes out of an inside pocket.

"Need a light?" Lock asked, her fingers grabbing for the lighter sharing her pocket.

He reached once again inside his coat and drew out a silver Zippo lighter and smiled slightly as he shook his head. Lock just nodded and eased back into her claimed place against the wall, drawing up her foot to perch under her. She once again ashed her smoldering cigarette before lifting it and took a drag.

"How's your friend?" she asked as she breathed out a lungful of smoke.

The man placed his unlit cigarette in his mouth. While with one hand he returned the pack to its place in his coat, the other holding the lighter. He scrapped it against his thigh and in one smooth movement, the lid flipped open and lit; a trick Lock had never been able to learn.

She watched as he lit his cigarette, still waiting for his answer as heavy rain pounded the roof above them.

"He's in good hands here," the man finally said, "He'll make a full recovery."

"Oh, that's good," Lock affirmed, taking another draw.

"Your deputy friend is a serious man," he announced casually, as if commenting on the weather.

"I guess so. I wouldn't know; I just met him."

"He's a leader among men. He's going to need someone to keep him anchored though. Evil doesn't care about willpower; it'll come for everyone."

Lock was a little confused by the man's statement, words clogging in her throat as she searched for a reply. *Um, okay.* She thought, but smiled at her smoking partner.

Then the man with the pony-tail said something that

caused Lock to take notice. "Are you up for a challenge?"

She lifted her cigarette once again to smoke, unsure of what to reply. "What do you mean?"

"Things are about to take a turn. Are you ready?"

Lock couldn't help but stare at the man. His eyes were bright despite their grayish color, and they were boring into her as if this was the most important question Lock would ever answer.

"I...uh..." she shrugged deep into her coat and shook her head, completely perplexed at the man's strange question. But the soft, even warm, expression on his face drew her back in and the silence between them, heavy with expectation, caused Lock to answer before she even thought it through.

"I always love a challenge," she said before clearing her throat.

This answer seemed to satisfy the man who's ponytail made him look like he belonged in a world war two movie.

He nodded. "Yes, you do," he mused.

He took a long draw from the cigarette as he took a slow step forward, then as smoke bellowed from his full lips, he watched his hand as he flicked the cigarette away into a flowing stream of water running along the curb. Then he kept moving past Lock, slipping his hands into his pockets, all the while Lock just staring after him in interest. Boy, was he weird.

"Better get inside," the man said over his shoulder, then looked out towards the mountains and nodded, "It's not safe out here anymore."

"Okay," Lock said, but was still very confused as to what just happened. Somehow things had just gone from sharing a spot on the sidewalk with another smoker, to receiving a very vague and mysterious warning as if she had some important role to play.

two bullets

She was still lost in her head, wondering who that man was, when the sound of thunder came to her. Her eyes quickly shifted to straight ahead to the edge of the forest, then up over the tops of the pine trees to a distant mountain peak. Mist clung to the uppermost peak, shrouding the side of the mountain that was black and brown from trees and rock formations. Then she realized that the thunder wasn't fading. It continued to rumble, and seem to be growing louder. She could almost feel the vibrations in her chest.

Then the words of the man who had just been with her came to her like whispers. *Evil. Are you ready? It's not safe out here.*

Time to go inside. Lock dropped her cigarette to the concrete under her and started moving. It was curiosity that caused her to walk to the front of the hospital rather than return inside through the side entrance. As she came around the corner, movement off across the front parking lot caught her attention. On the road that ran past the front parking lot, a line of motorcycles and riders came oozing out from between a pass between two hills, as if the men were being born out of the inner mountain.

Something about the sight gave Lock's heartbeat a spike. She didn't know why, but there was something very wrong with this scene. But she shouldn't worry, right? Just 'cause a bunch of men riding motorcycles were coming up near the hospital didn't mean anything. It wasn't like they were wearing masks and wielding shotguns, coming for the souls of the dead.

And yet, something inside Lock spurred her on and she began to run.

I'm just hurrying to get out of the weather, she rationalized internally. *I'm not scared.*

And yet the closer she got to those automatic doors with the rumbling of motorcycles behind her, the more her speed increased. She paused only long enough for the doors to make a human size break as they opened and she slipped in. She glanced back and saw the lead rider of the group turn into the hospital parking lot.

From the hallway that ran into the building straight ahead from the entrance, a tall man of Native American descent in a black Polo shirt came towards her. She recognized him as the man that had made the snide comment to Bass earlier in the ER. His hand rested on his belt, a black holster holding a tazer was clipped around his thigh.

"Where's the fire, babe?" He asked, face expressionless.

Lock opened her mouth to answer, but was cut off by the echoing sound of some thirty Harley Davidson motors come pouring in to the parking lot, their loud engines rattling the windows.

"They with you?" the guard asked, stepping up towards the windows next to the doors and peered out curiously. A long black braid hung down his back, tied off with a blue feather.

"No," Lock wheezed, short of breath. She was regretting her sprint. She slipped her hands into the back pockets of her jeans, standing in front of the entrance, unsure what to do now. Her eyes went out to the bikes coming closer.

The guard reached his hand up to a clip on his shirt color and pressed a button, then spoke into the chord hanging from his ear, "They're here."

Lock stepped up to join him at the floor to ceiling window, following his gaze out to the parking lot. "Who are they?"

The man with a strong jaw and wide forehead gave her

a glance out of the corner of his eye before looking back out the window.

"Ma'am, I don't mean to frighten you, but there's a patient here who claims he was attacked by a biker gang. They promised they'd find him and kill him and anyone else who got in their way." He said all this with a stern, blank face, giving his speech as if reading it from the glass window.

Lock scoffed, "Well thank you for not wanting to scare me..." But she wasn't scared. A familiar tingle rose through her body.

The man of stone gave no indication of hearing her. She could hear the voice coming through his ear piece; "Lock it down. Don't let them inside."

Outside the window, the gang of motorcycle riders were in the process of rolling up under the awning of the main entrance, pulling in backwards to park in a neat, nearly perfect line all the way down the sidewalk. Lock couldn't help but notice and appreciate the beauty of the machines. Some were blue, some painted black with white wisps of smoke, others were orange. Custom paint jobs that probably hadn't come cheap.

Not a helmet was worn by any of the riders. Lock looked from man to man, seeing their scraggly beards and long hair. A few wore stud earrings in their ears, one had a small hoop hanging from his eyebrow. A rough bunch of men if she'd ever seen one. All of them wore leather or jean vests with multiple patches. They were all flying colors, a symbol that told their biker affiliation with one look. Theirs was a red pitchfork with blood dripping from the sharp points. In bold letters underneath was printed the name, "Demon Troop."

As the bikers began to dismount, the security guard sucked on his teeth, eying one of the men through the glass.

"Guess I should go lock those doors," he said dryly.
"You think?!"

✳   ✳   ✳   ✳

Lock had moved herself down and around the corner
near the elevator cove, peering back around at the front
entrance. She claimed to be waiting for Bass and the sheriff to
arrive, but she was really hiding. Not because she was scared,
but because she didn't like being seen by a bunch of bikers who
were mad about not being let inside the hospital.

Braid, the nickname she'd given the security guard, on
the other hand hadn't moved from his spot in front of the
locked doors. He had no problem standing there in front of the
angry crowd, feet planted and arms crossed. He glared through
the glass at a man in a leather vest who was pounding on the
door with his fist, his biker friends standing behind him yelling
and making crude gestures with their hands. But Braid was
unmoved.

The guy had nerves of steel.

The sound of footsteps came up quickly behind Lock
and she straightened, turning around to see Deputy Jones and
the sheriff.

"Hey," she said in a whisper, though there was no one
else around.

"How's it going out there?" Sheriff Cassidy asked
softly as he stepped past her to peer around the corner.

"Well, they're not happy about being locked out," Lock
replied.

"Well, that's what happens when you threaten to kill
someone," Cassidy said with a quick dip of his chin. Then he

started walking away. "Alright, let's go see what they have to say."

Bass fell in step next to him and Lock hurried to keep up with their brisk stride as they made their way down the hall towards Braid.

"Open the doors, Jack," Cassidy instructed with a wave of his hand.

"I'd rather not, Sheriff," Braid replied calmly, his steely gaze still set straight ahead on the crowd outside.

"Not the big ones; open the side door," Cassidy replied, motioning to the single panel door next to the automatic doorway.

Jack grumbled his disagreement, but dropped his hands from across his chest and stepped forward. "You're the boss."

"What are you going to tell them?" Bass asked.

"Just going to have a friendly chat," Cassidy said with a smirk. "Give them a chance to explain themselves."

Lock liked the way the he seemed unintimidated by the angry mob.

Jack pulled out a key card connected to a string on his belt as he walked up to the small door, sliding the card across a little pad that lit up with a green light. The sound of the lock releasing seemed to echo in the empty lobby. He stepped back out of the way and Cassidy replaced him, pushing open the door slowly, keeping his hands on the door as he only let the left half of his body step out unprotected. With his head bent out around the frame of the door, he called to the gathered men, "Gentlemen, I'm Sheriff Cassidy. I'm sorry, but we are not permitting anyone entry right now."

Lock stood next to Bass directly behind the sheriff. Though neither said as much, they were prepared to yank the sheriff back inside if the need arose.

Jack had taken out his cell phone and now, without any sense of tactfulness, held it up to the window, recording a video of all the bikers.

"Let us in, Sheriff!" A man with curly black hair and a beer belly turned to walk towards Cassidy, waving his hand at the doors. At his antagonistic approach, Bass and Lock hunched up and moved their hands up in preparation behind the sheriff. It was a bit dramatic, but one can never be too careful.

Cassidy considered the confrontational man carefully, biting his lip as he turned his head slightly to the side, "I can't do that. And your name is?"

"Heinous," the man declared with spit off to the side.

"Well Mr. Heinous, I'm gonna have to ask you and your men to disperse."

"Why?" Heinous demanded with a furrowed brow, then his anger betrayed him. "Did that little punk say something?"

"I'm not going to ask you again," Cassidy warned in a low, even tone.

"Well, we're not going anywhere," Heinous snapped.

Cassidy shrugged. "Well, okay then."

He stepped back inside, pulling the door shut with him. The lock engaged with a solid click.

Heinous had started for the closing door but had been too late, and now kicked it hard with his boot. He yanked on the handle and rattled the door, yelling angrily, slamming his fist into the glass.

The door held in place, and Lock prayed it would stay strong.

"Jimmie's back. He's on his way," Bass announced, having glanced at his phone.

Cassidy nodded, turning to look for Jack. "Hey," he

called, "you done over there?"

Jack nodded, tapping the screen of the phone and then pulled it down. "Got all their faces on video."

The hoard outside no longer hid their agenda and were now pressing up against the doors, shouting and pounding like zombies desperate to get in. Lock and the others stood back from the entrance in a tight circle, discussing what to do next.

Up the side hallway from the direction of the ER, a young man wearing a sheriff deputy shirt came walking with a black duffel bag. He gave the hoard outside a curious look as he moved to the wall and set down his bag.

"This looks promising. Jack, what did you do this time?"

Cassidy and Bass moved away to talk to him, but Lock was keeping her eyes on the doors, not ready to look away for fear something would happen if she did.

One of the bikers had stepped away towards the bikes, and she was trying to keep an eye on them through the crowd.

"So you're Sly's niece, huh?" The security guard named Jack said from beside her. "The one that got shot?"

Lock glanced up at him without moving her head. "That's me."

"Why are you here?"

Lock snorted. She turned her head to see Jack wasn't laughing. She cleared her throat and turned back to the doors and nodded. "Taking in the sights."

Just then she saw the biker who'd walked to the bikes return, the others around him moving out of the way like the parting of the Red Sea.

In his hands he carried a sawed off shotgun.

"Gun!" Lock said, immediately stepping back, then she yelled it again, "Gun, gun, gun!"

two bullets

Everyone spun around at her call just as the man lifted the muzzle of the weapon up to the door. Everyone dove for cover, flattening themselves against the nearest wall, while Lock still stood front and center, only a pane of glass between her and the man about to fire.

Jack saw her frozen, unable to move, and lunged for her, tackling her out of the way just as the first blast exploded into the glass. It didn't shatter, only causing the thick glass to spiderweb in a circular fashion from the blow. The concussion echoed in the high ceiling room.

"Everybody back!" Cassidy yelled. Jack helped Lock up from the floor and pushed her into Bass. The deputy threw his arm around her and they rushed after Cassidy towards the unmanned desk there in the shallow lobby, taking shelter behind it.

Cassidy and Bass both wore bullet proof vest, and threw themselves over Lock to protect her as multiple gunshots were fired into the doors, a few bullets breaking through and whizzing overhead.

Jack took a running leap and flew over the desk, clearing it and landed on his feet, using Bass and Cassidy to keep him from slamming into the wall. Lock winced as she was pressed harder into the wall, the smell of three different colognes mingling in the tight space.

Lieutenant Reeves had taken shelter in a room off the hallway, across from the desk and now called to Cassidy. The sheriff shifted his feet and turned as Jimmie shoved a gun across the slick floor. He sent two more from the duffel over and Cassidy passed them on to Bass and Jack.

"That glass isn't going to hold!" Jack said, taking the shotgun up into his hands. He was crouched up near the chair at the desk, stealing glances up over the counter. As if in response, more bullets broke through the weakened glass, punching holes in the sheet rock above those hiding.

"We got to move!" Bass Jones roared, still shielding Lock with his back as he crouched in front of her, rifle in his hand. Lock stayed tucked up against the wall, arms thrown over her head.

"Get down the hall," Jack called, popping up to fire over the counter. The members of the Demon Troop were moments away from busting all the way through. Chunks of the spider-webbed glass fell inside on the floor as two men jammed the butts of their guns into the weakened barricade.

Lock managed to get her feet underneath her and wrapped a trembling hand around Bass's bicep, the other grabbing at his shoulder. She quickly patted his back so he knew she was ready.

Jimmie and Jack both stood at once and began laying cover fire for the others as the others broke away and raced down the hallway into a cross section of more halls.

Lock rounded the corner, Bass and Cassidy diving in after her as gunfire rocked the hospital. Jack slapped a button as he cleared the doors and the powerful metal doors swung shut, locking in place. For a brief moment, the air was eerily quiet.

Lock was shaking as she slid down the wall and took a seat, fighting hard to keep from losing it. Her hands were over her face, elbows to knees, eyes squeezed shut. Adrenaline coursed through her veins like electricity, everything around her moving in slow motion. She couldn't hear anything clearly, it was like her ears were plugged.

Just breathe. Just breathe. It's gonna be okay. Pull yourself together!

Fear is a curious thing. It takes a hold of you like an

assailant trying to choke you. It decides what you're going to say. It tells you how the story ends and makes you very aware of just how weak you really are.

Lock didn't want to be afraid. That's not who she was. At least, it wasn't who she used to be. Up until a month ago, bullets and gunfire had never done anything to her. Four months of police training and three years on rough streets had taken care of that. But because she'd been shot, she had a new respect for murderous intentions and guns. Or more specifically, a new fear of them.

This was the first time since her incident that she had been faced with the very thing that had tried to take her life. And her nerves, her mind, and her emotions had taken on a foreign reaction, leaving her body paralyzed. Terrified. Completely unsure of herself.

Images of her ex partner Shane Danson holding a gun on her flashed through her mind. She clenched her jaw, her teeth grinding together. She wasn't ready to face what was coming through those doors down the hall. She wasn't ready to be brave.

But courage and bravery never wait until your ready.

Suddenly everything became very loud as gunfire exploded outside the crossroad of hallways. She didn't have the luxury of being afraid.

Someone was saying her name.

"Lock!"

She turned her head to the left to see Bass at the corner, his back up against the wall. He held out a handgun to her. His eyebrows were raised. "Are you with me?"

She nodded. "I'm with you." She took the gun, her mind rushing to remember what to do with it. Then her training kicked in and she yielded to its control.

It was then she realized the double doors had been shut and the shooting had been isolated to the other side of the doors. The bikers were now inside the hospital, trying to get to those hiding like rabid dogs.

Jimmie and Jack were no where to be seen, probably to secure other areas of the hospital. Cassidy was down the hall to her left, talking on a phone anchored to the wall in a red box. It was just Lock and Bass now.

"Are you okay?" Bass asked, bending his arm back to touch her arm. His concern was warranted, but Lock was ready now. She was still a cop, if not on paper then in her heart.

She quickly nodded, hands rushing to chamber a round. The metal on metal sound echoed, affirming that she was ready.

"I have to go. Stay here." He said. She nodded. He waited until she met his eyes, then he gave her a nod and pushed himself off the floor. He tore off down the hallway, pausing briefly to talk to the sheriff who was still on the phone.

It sounded like World War 3 on the other side of the closed doors. *Boom! Boom!*

Facing the corner in a crouch, her weapon held down in front of her, Lock took two deep breaths to prepare herself for what lay ahead. She needed to be what the others needed her to be.

Today she needed to be a cop again.

two bullets

Chapter Five

A lock down was initiated, automatically causing all of the quarantine and hallway doors to release and swing shut, sectioning off hallways and floors into isolated areas. All access into the main hospital from the front hallway was cut off, keeping the bikers contained out front.

Bass caught up with Jack Stone inside the now empty and quiet ER. Everyone had been moved deeper into the hospital only minutes ago. Lieutenant Jimmie Reeves stood guard at the closed ER doors, and would stay there until further notice. Ezra was upstairs in surgery, and it was the duty of Bass and the others to make sure the bikers didn't make it that far.

There were three different entrance points from the main hallway at the front of the hospital, all of which needed to be checked and secured. If the bikers broke through, there was very little keeping them from overtaking the entire hospital, and finding Ezra. Cassidy, Jack, Jimmie, and Bass would have to fight the battle on their own; three other hospital security guards were back with the hospital staff and patients and were instructed not to leave their posts.

After checking in with Jimmie, Bass and Jack took off together to get around to the west end of the hospital, checking the doors along the way to make sure no member of the Demon Troop had managed to slip past before the lock-down had taken effect.

"Beautiful day for a shootout." Bass said as he sprinted through the maze of halls.

"Any day is a good day for a shoot-out!" Jack replied

with a grin. He was also a reserve deputy, and loved when action came to their sleepy small town. He lived for days like this.

They pulled up as they took the corner, then continued running towards the front end of the hall and the final set of doors. They were now on the complete opposite side of the hospital from the ER and Jimmie. Cassidy and Lock were somewhere in the middle, holding down the fort.

First Bass, then Jack stepped up to peer out through the small window in the door and the length of hallway that ran the complete width of the building end to end. It appeared quiet and Bass saw no one from his small window. But Jack had a different angle, and he suddenly cursed. Bass moved to look.

Out in the hallway, a young woman was huddled with her small child behind a pillar near the windows. There was no way to know if there were any bikers around, but Jack didn't care. He swiped his card over a keypad next to the doors and said, "Cover me. I'm going to get them."

"Be smart," Bass whispered.

Jack nodded and pulled on the door. It clicked open. He slipped out through the crack with his gun pointed down the hall to his right, away from the mother and child just off his left shoulder. There was a curve in the long hallway, and he couldn't see very far. But the area was clear, though he could hear yelling and banging from up ahead.

He sidestepped out further into the open, angling back towards the pillar while he faced the opposite direction, walking backwards until he was even with the woman and child.

"Hey," he hissed as he crouched down. The woman gasped and pushed her child behind her at the sight of the strange man.

"I'm hospital security," he said, twisting away from her so she could see the words printed on his back. "You need to come with me right now."

The woman relaxed, tears streaming down her face and she nodded. The coast was still clear and with a look to Bass, Jack knew he was covered. He lowered his weapon and reached for the woman to pull her to him. The mom grabbed for her son and lifted him up into her arms, ready to run.

"Stay behind me," Jack growled as he rose. He kept his gun out in front of him as he held the woman closely behind him and shuffled sideways back up and over to the door that Bass was holding open.

Just as they were in the clear and about to go through the door, the mother suddenly gasped and spun around. "My purse!"

Jack firmly shook his head and shoved her back, "Forget it."

"But Isaac has asthma; his inhalers in my bag," the woman pleaded.

"Ma'am, this is the part in the movie where you do what I say. We can't risk going back out there."

The woman sobbed, clutching her baby's head to her chest, but Jack was unmoved. He knew the second he went back for the purse, bikers would round the corner and he'd be a sitting duck there in the open. This was a hospital for crying out loud; they'd find another inhaler

He crowded the woman and urged her back through the doors. She complied but she wasn't very happy about it, continuing to argue and demand that he go back after her purse.

Never get between a woman and her child's inhaler

When the woman was seated on the floor with her child

two bullets

in her lap, Jack turned back and reached out to tap Bass on the shoulder.

"You ready?"

"Hang on," Bass hissed back, "I hear something."

Three heartbeats passed, and there came a sound of jangling chains rattling in tandem with heavy footfall. Then from around the corner appeared two men in biker leathers wielding pistols and a shotgun.

Jack and Bass slipped back in behind the doors as quiet as mice. Bass moved and quickly grabbed the woman and child up off the floor and told them to run, following right behind them as he directed them down the hall and around the corner, leaving Jack at the doors.

The door hadn't completely closed and hung open, and as the bikers drew near they saw this and moved to investigate. They carefully pushed open the door, thinking they had found a way in to the otherwise locked down hospital and filed through the door one at a time. Jack had been hiding behind the door and when the last man was through, he pushed the door shut with his hand and it made an attention grabbing crash. The bikers spun around and Jack lunged forward, slamming the first man's hand out of the way and landed a closed fist to the man's jaw, and he fell to the ground. The second man went down a little harder, but Jack was no stranger to brawling and was much quicker and swift. A final round house kick sent the second biker flying and sprawled on the ground.

It was then that Bass came running back up the hallway. He slowed as he approached, looking down at the two unconscious men on the floor.

"I see things went well in my absence."

"Help me get 'em into that closet over there."

two bullets

Jack stepped around to get to the head of the first guy, while Bass hurried to get the man's feet. One at a time, they carried the men to the linen closet and tossed them in, securing the door behind them. Jack ran back to the doors and slipped out, sprinting for the pillar where the mother and child had taken shelter, and swiped up the brown leather purse from the floor. There was movement outside the window and he paused, hearing the muffled sound of engines at the same time he saw five men on motorcycles drive past.

"That can't be good," he said.

Clutching the purse, he ran back through the doors and slammed them shut, swiping his key on the pad and the lock engaged.

"A bunch of our friends just rode off around the corner of the building," he announced.

"Where are they going?"

"To get a pizza," Jack retorted. "Which actually isn't a bad idea. Think they're taking requests?"

"They're probably heading around back."

The two men started back down the hallway. Before taking off for the back, Jack found where Bass had stowed away the mother and child in an empty room and gave the mother her beloved purse. She cried tears of joy and thanked him, but Jack just grumbled something about staying quiet and then left the room. He nodded at Bass as he shut the door behind him and they took off running.

"So," Bass said, pulling up for a corner, "what do you think about Sly's niece?"

Arms pumping, Jack shot Bass a skeptical look, "Um, she's nice?"

"I know that, but what do you think of her as a person?"

two bullets

"Seriously?" Jack puffed.

"Yeah!"

Jack held out his arms in front of him, "Well, she's a girl, so..."

Bass frowned, still running. "You don't like her?"

"I don't think now is the best time to be discussing your new found infatuation!"

The sound of distant gun shots could be heard back behind them. Bass grabbed his radio. "Sheriff, you there?"

"Go, Bass!" Cassidy's voice yelled back.

"They're trying to get around back..."

"You got it covered? We're a little busy here!" Cassidy replied, followed by a popping sound.

"Call you in a minute." He had slowed down, now in a dark area used for bringing in deliveries for the kitchen. Jack was ahead of him at the narrow door, peering out the window. Bass came up behind him. "See anything?"

"I think I hear 'em," Jack said, nose pressed to the window.

The small window to the outside revealed a limited view down a walled off pathway that led out out into the back parking lot. They heard the motorcycle engines first and then saw the bikes and riders come into view. Jack and Bass ducked, then popped their heads back up slowly. Two of the bikes came back by from the other direction, then turned and went back.

"They're circling up on us."

"What do they think they are, a war party?" Jack asked, sounded disgusted.

"Looks like they took a play out of your ancestors playbook." Bass said, causing Jack to scoff. "This is seriously all because of one kid?"

two bullets

Bass shrugged, "They apparently don't like leaving witnesses."

"Seems a little excessive, don't cha think?"

"I've heard of these guys," Bass said, still peering carefully out the window. "Down in Reno last year they beat up a married couple just walking down the street. Killed them."

"Let me guess; one was white and one was black?"

Bass gave his friend a knowing look. "Sound familiar? They probably saw Ezra with Terri at the campground and decided they needed to be taught a lesson for "mixing races.""

Jack just grunted, his anger evident in the way his jaw shifted side to side. Bass turned his back to the door and lifted his radio to his mouth. "Jimbo, you copy?"

"Copy."

"They're circling the wagons at the back of the building. Can you get to the roof and slow 'em down?"

"Shoot out their tires?"

"That'll work."

"I'm on it."

Bass clipped the radio back to his belt and readjusted his grip on his pistol as he gave one last look out the window at the passing bikes.

"Cass and Lock need us. Let's go. Jimmie's got this." He smacked Jack's arm and motioned for them to go, and the pair took off running back down the hallway.

"So, you like Lock, huh?" Jack asked, running next to his friend.

Eyes sparkling, Bass grinned sideways at him.

＊　　＊　　＊　　＊

two bullets

The doors held on as long as they could, but a couple of shots from a shotgun destroyed the locks. Cassidy and Lock scrambled to get out of the way as bikers charged through the now useless security doors. Forced to separate as they ran for cover;Lock ran to the left and hid behind a section of wall jutting out, while Cassidy ran straight up the hall and into a break room.

The first line of defense into the hospital was broken. It was up to Lock and Cassidy to make sure this was as far as the group got.

Despite their numbers and artillery, the murderous gang weren't fast or skilled, but they apparently had no shortage of bullets. Lock could only manage to get off a few shots at a time. The shooters knew where she was, and paint chips and pieces of plaster flew through the air as bullets ravaged her hiding place.

Determination had replaced Lock's initial reaction of terror and shock. Now she was in her element, and there was no way she was going to let these bikers finish what they had started. Even if she was killed, she would do whatever she could to not let these guys get past her and find Ezra.

Her ears were ringing, her nose stung from gunpowder, and her body ached, but the adrenaline pumping through her was enough to keep her strong and in control. As long as she stayed moving.

A handful of bodies now lay out in the middle of the tight space, their deaths the result of being the first ones to enter. Cassidy continued to return fire from his spot down the hall to the left and behind Lock's position. She was hidden just out of sight from the entrance. With a quick glance, she noted that there were two men shooting her direction from up the hall, while the others were out of sight through the double doors. They were keeping Cassidy pinned down. The rest had fled, looking for a easier way in.

When a break came in the shooting, Lock took a knee and swung herself out into the open. She immediately had her shot lined up, and she fired at the man facing her from down the hall. His head snapped back and he collapsed to the floor. Dead.

Her gun clicked with her final bullet. She stood and returned to hiding.

"Lord, help us!" She prayed, pressing hard into the shallow corner. Bullets popped into the other side of the wall next to her ear. She heard the whine of multiple shots pass by her face. She was a sitting duck.

She looked over to her right, seeing through an archway an open door about ten feet away. She imagined herself running and sliding in through the door, but then what? She was out of bullets. And to run would take her out into the open and directly into the line of fire.

Over the blasting gunfire, Lock heard something clatter then roll across the tile floor. She managed a look out from her hiding spot just in time to see two grenades roll into the center of the crossing halls. She instantly yanked herself back from the corner and dove to the side in the fetal position. Hands over her head and ears, eyes squeezed shut just in time for the two concussion grenades to explode. The building shook with the blast, rocking and rolling as glass windows shattered and pictures fell off their hooks.

Those who hadn't collapsed and fallen from the shock of the concussion grenades were standing with their hands over their ears, mouths open, stunned as they tried to get their bearings.

There was no time to waste. Lock pushed herself up

off the floor, staggering to her feet, then ran straight towards the closest man she saw. Cassidy, joined now by Bass and Jack, appeared and quickly began taking advantage of the stunned men. It took only a matter of seconds for Lock and the others to have the situation under control.

With her knees digging into the back of the man under her, Lock took a moment to catch her breath, surveying the carnage around her. It was a beautiful sight for the good guys. At least half a dozen bikers were down on the floor with the hands behind their backs, surrounded by their fallen comrades. Dark pools of blood grew across the white tile. The walls were pitted with gaping bullet holes. The air was thick with sheet rock dust that seemed to just hover around them.

Lock was still alive. The good guys had won.

"Someone had to hear that," Lock heard Cassidy say.

"Lock," Bass called as he stepped towards the entrance, "you're with me."

She rose off the man she had been keeping on the floor, Jack coming to tie his hands with a black zip-tie. She needed a gun, and Jack was quick to give her his.

She hurried out towards what was left of the ravaged lobby, Bass a full stride ahead of her. When he came to the corner, he stepped out wide, pointing down the east section of hallway.

"On the ground now!" He shouted.

Lock came around the corner, her weapon up, prepared for whatever awaited her on the other side.

Before her stood a surprised number of bikers who had been on their way to check on their friends, having heard the blast. Bass and Lock had the upper hand, and the bikers knew it. One by one they dropped their weapons to the floor and got down on their knees.

Bass glanced over towards Lock. "Welcome to Barrier Ridge, Love."

two bullets

Chapter Six

After thriving on such an incredible adrenaline high for the past half hour, Lock's system began to crash. She was exhausted and could feel every single pin-prick of pain; between running, jumping and diving, her body screamed with fresh waves of pain. Her mind spun like a green rookie on their first day.

She was able to hold herself together long enough to be reunited with her uncle and make sure he was okay, but with each passing second she became more aware that she needed a moment alone to collect herself. There were people everywhere, a deafening jumble of a hundred voices talking at once, and her neck under the collar of her shirt was getting warmer and warmer by the second. She was no longer listening to Bass and Cassidy talking to Sly; she was searching for the nearest exit.

She managed to excuse herself and and made a quick beeline for the doors and fresh air. Outside she turned away from the now parking lot full of paramedics, doctors, reserve sheriff deputies and their vehicles. She dodged a newspaper reporter who had snuck inside the police tape and walked through the rain to the west end of the building. She slipped out of sight around the corner and stopped.

Finally alone and out of sight, she let out a deep, heavy groan of pain and aggravation, flattening herself against the smooth wall and closed her eyes.

Her body involuntarily shook as she slid to a seat down into the wet grass, back pressed against the building as the rain continued soaking through her hair and clothes. But she barely noticed it. She wanted to cry, though she didn't know why. She wanted to laugh, she wanted to scream, anything to release the pressure in her chest that felt like it was going to suffocate her. But her mouth stayed clamped shut, her arms hanging out over her knees pulled to her chest as she stared out through the rain. How quickly she had forgotten what being in shock felt like.

Lost in a haze, she barely noticed when someone found her hiding spot and walked around in front of her. The legs walking by and moving up to her left side could have belonged to anyone.

When the person sat down next to her in the wet grass, she saw a blur of black. Maybe Jimmie, maybe Jack. She was too lost in her own head to really care about turning to look.

Whoever the person was didn't say anything, which was fine with her. She wasn't even sure she would be able to talk if she tried. It felt like a rock sat in her throat. She continued to stare at the running water flowing past on the other side of the curb, watching as little bits of trees and leaves and grass spun and floated along.

Finally, after a good five minutes had passed, Lock's thin voice broke the silence. "It's funny. I've watched men jump off of buildings and helped clean up the mess. I've held dying children in my arms because their druggie parents were too high to remember to feed them." She scoffed and shook her head. Her fingers played with a thin blade of grass she plucked out of the ground next to her. "Guess I'm not that person anymore."

"Well, we had a hard day," came the casual response.

"It's been a hard month," she replied quietly, biting her lip.

She remembered something Danson used to tell her when she got emotionally invested while on the job; "This is why hiring women is the dumbest thing the brass ever decided to do. Women are nurturers- soft and compassionate. There is no place for a woman on the street. That being said, you did the training, you took the test, and you pledged the oath. You're a cop now, so quit being a girl and act like one."

Like a slap in the face, Lock was suddenly aware of just how overly emotional she was being. She cleared her throat, then quickly rubbed her face and smoothed back her hair in an attempt to appear normal, even managing a weak smile as she turned to look at the man sitting next to her. She was surprised to see the dark skinned security guard named Jack, his head resting back on the wall behind him, a ball cap low over his slit-like eyes.

The last person Lock would have expected to give a darn about her had not only come and found her, but was sitting with her out in the rain getting completely drenched.

Her lips twitched with a smile as she said, "You're all wet."

"So are you."

They continued to sit there, clothes completely soaked through, staring at the grove of trees in the lot next to the hospital, neither one of them speaking.

Jack wasn't there to fix her. He didn't see her as a broken, tortured soul; he saw her as an equal. Someone who had stepped up to the plate and fought, and needed a minute to decompress. She had earned his respect today, which wasn't an easy feat. She didn't know him, and he didn't know her, but they had gone through the day's events together, and right now that was enough.

"We should probably go," Lock said, feeling a little

uncomfortable as her mind settled back in reality.

Jack made no attempt to move. "Are you ready to?"

Lock didn't know him very well, but her first impression led her to believe this kind, thoughtful approach of his wasn't typical. Jack was a no nonsense, impatient man with his own opinions. Having him be the one to offer moral support had to mean something when it came to God's sense of humor. She would have felt awkward if it had been Bass or Sly to find her. Jack's presence made her quickly dig deep and find a strength she had forgotten about.

In answer to his question, Lock nodded her head and began to push herself up off the ground. But about halfway up, her body protested and she winced, groaning as she let herself fall back down and take a seat.

"Maybe in a minute," she grumbled.

Jack had brought with him a plastic evidence bag, and lifted it up now from where he'd set it next to him, and held it over for Lock to see. "Found this in the mess."

Lock took it from him and examined the bag's contents, rolling it over in her hand. It was a rather large knife with a leather handle, words burned into one side.

"Demon Troop; For God, for purity of blood, and Victory."

"This is one of theirs?" Lock asked.

"It's definitely not mine."

"Pretty ironic," Lock said as she handed it back, "they came to kill a kid who just happens to have the wrong skin color, and they died for the same reason. Some victory."

"That's the job," Jack said, thoughtfully looking down at the knife. "We fight bad guys and sometimes like today we get to win. Not some bigot race haters; we did. You were a part of that."

Lock nodded, flashing him a tight-lipped smile. "Thanks."

He groaned, rolling his eyes, seeming a little embarrassed. "Let's not make this a thing," he said, which made Lock laugh. There was the Jack she knew.

He roused himself and hopped up onto his feet. Standing over Lock, he reached down a hand, holding his palm up for her to take. "You should probably get yourself checked out by the medics. You look like crap."

$$*\quad*\quad*\quad*$$

The parking lot had been converted into a makeshift triage center. Volunteers and first responders had set up canvas tents and were helping nurses and doctors treat the wounded, which were mostly bikers, under heavy guard from off-duty reserve sheriff deputies. Under one of the tents, Cassidy had rallied a team, preparing to execute a county wide search for Heinous and the others who had managed to make a get away. Bass was there, sitting on an overturned bucket as he listened to the sheriff speak. The sight of the young deputy made Lock catch her breath, and she quickly ducked her head in hopes of avoiding being seen.

She went on her way to a different tent that, for the moment, had no patrons. An ambulance was backed up under a canvas tent. A young female paramedic sat in the back doing some paperwork.

Lock approached and called up into the vehicle, "Do you have a minute?"

The young woman with purple hair and red lipstick

immediately looked up from her writing, taking in the sight of Lock; hair flat and wet, clothes soaked, body language saying she was in pain.

The medic quickly set aside her clipboard, "Yeah, come on up."

Hand pressed into her side, Lock winced and shook her head, knowing she couldn't make the climb alone. "Can I stay down here?"

"Sure, have a seat on the bumper there," the woman said as she grabbed a duffel bag off the gurney. Then she hopped down onto the ground as Lock leaned back on the bumper and pulled up her t-shirt. The medic slipped on a pair of gloves and moved closer to Lock.

"Alright, let's have a look here," she said, beginning to pull back the bandage. Lock hissed under her breath as the stickiness pulled at her tender skin.

A perfectly manicured eyebrow arched as the woman said, "This looks old. How did you say it happened?"

"I was shot," Lock said, flashing a quick smile. "Not today, obviously."

The woman smiled brightly, turning back to her bag. "I'm Aria."

"Elizabeth."

Aria moved back in and bent down for a closer look. Lock looked over the woman's purple pony-tail, her gaze fixed on a screw in the pole holding up the canvas roof.

"So were you in there today?"

Lock nodded. "Yeah. I'm came to work with my uncle today."

"Wow. Wrong place, wrong time, huh?" Aria chuckled and Lock smiled, "Story of my life."

"And who's your uncle?"

"Pastor Malone."

Revelation caused the woman's eyes to widen and her lips parted slightly, then her eyes briefly glanced up.

"Wait, you're Lock?"

"You know me, huh?

Aria nodded. "Yeah, Sly talks about you all the time." Then her brow furrowed. "He was in there? Is he okay?"

Lock saw something flash across Aria's face, and it made Lock think she might be carrying a small flame for the preacher. She nodded as she assured Aria, "He was back in the chapel with some people. We never let the bikers get that far."

"Good," Aria said with a nod, adjusting her stance as she visibly relaxed. She brought her attention back to Lock's side.

Lock guessed the bold and cheery paramedic to be a littler older than herself, probably late twenties. She was absolutely beautiful with perfect skin and bright eyes that were set off by her brightly colored hair. She was one of the few people Lock had met who could pull off such a look.

"Okay," Aria suddenly said, "You've got a pretty bad infection going on. I'm going to have to give you a shot. I'm not going to lie; it's going to hurt..."

Lock sucked in a deep breath through tight lips and nodded, mentally preparing herself. Aria offered a reassuring smile, touching Lock's arm as she stepped back up to her bag of tricks. She pulled out a small, clear bottle and a packaged syringe. Ripping the protective sleeve off with her teeth, she turned the bottle upside down and stuck the needle up through the lid. Lock felt herself begin to panic at the sight and quickly turned her head away, blowing out a short burst of air, clearing her throat nervously.

Aria noticed and asked gently, "Not a fan of needles?"

two bullets

Lock coughed nervously, laughing at her own silliness as she shook her head. Aria walked back around in front of Lock, purposefully keeping the needle hidden down by her leg. "Sly said you live in Cincinnati? You didn't grow up there, right?"

"No, I moved there a couple years ago to go to college and go through the police academy."

"I instantly pegged you as a cop when you walked up," Aria said and bent down in front of Lock, keeping the needle as out of sight as long as possible.

Lock gave a muffled scoff. "A cop with the knack for getting shot at apparently."

"Doesn't that mean you're good at your job?" Aria grinned.

Lock laughed and had to nod. Then she felt the needle break skin and she gasped, tensing as she braced herself hard against the bumper. She cursed as she gritted her teeth.

"Sorry," Aria hissed, grimacing in sympathy.

Fire shot through Lock's stomach, causing her lips to curl inward as she bit down hard against the pain, holding her breath.

"Breathe," Aria encouraged.

Lock tilted her head back to stare up at the bright white roof above her as she breathed in thin, rapid bursts of air. Aria then spread a thick salve across the wound and applied a fresh bandage.

"You must be freezing. You need to get out of those wet clothes."

Aria climbed up into the ambulance and pulled out a bag from under the front seat. She returned with a pair of sweats and a sweatshirt for Lock, then set up a privacy curtain around her so she could change. Topping off the outfit was a heavy coat that read "**paramedic**" on the back.

Thankful for the borrowed, warm clothes, Lock quickly changed, then pulled herself up inside the ambulance and took a seat on the floor. She stared outside at the rest of the parking lot as Aria began to clean up her supplies and trash.

Everything was damp and cold as the rain continued to fall from dark clouds, but there was an electricity in the air that Lock couldn't quite put her finger on. These people should be traumatized, chaotic at the notion that a biker gang had just rode in and attacked the hospital. But all Lock saw were calm faces and steady hands, and even heard a few laughs over the distant murmur of conversation.

"Do you guys get a lot of days like this?" Lock asked.

Aria was back behind her inside the vehicle, replacing the things she had used in her bag with replacements from the cabinet. "Days like what?"

Lock motioned out towards the hospital. "Shootings. Massacres. Bad days..."

Aria surprised Lock with a laugh. "No, I can't say that we do."

"But you all are so calm! The hospital is riddled with bullet holes, and you don't seem the least bothered by any of it."

There was a soft grunt as Aria hopped down out of the vehicle to the ground, her uniform jacket rustling as she reached up to fix the tail of her pony-tail, pulling the strands tight. "Let me ask you something. Why did you take up a gun and fight to defend strangers that you never met before in there?"

Lock shrugged, "What else should I have done?"

"Well, you could have run. You could have hidden in a

corner somewhere until the danger was over. Why didn't you?"

Lock shrugged, stammering to answer such a blunt question. "I don't know. I...I don't run away. After the shock wore off, I just wanted to help."

"You weren't scared?"

"Of course I was. But there were lives at stake. I did what I was trained to do."

Aria nodded firmly. Then she zipped up her coat, stuffed her hands in its pockets and turned around to lean up on the vehicle next to Lock's knees. "If you are in this town long enough, you'll learn a few things about the people. Bad days don't mean it's the end of the world. The people around here are trained to fight and win. We don't give up when things get hard. Our faith makes us strong, and we aren't afraid of the unknown."

Her words were foreign to Lock. This was small town Washington; not a country from the middle ages who were trained for evil days of war.

Lock could only shake her head. "That's absurd," she finally said with a scoff.

Aria just shrugged, sniffing against the cold as her eyes moved to a group of people in the next tent. "That's Barrier Ridge. Years ago, a group came to the area with their shaved heads and hate filled teachings that made everyone cold and heartless. It was your uncle that helped teach about courage in the face of evil. Unity in the face of division."

Lock was rethinking her opinion of Aria now. This girl was crazy!

"Not everyone here can feel like that."

Aria shrugged. "No, but if you knew the town before...well things are different now. I know it takes a while to get used to," Aria continued, "but if you spend more time here, you'll see that these people are very firm in what they believe. It's what drives them. Danger and terror can't thrive here. There's no place for it. Do you have faith, Lock?"

Lock was caught off guard by the question and she struggled to grasp where this topic of conversation had gone.

"I used to," she answered truthfully, but she wasn't sure what that had to do with anything.

Aria turned her body slightly towards Lock now, casually looking at her. When Lock looked down to meet her gaze, she saw a soft smile under a strong gaze.

"You've been hurt, haven't you? Your spirit is broken."

There was something about the way Aria said this that caused a memory to flash before Lock's eyes. She recalled the man with the blond pony-tail who had spoken so strange and bluntly to her when she had been smoking not an hour before. Was everyone in Barrier Ridge out of their minds?

Lock could only nod, brow furrowed as she looked straight ahead, shrugging her shoulders as if that would cause Aria to back off now that she had received a reaction. But Aria wasn't done. "Is it so strange to see a community rise above their circumstances and come together to help others?"

"Yes! People are selfish and only care about themselves. We're all human, and trouble and pain brings out the worst in people."

Even as she said this, Lock saw that the people around her were an exception to this observation. But how?

"Not here," Aria went on. "We are a people set apart. We choose to overcome and walk through fire. But it's not because of us, it's because of Who is in us."

Lock knew the woman was referring to a belief in Jesus Christ, but though Lock had been raised as a Christian herself, she had never seen a society come together in the unity of their faith with such strength. Not this strong. Not this overpowering.

"Incredible," she breathed, still shaking her head. She flashed Aria a smile, who shot her one back. Then they both sat there together, watching the scene play out before them as rain continued pelting the pavement, creating a veil of glistening beads.

Chapter Seven

In the days that followed the violent and sudden attack on Carlyle Medical Center, results in the man hunt for Heinous and what was left of the Demon Troop was slow going. The mayor had called on Canyon City SWAT and the US Marshals to help, but even with their added numbers to aid in the search, there were no strong leads. There were hundreds of miles of mountains and forests out there surrounding Barrier Ridge, with hundreds of good hiding places far from modern technology.

The remaining bikers that had been arrested weren't talking. They were a hard and very loyal group of men who didn't find the threat of returning to prison reason enough to turn rat. The sheriff's department ran the names they had through databases for known associates in hopes something would pop and reveal where the fleeing bikers would go to hide, but so far there was nothing. But Sheriff Cassidy and the police in the surrounding three counties weren't giving up.

Once again, Lock was back out at Sly's. Once again unsure what to do with herself. With nothing but time to think and rest, she spent most of the hours sleeping, hoping to sleep away the incessant ache that had settled into her weak body. Running, jumping, falling, and tension had taken its toll on her already less than healthy body. When she was awake, with the house to herself, she stayed in the living room where she'd made a nest on the couch and watched TV.

It was weird to think that just a few days prior, she had been entrenched in a heated gun battle, fighting to protect a hospital and a boy she'd never met. The memories came in vivid color with mixed emotions to match. She could see herself in her minds eye, flying around corners, returning fire at the enemy that never seemed to run out of men, or bullets.

The thought made her grin.

She reworked the shooting over and over in her head, analyzing every little move she had made, reliving every emotion, wondering if she should have done something better or differently. She saw visions of red, blood everywhere, and would find herself staring, her ears filled with the deafening sound of gunfire. When these visions overwhelmed her, she would go back to sleep. But her dreams were no better than being awake and she would soon wake up, drenched in sweat, shaking from yet another nightmare that had brought images of Danson.

Her conversation with Aria was always close at hand. She found herself going over and over the woman's words, remembering the smiling twitch in the girl's red lips as she spoke about faith and a community who wasn't afraid. It intrigued Lock, and made her wonder if Aria had seen one to many Sci-fi movies...but in the end, she couldn't help but see the truth of the woman's words.

Even though Bass, Cassidy, and the others worked in a town with one stop light, where the biggest emergency was rogue skunks in the town square, their cool and calm demeanor in the midst of a fire fight was something that couldn't be trained. There was a strong, confident air about them that was motivating.

In her years on the force, Lock had seen many a man break down and cry when the odds were stacked against him,and the smell of death hung in the air like smoke. Men who thought they were tough, but when it came down to it, they just couldn't handle the trauma. She'd watched good men become so overcome with grief that they could no longer perform the duties of the job. It was inspirational to have seen first hand the Barrier Ridge sheriff's department respond to such horror with such grace and bravery, and the town behind them respond the same.

Friday morning, two days after the shootout, Lock wandered through the house and found Sly on the back deck, spending some alone time studying and preparing for his sermon on Sunday. He had his work plate full with meetings and wellness checks, and he and Lock only had a few hours here or there to talk in the short time he was actually home.

"Good-morning." He said as she stepped through the french doors out onto the deck.

"Mornin'."

He lifted his leg and kicked out the chair across from him under the table. Lock slowly made her way to the chair and lifted herself up into the high seat. "Whatcha doin'?"

"Just going over my notes for Sunday. Still trying to figure out what I want to talk about."

"Don't you usually have that stuff planned out in advance?" She asked, motioning for his coffee cup.

He pushed it across the table as he grinned, "Well, the church board wishes I would so they could decide if they like the topic or not. But I don't work that way." He gave her a mischievous smile, "I like to be spontaneous."

"Keep 'em on their toes." she added and he nodded, "Exactly."

Looking at the open Bible in front of him, Lock could see that words in both columns on the open pages were highlighted in at least three different colors, and tiny handwritten notes cluttered the margins. Sly's passion for studying the Bible put any other person's to shame, and it made her proud to have Sly as her uncle. He was the real deal, so in love with the Word that even if he wasn't a pastor, he'd still pore over his Bible with just as much conviction and heart as he did leading up to a service.

This fact made her feel guilty for her own neglect of Bible reading, or anything really having to do with God. Between long days on the beat, and long nights out with Danson and their friends, she had become too busy the last few years to take a few minutes to pray or study the Bible. She honestly couldn't even remember the last time she had stepped foot in a church. She'd put God on the back burner for a long time and she wasn't even sure when or why. It had just...happened. It hadn't bothered her at the time, but since being in Washington, it had stared her in the face and made her self-conscious.

"So I have a question for you," Lock said, curling her fingers around the coffee cup. She went on to tell him about her talk with Aria, the paramedic, and asked him to clarify her explanation of the town's reaction to trouble.

"Well I never heard it put into those words," Sly said thoughtfully, "but Aria explained it pretty good, I guess."

"But how?"

"I don't know if you remember why I moved here but, besides there being an open position for a pastor at the church, there had been a big crusade that had swept through the area around the time. A friend of mine had invited me out to attend it and help out behind the scenes. Barrier Ridge looked a lot different back then than it does now. The people were lost and didn't have much in the way of moral convictions. In the late eighties, this area was descended upon by a White Society group that brought hate and crime with a vengeance. It was a slow take-over at first, but by the time anyone began to figure out what was happening, it was too late. For years, crimes ranging from petty theft to human sacrifices was the norm. No one respected each other, and the hearts of men were cold. No one ever came through here because they knew Barrier Ridge was an evil place, having heard the "ghost stories."

"Anyway, almost ten years ago a man named Anthony Avelina felt like he heard the Lord tell him to start these Christian crusades all across Washington State. He started south and worked his way up and back again, going from town to town with a team of just four men and their wives. They'd rent out fields near the towns and set up tents, inviting everyone to come out. It grew with intensity and became a phenomenon that no one could explain; it was a supernatural fire that caught and couldn't be stopped. The word of God was preached and people by the hundreds turned from their old ways and accepted Christ. They repented and their hearts changed.

"When it came to Barrier Ridge, after a few years of Avelina holding his meetings here, the people were ready. These people knew what evil looked like. They know what sin and death could do, and how it can ruin communities. They had lived under a dark cloud, one they could literally feel, like a haze of smoke, and they don't ever want to go back to that way of life. Obviously, there were a few who were skeptical and stuck to their old ways, and there still are, but I'd say eighty percent of the town was changed and turned back to God. As a community, they purposed to change the reputation of their city and for the last ten years have cultivated a unique and beautiful atmosphere that draws in people from all over. Where no one even dared to drive through before, now people come from all over to sight-see and vacation. The Bible and faith in God have completely changed this place. I've been able to witness it all first hand."

A shiver danced down Lock's spine as Sly told the story with a fiery passion in his eye. It was contagious, this feeling of hope that underlined every word he spoke. She understood now; these people weren't crazy, they were heroes! She couldn't imagine what a place like that must have been like back during the time that Sly spoke of. She had gone on many calls to homes that upon entering, there was a shift in the very air she breathed. It was as if evil occupied the space and hid in the shadows like demons ready to pounce. It was after such calls that she drank a lot of alcohol and never wanted to be alone. It was a heavy feeling one couldn't shake, as if her very skin carried the whispers of monsters.

She couldn't imagine an entire community being that way day in and day out. It was no wonder Aria had spoken the way she had about her home town. Barrier Ridge had become a light in a dark place, where goodness and love thrived. These people weren't oblivious to the big bad world; they had *been* the big bad world.

Now that she knew all of this, Lock realized that there had definitely been a shift in the atmosphere when she'd arrived. A warm, life exuding feeling, though at the time she'd barely given it a second thought, since she had been only interested in her own pain.

Her heart began to sink then. Barrier Ridge, and the beautiful people here, reminded her just how weak she had been in the face of temptation. How easily she had caved to worldly pleasures and darkness. The light that had at one time been in her had all but dimmed. Her heart had grown cold and the flame nearly snuffed out. These people, so strong in the faith, merely reminded her of something she had once been.

two bullets

She was a stranger here, a clump of dirt in a sea of diamonds.

She had been like them once; happy and carefree and strong. She remembered the feeling like a long lost dream. In the last few years, she had lost her self without even realizing it. She'd made friends with people who made fun of her "antiquated beliefs,"and in an attempt to fit in and make them stop calling her "that weird religious girl," she'd abandoned her personal morals and convictions. But when all was said and done and all the chips lay on the table, she had nothing to show for her choices. Her friends had abandoned her without a second thought, and she didn't have a faith to fall back on.

Was it worth it? she asked herself. Had selling her soul for attention and affection been worth the pain and emptiness she lived with now?

Sunday evening came around with clear skies and a brilliant sunset of gold and purple, the early onset of dusk setting in before dinner. It was Sly's turn to host a men's bible study, which meant Cassidy, Jimmie, Jack and Bass were all coming over. Lock was looking forward to some social interaction, and getting to see everyone again. Hopefully this time would be a little less exciting with less gunfire.

As six o'clock neared, Lock waited out on the front porch for Sly's guests to arrive, smoking a cigarette while she held a ice pack up to her shoulder with her free hand. As she watched the last glimpses of sunlight fade beyond the trees, took a breath of the fresh night air, savoring the few minutes of solace. It was quiet out here, far away from the lights of town. She would have liked to admit that she was doing some deep introspection in those few moments alone, but all she could find herself thinking about was the ridiculously tall Deputy Sheriff with brilliant blue eyes.

She didn't have to wait long; headlights cut through the last moments of hazy dusk as a pickup rumbled up the driveway. She quickly put out her cigarette in a coffee can-turned-ash-tray on a small table next to the porch swing. She watched the shiny black diesel pull up in front of the garage and parked, the engine cutting off as the lights went out. She slowly moved to stand and watched the doors on the pickup open. Bass stepped out first wearing fitted, dark wash jeans over boots, a long-sleeved white shirt tucked into the waistband, and a bible in his hand.

Lieutenant Jimmie Reeves, climbing out of the passenger seat, wore black all the way down to his boots; black ball cap, black t-shirt, black jeans.

Jack Stone was surprisingly a little bit more fancy; wearing black wranglers and a maroon dress-shirt under a very becoming black vest with three gold buttons, the chain of a pocket watch strung from the shallow pocket on the vest. His black hair was in a pony tail, pulled tightly back from his large forehead, not a hair out of place.

Lock's tummy took a few nervous spins at the man she barely knew and she waved. She went to meet them at the front door and led them inside. Sly was cleaning up some papers from the island as everyone filed in. Cheerful banter and loud voices followed Lock as she slipped off to her bedroom to deposit her belongings. When she was done, she turned around and walked back into the living room.

"Help yourself to the coffee, guys," Sly was saying. "Cassidy should be bringing something to eat, but there's donuts just in case."

"Stuffed?" Jack asked.

"It's not a pizza, Jackie," a voice belonging to Jimmie replied.

Lock eased herself down into the recliner as the talking and teasing continued in the other room. After a minute or two, Jack stepped into the living room with a hot cup of coffee and a donut in his hand. He saw Lock and nodded his head. "Cincinnati."

The nickname made her smile.

"Jack," she replied.

Jimmie entered then with Sly, the pair talking about something to do with a car engine, and Lock saw her chance to go get something to drink before everything started. She was already pushing herself up when she noticed that Bass had come to the living room and was standing over her, leaning against the side of the arched doorway between the two rooms. She covered her surprise at his closeness to her by giving him a quick smile, then slipped past him into the now empty kitchen.

She rounded the island in the middle of the floor and headed to the dimly lit corner of counters and cabinets near the sink. She cleaned up a little before starting on her own drink, wiping up the spilt liquid and powdered creamer with a damp wash cloth. Returning the cloth to the sink, she stepped back to the counter and started reaching up to the cabinet where Sly kept the mugs. As she lifted her arm over her head, her shoulder protested and she jerked it back, sucking air at the shooting pain.

"Here, I got you," came a low voice. It belonged to

Bass. He reached over her into the cabinet, his height making it barely a stretch for his arm as he gabbed down a mug. He edged her out of the way as he reached for the coffee pot. She thanked him and watched, absently rubbing her left shoulder with the opposite hand, trying hard to resist scratching at the healing scar.

Bass saw the movement out of the corner of his eye. "Have you ever tried putting Emu oil on that?"

"Emu oil? What's that?"

"Aboriginals swear by it. Use it like a cream, just smear it on and it'll get to work right away."

"Huh. Who knew?"

"I'll get you some." He assured her, returning the carafe to the coffee maker.

Amused, Lock asked, "You just have Emu oil just lying around, huh?"

Bass's eyes sparkled with humor. "It's the only thing I have in my first aid kit. My mum sends me the stuff once a month, I swear."

"Does she get it from Australia?"

"Natural Surplus in Louisiana," he replied with a mischievous grin. Lock laughed, then cringed at the tug in her stomach. Bass picked up a spoon and used it to point down at the cup. "Do you take creamer and sugar?"

"One of creamer, three of sugar."

At this, Bass glanced sideways at her amused, "Are you sure you don't just want to take the sugar bowl and eat out of it instead?"

She laughed, but gave a firm shake of her head. Dishing out the correct amount, he then dropped the spoon into the cup and gave it a few stirs before handing it over. She thanked him and took a sip. It was perfect.

two bullets

Bass turned himself towards her, leaning on the counter with his hand, a twinkle in his eye as he teased, "I bet you eat cookie dough raw too."

She looked up at him with wide eyes, licking her upper lip. "What's wrong with that?"

Quickly dropping his eyes, he shrugged absently. A smile made his lips twitch. "Just making an observation."

"Oh," Lock countered, "so you've never eaten cookie dough? You wait like a good little boy until they come fresh out of the oven?"

Knowing he was caught, Bass leaned deeper into the counter as he replied shyly, "Maybe..."

Lock took another drink, then smacked her lips together, "You're missing out."

"Hey," Bass said, suddenly straightening up, "you make the cookies, I'll eat the dough. Just for you."

Bass oozed with charm, and she knew she had fallen prey to it. But, she had to remind herself that with looks like that, he probably laid it on thick for all the girls. She couldn't get caught up and lose her head over a few flirty remarks here and there. He followed her back into the living room and took his position against the archway wall as she returned down into the recliner. She liked the feeling of having him near, standing over her like a lookout watching her back.

"I guess we can go ahead and get started," Sly was saying from his seat in the chair he'd taken from the dining table and set in front of the fire place, facing the couch.

"What about Cassidy?" Bass asked, checking his watch.

"Well, if you would have been in here instead of flirting in the kitchen," Jack replied mockingly from where he sat on the couch, "you would know that our dear Sheriff is running late. As usual."

"Hey, Jack, I think you've got some jealousy right there on your chin." Bass retorted, rubbing his own chin.

"Why would I be jealous? I'm the one that got to tackle her to the ground. It was a special moment for us."

Sly held up a hand to interrupt as he protested loudly, "Guys. I'm right here!"

Lock's face was nice and red and she sank down further in her seat, hiding her face behind the bulk of her coffee cup.

"Sorry, Preacher." Jack said, "We're just messing around. You may continue."

With a dramatic bow of his head, Sly thanked him. "Now," he said, "who read this week's chapter?"

Hands instantly went to find the personal copies of the book.

"Well, we all know Jimmie didn't read anything." Jack said, pulling out his book like a good student sucking up to teacher.

"Do they even teach reading on the reservation?" Jimmie retorted. Apparently the pair were close enough friends that this wasn't an actual insult, but it still received a cold glare and low "ooohs," from the others.

Sly just looked over at Lock with a perplexed look as he motioned to the others, "They resort to their fourth grade manners in the presence of a woman."

She giggled, slurping on her coffee as the arguing continued. She stole a quick glance up at Bass. He was watching his friends argue with a wide grin and a chuckle bobbing his shoulders up and down. Life. The house was full of it.

The front door opened and the sound of Cassidy's voice

called over the noise, "Party start without me?"

All arguing stopped and the sheriff was greeted with a resounding, "Hey!"

"I brought pizza."

Like the gates were opened, everyone rushed to the kitchen, shoving each other out of the way in a fight to claim a piece of pizza. It took awhile for everyone to come back in and settle down in the living room, but now with Cassidy there, the deputies seemed to rein themselves in and finally Sly was able to start.

Despite there being an open seat on the couch between Jack and Jimmie, Bass grabbed a chair from the kitchen table and pulled it up near Lock's feet stretched out on the foot rest. She found herself tensing just a little, distracted by his nonchalance and dared not to look at him directly. She knew she shouldn't think he meant anything by it, but since their first initial meeting, he had seemed partial to being near her and it was hard not to read into it. She carefully stole a glance at the guys on the couch to see if they had noticed Bass's change in position, but they were concentrating on listening to Sly as he gave an overview of the chapter they were supposed to have read.

The book they were studying Lock was only slightly familiar with, having heard about the study for men only through church back in the day. As each man took turns reading through the chapter, Lock realized she was in a unique position, getting to hear first hand from the lips of those reading what this author had felt was vital for men to understand about themselves. There aren't a lot women who get to have such unfettered back stage access like she had tonight.

She hung on every word. The ratio of men to women

she had spent time with in life was greatly uneven, having spent most of her life drawn to men because of the lack of drama. Growing up with Sly, she felt like she understood men pretty well, but after hearing just a little from this book, she realized she had a lot of preconceived notions about men that simply weren't true. She would have to work on that.

Eventually, the study came to a close, and Sly asked Jimmie to say the prayer. Lock was surprised to see him reach for Jack's hand, and amazingly Jack didn't slap it away. Cassidy rose from his chair to get close enough to take Jimmie's hand, then grabbed Bass's. Bass held his hand down to Lock and she took it, staying where she sat as Sly took her other hand. Everyone then together bowed their heads, and Jimmie led them in a simple closing prayer, adding on a mention for Lock, thanking God for her being there.

She smiled, touched by his words, feeling Bass gently squeeze her hand.

Immediately after Jimmie said "amen", Jack announced he was ready for a rematch in a game of cards that apparently was a favorite for the group. Reading material set aside, the coffee table was cleared and chairs were moved in closer. Cassidy's cell phone rang then, and announcing it was his wife, asked the others to wait to start the game until he returned, then left to step out on the back porch.

Lock felt a nicotine desire coming on and rose up to go to her room to retrieve her things. Not wanting her bad habit on display, she hid it near her leg as she walked back out through the living room.

She took a seat on the porch swing and pulled out a cigarette. As she watched the white smoke disappear out over the porch and dissipate in the night air, the front door suddenly opened. Startled at being discovered, she instinctively hid her hand with the cigarette down by her thigh as she looked towards the door. The light from inside bled out into the dark and a shadow filled the doorway. Her pulse spiked at the familiar form of Bass stepping outside, quietly closing the door behind him. How was she going to talk herself out of this one? Wisps of smoke filtered up over her leg, the strong stench of tobacco anything but hidden.

His low voice offered a question in the same way he had asked to sit next to her in the ER. "Mind the company?"

"Um, no, not at all," she replied as if she wasn't hiding a sin.

"Sorry about the guys. They mean no harm. They're just... exuberant."

Lock chuckled but shook her head, "It's all good. It's nice actually. It's nice to see people get along so well."

Bass walked out to the railing, hands in his pockets all causal like, looking out into the dark. "Beautiful night, huh?"

Out of habit, Lock flicked her fingers to ash the cigarette, covering the snapping sound by saying, "Absolutely."

Would he think less of her if he knew?

Turning to face her, Bass rested back and leaned against the wood railing. His eyes smiled as he asked, "So how ya doin'?"

"Good," she said with smile. She moved to cross her legs as she said, "How about you? Any news on the Demon Troop?"

"Not yet. But we'll get 'em."

Lock nodded her head, wishing desperately she could take a drag off whatever was left of her smoke, but as long as she kept it hidden, she didn't have to admit to having a bad habit.

two bullets

"Perks of the job; having to wait around," she mused to fill the quiet.

"How has the rest of your visit been? Been able to actually relax yet?"

"Oh yeah." Her fingers flicked the cigarette again. She had to be down to only a couple drags left, but talking to Bass made up for it. "Not much else to do," she added with a laugh.

"It's not so bad here when you get used to it. We have our own kind of fun, but you're going to have to heal up a little bit before I can show you."

She could hear his smile and she matched it with her own, nodding as she absently touched her side at the mention of it.

"I never got the chance to thank you for all your help Wednesday."

She waved him off. "Oh, it's no problem. I'm glad I could help."

Bass chuckled, crossing one booted foot over the other as he crossed his arms. "You did more than that. If those guys had been able to get past you into the ER, the outcome would be a lot worse."

Lock just nodded, remembering the moment her courage had returned and she'd opened fire on the group bound to push past her.

"It was a good workout," she joked.

"You should think about talking to Cassidy about coming onto the department."

Lock shuddered at the thought, "Oh, I don't know about that."

"I'm serious. He only hires the best, and from where I stand, that would be you."

Looking up at him, Lock could see he was completely

serious. Not sure what to say, she just nodded. "I'll think about it."

The she turned to the side and quickly tossed the dead cigarette into the coffee can next to her on a small table and slowly got to her feet. "We'd better get inside. They're probably getting impatient."

Bass walked ahead of her to the door and held it open for her.

"Finally!" Jack called out as they walked in, a deck of cards in his upheld hands. "Lock, you're on my team. I hope you're prepared to win."

Lock smiled and walked around to the other side of the coffee table and took a seat on the couch near Jack. He began an animated explanation of the game and she listened intently. Cassidy stepped inside through the french doors of the back porch, and the game began.

Lock took a moment to look around the table at the happy faces and relished the warmth the sight brought. This was a dramatically different get-together than their first meeting, but she thought it probably wouldn't mean as much if she hadn't seen them all on one of the worst days. They had proved themselves gentlemen and heroes, and she was proud to be included. Sly was like a brother to her, and she couldn't help but feel like she had found four more.

Then Bass caught her eye across the table and he winked, then laughed along with the others at something Jimmie had said.

She melted instantly and her cheeks blushed.

Well, maybe only three brothers.

Chapter Eight
Monday Morning

Lieutenant Jimmie Reeves walked towards the front of the mechanic's shop, seeing a familiar face waiting for him at the door. Jack Stone was on shift today as a reserve deputy, and it was he who had made the courtesy call to Jimmie.

Jack stood like a guard in front of the open door, his hands relaxed in front of him, folded over his gun-belt. Dark sunglasses hid his eyes making him look like one of those robots in the Terminator movies. Jimmie removed his own pair of sunglasses as he stepped into the cool shade of the awning.

"Where is he?"

Jack nodded over his shoulder in through the mechanic's shop entrance. Once inside, Jimmie saw his brother-in-law Dane Kurtz sitting on a metal chair, a pair of handcuffs keeping him secured to the armrest.

"Dane," Jimmie said, his irritation evident. Dane looked up with a start, instantly stating his case.

"Jim, come on! It was just a scratch! The old guy didn't even feel it. I told them not to call you."

Jimmie's eyes went to the broken window behind Dane, then on out to where a man sat with a paramedic holding a giant piece of gauze up to his forehead.

"You threw a man through a window, Dane. Of course they're going to call me." He hung his sunglasses through the collar of his shirt.

"The window was already broken. I swear I just barely pushed the man and he fell back into it and suddenly the glass shattered."

"You hit your boss in front of witnesses. That's assault." Jimmie looked back at Jack and asked, "Is Steve pressing charges?"

Jack dipped his head slightly. "Yep."

Jimmie just shook his head, unable to look back at his brother-in-law just yet. Dane, who's sand colored hair was cut into a shaggy Mohawk strained against his restraints. "Boys, come on, it's me. Your sister's husband! There's gotta be a little grace!"

Dane was desperate and apologetic, and Jimmie almost felt sorry for him. "This is your third fight in as many months, Dane. You're lucky this is the first time someone is pressing charges."

Dane's shoulders drooped, desperation in his face as he looked pleadingly from Jimmie back to Jack. But both men were stone cold serious and he found no sympathy.

"What was the fight over this time?"

Dane flopped back in his seat, tired of trying to get sympathy. He threw up his free hand. "What do you care?"

"I care because like it or not, we're family. Did Steve say something to tick you off?"

Dane looked off to his left, shrugging.

Jimmie eyed him, waiting for an answer, but Dane wasn't in the mood for talking if it didn't involve him getting out of going to jail.

"Alright," Jimmie said with a frown, "have it your way. I'll tell your wife you said hello."

He turned on his heel and heading back out the door, Jack turning in behind him to follow. Neither spoke until they were at Jimmie's vehicle.

"You gonna go see Jamie?"

two bullets

98

Jimmie groaned, but nodded. He glanced up at the man who had been a part of the Reeves family for the last twenty years. "She's your sister too. Wanna join me?"

"No," Jack sneered. But despite his words, he turned and walked around the front of the pickup to the passenger side.

Jimmie was one of the few who understand and could deal with Jack. The man had been through a lot; his birth mother had beat him on the regular after his father had died. It had been Jimmie's father who had treated his many injuries at the hospital. The Reeves had taken Jack in and eventually were able to make things official and adopt Jack, despite his Native American heritage. Since the Reeves were white and from Washington, and Jack was originally from a reservation in Arizona, the tribal court had fought hard against the adoption, thinking it better for Jack to stay with someone who was of his heritage. But Jack's mother had been more than willing to give up her son, and by the grace of God, the courts had finally approved the adoption.

Jimmie was also grateful to not have to go give his twin sister the bad news about her husband alone. Not that having Jack along would ease the tension, but they were all family after all.

Jamie Reeves-Kurtz suffered from depression brought on by her first husbands death. Despite ten years having passed, she'd never really gone back to her old self. Of course, Jimmie didn't blame her; it had been Jamie who had found the body after Craig had put a gun to his head and pulled the trigger in their garage. She lived with not only the trauma of finding her husband, but also with the guilt of not seeing her husbands pain. She had been pregnant with twins at the time, but hadn't had the chance to share the news with her husband

two bullets

before he'd killed himself, and she tortured herself with the thought that if she had found out sooner about the pregnancy, Craig might not have felt the need to end his life.

While Jimmie had been off serving his country in the United States Marine Corps, it had been Jack who had looked after Jamie during those tough years. Jimmie had known his twin was struggling, but it never occurred to him things would become as bad as they were. Part of him always wondered if their family would be in the state it was if he hadn't left for eight years.

Jamie had eventually remarried, marrying Craig's best friend Dane and for awhile, Jamie's life had been normal on the surface. They now had four children, but Jamie's demons were never far out of reach, secretly isolating her. Over the years she had slowly lost her ability to function in the real world. She was fine if she kept herself busy around the house, but that only worked if she actually got herself out of bed. Anymore all she could manage to do was get out of bed sometime in the afternoon, maybe do some laundry or the dishes, then as soon as her husband got home from work, she'd take a book and a bottle of wine and retreat into the bedroom, leaving her kids to fend for themselves.

Jimmie hadn't needed Dane to tell him what the fight with his boss was about; it was the same story every time. Dane had a short fuse to begin with, but with the added strain between he and he wife at home, and the pressure to provide for six mouths and a house payment, any off color remark would set the man off.

On the north side of town, Jimmie pulled into his sister's driveway behind the family minivan and cut the engine. As they climbed out of the pickup, two young boys came running across the yard.

"Uncle Jack, catch!" Watson, the oldest boy, called and launched the football up and over to where Jack was coming around the front of the pickup. Jack caught it, then told the young boy to go run for a pass. The nine year old boy quickly sprinted back across the yard, looking over his shoulder in anticipation as Jack sent the spiraling football flying through the air.

Jimmie walked through the waist high gate, cheering on his nephew as he caught the ball. Up the side walk to greet the two men was Watson twin sister Phoebe, her dark hair long with a small braid weaved through her bangs. She smiled and gave Jimmie a hug.

"Hey, Carrot," Jimmie said, ruffling the girl's hair. She had her mothers eyes and her father's spunk. Craig sure had missed a lot, never getting to meet his kids.

"Mama inside?" Jimmie asked, now walking with the young girl under his arm.

"Yeah, she got a cleaning bug and tore the house apart. Dad's gonna have a fit."

Phoebe was mature for a nine year old. She was well aware of her mother's mental state and had taken on the responsibility of being a second mom to her three siblings. Jimmie hated that she had missed out on a normal child hood, having to practically nurse her mother back to health numerous times when Jamie slipped away from reality. Jamie constantly blamed her pain on her two oldest, seeing them as just reminders of her dead husband.

"She's still taking her medication, right?" Jimmie asked, and Phoebe nodded.

"She fights me constantly, but she always ends up taking them."

Jimmie stopped at the bottom step of the front porch

and looked back behind him, watching Jack and Watson playing in the yard.

"Are you and Uncle Jack here to take us to grandma's?"

Jimmie looked down at the young girl. "I guess it is Friday, isn't it?"

"Uh-huh!"

Jimmie smiled and patted her head. "Have you had a chance to hang out with your friends this week at all?"

Phoebe smiled but shook her head. "You know how mom gets."

Jimmie dropped his arm around the young girl's shoulders and tugged her into his side. "I know. But you're still just a kid. You need to have some fun. Get in to trouble."

Phoebe grinned. "How much trouble can I get in to when you're always around?"

"You're smart. You'll find a way," he winked. Jake, the second oldest after the twins, called to him just then and told him to watch him throw a pass. It was a perfect spiral.

"Atta boy, Jake!"

"Kid's got quite the arm," Jack said, his voice drifting over the yard.

From under Jimmie's arm, Phoebe spoke quietly. "Something's wrong with daddy, isn't it?"

Jimmie quickly looked down at her with a frown. "Why would you think that?"

"Dad was suppose to come home on his lunch break and take us for ice cream to meet grandma and grandpa. He never came." A shadow passed over her face and she looked down at her feet.

Jimmie saw no reason to lie to her. "I'm sorry, Carrot. Dad got into some trouble. After I talk with your mom, Jack

two bullets

and I will take you guys for ice cream. How's that sound?"

The shadow passed from the girl's eyes and she nodded up at him excitedly.

"Go get your stuff."

"It's already packed." Phoebe pointed to the pile of backpacks up on the porch.

"Alright, wait for me out here."

She gave him a quick hug and then ran off to play with her brothers and Jack. Jimmie motioned to Jack that he was going inside, then headed up the stairs.

"Jamie?" He called as he pushed open the front door. He stepped inside the dimly lit house, eyes adjusting to the sight before him. Laundry was strewn in piles all around the living room, along with various piles of boxes packed with garage sale goods cluttering the entry way. A Disney movie was playing loudly on the large screen TV, DVD cases and LEGOs carpeting the middle of the floor.

Irene, the two year old toddler was standing amidst the chaos in only a diaper between the couch and coffee table, a pair of scissors in her hands, the sharp end acting as a pacifier as she stared up at the TV

"Irene Babe, what are you doing?" Jimmie called quietly so as not to startle the little girl and make her stab herself. At the sight of him, Irene broke into a wide grin and dropped the scissors to the floor, waddling towards him with her arms up to be held. He swooped her up and looked her over, wiping a smear of jelly from off her arm with his thumb.

"Where's mama, huh?" He whispered into her ear as he gave her a little bounce. "Where's your mama?"

The dark headed baby threw out her arm behind her towards the back of the house in answer.

"In the kitchen? Okay, let's go find her."

Cradling Irene against his chest, Jimmie stepped over to the couch and swiped the scissors off the floor before crossing the sea of toys to the back of the house. He set the scissors in a cup of pens on a small shelf hanging on the wall.

"Aimes? You back here?"

He passed from the living room into the small dining room, then turned to the right into the small kitchen. Jamie stood with her back to him, elbows deep in soapy dish water as she chatted away into the cordless telephone tucked between her head and shoulder. She was dressed in a pair of her husband's sweats and an over sized t-shirt, her uncombed short hair going in all different directions.

Jimmie carried Irene over to her high chair at the table and buckled her in, Jamie still not turning from the sink. He walked towards his sister, and upon reaching her, snatched the phone free from her shoulder.

"Hey!" Jamie shrieked, turning her head around to look at him. "Jimmie! What the..."

He looked down at the phone and pressed the END button with his thumb and the line went dead.

"Um, excuse me!" Jamie said, pulling her hands up out of the water as she turned to face him.

He waved the phone back and forth at her. "You didn't even hear me come in. What if I was a robber, huh? Or a crazy psychopath here to kill you and your kids? Speaking of your kids, I walked in to find Irene with scissors in her mouth."

"Oh, come on Jimmie." Jamie said, drying her hands. "You're being a little dramatic don't you think?"

"I'm serious, Jamie."

"I heard you come in, Jim. I'm not an idiot."

"And Irene sucking on scissors? You knew about that too?"

"She's a big girl. She'll learn not to do that again if she hurts herself."

Jimmie balked, face wrinkling as he cringed, "Are you kidding me right now?"

Jamie rolled her eyes, walking over to the fridge near the door. "I hope you brought some grocery money with you this week. We're almost out of food."

Jimmie heard the front door open, and a couple seconds later Jack appeared, surveying the scene in the kitchen as he slowly leaned against the door-jam. Jamie hadn't seen him come in, and as she rose from looking through the fridge, her face lit up.

"Jack!" She exclaimed in happiness, reaching out with her arms as she moved to wrap her arms around his neck. Jimmie tried not to be offended. He got yelled at and asked for money when he showed up, but Jack got a hug.

Jamie pulled out of the hug, giving Jack's shoulder a thump with her palm. "How are you?"

Jack smiled slightly, then his eyes went past her to Jimmie. Jimmie shook his head; he hadn't told her about Dane yet. Jack looked back at Jamie and smiled. "I'm alright."

"Jamie," Jimmie said as she turned back with the jug of milk and walked to the counter. "We need to talk. It's about Dane."

"What about him?" Jamie asked in an absent voice. She had left the refrigerator door hanging open, and Jack reached out his hand to push it shut.

Irene whimpered in her high-chair. Jamie hurried over to pull her out, settling the girl on her hip. She looked expectantly at Jimmie, then to Jack as she waited for an explanation.

"Dane got in a fight today," Jimmie said.

Jamie threw a hand over her head and marched back to the counter where she had left the milk. "What's new?"

"Jamie... we had to take him in."

She spun around. "You did what?!" She cried.

Her sudden change in tone startled the baby in her arms so badly that the little girl suddenly began to cry.

"He said we had to arrest Dane today!" Jack informed her, yelling to be heard over Irene.

Jimmie quickly hurried forward to take Irene from his sister's arms and handed her off to Jack.

"Are you kidding me right now?" Jamie was saying. Jimmie and Jack shared a look before Jack stepped out of the room to try and soothe the child. Jimmie took a deep breath before turning to face his sister. Jamie's eyes were wide as she held out her hands, demanding an answer from him for this horrid thing he had done. Jimmie could see clearly now the woman's unkempt black hair and the dark circles under her demanding eyes. This wasn't his sister. Someone else had entered her body and ravaged it. She didn't even sound like herself anymore.

"I'm sorry Jamie. He got into it with Steve and threw him through a window. I had to bring him in."

"No, you wanted to." Jamie challenged. "Why couldn't you just let it go?"

"This makes three fights for him, Aimes. I can't keep giving him passes."

"I can't believe this!" Jamie moaned, walking to the sink. "How could you?"

Jimmie was irritated now. "Hey, I'm not the bad guy here! Dane did this to himself. And I'm going to ask you not to post his bail."

"I am his wife, Jameson!" Jamie said, gasping at him

two bullets

appalled. "You expect me to leave him there?"

"Yes, I do. Have you even considered how this will affect the kids?"

"I could ask you the same question," she snapped. "You put the cuffs on their father, not me."

Jimmie walked the short distance up to Jamie, attempting to comfort her. She turned away from his touch, walking to the other counter, slamming doors closed and tossing dirty dishes out of her way.

"Aimes, I-"

"Don't you dare 'Aimes' me, Jameson Reeves." She said, still turned from him shaking her head. "You know I don't have the money to bail him out. And now, now he has a record! What if he loses his job? What then, hot shot?!"

Jimmie was in the process of coming up with something to say that wouldn't add fuel to the fire when Jack returned to the room.

"Don't blame him, Jamie." Jack said. "I was the one to arrest Dane."

Jimmie noticed a candle burning on the counter near him, and the pile of rags directly next to it. He quickly crossed the distance and blew out the candle, irritation now crawling through him. Jamie and Jack were arguing now behind him, Jamie's shrill voice matching Jack's deep, growling one. Jimmie took a moment, asking for strength.

Jack must have run out of tactfulness because Jamie suddenly exclaimed, "Just because my family adopted you doesn't mean you have any right to speak to me like this!"

"Speak to you like what? I'm just saying-"

"Get out!" She looked at both men as she waved her hands. "Get out of my house!" Then to emphasize her point, she turned around and grabbed a dirty glass off the counter. She threw it to the floor and it shattered, spewing tiny shards of glass and old kool-aid everywhere.

"Nice. Real nice." Jack muttered, turning to look for something to clean up the mess.

Jamie's eyes were glowing now with malice. "I hate you! I hate both of you."

Jimmie scowled, but tried to keep a civil tone as he said, "Jamie, that's enough. There's no need to act this way."

"You!" Jamie said, seething as she turned her wrath on him. She pointed sharply at his face. "You don't get to speak. Now you go down to the jail and you get my husband out of there!"

He shook his head. "Ain't going to happen. He's gonna stay there over night."

"Lord knows I would stay," Jack said, crouched on the floor as he mopped up the sugary mess with a towel.

"I can't do this. I can't." Jamie stormed out of the room then and disappeared, the sound of a door slamming coming a couple seconds later.

"Go after her, I got this," Jack said, not looking up from the floor.

Jimmie sighed and grabbed a towel and moved over to the mess on the floor. "I'll give her a minute to calm down."

"Make it more like a couple days. I swear, I've never seen her this bad."

Jimmie had just been thinking the same thing. From where he crouched on the floor, he noticed something under the counter, just under the lip. He lunged out his leg over a puddle of kool-aid and reached for the object. Pulling it out, he saw that it was a cork, probably out of a wine bottle. The bottom was still cold. He hissed.

Jack looked up at the sound, eyes going to the cork.

"She's drinking while on her meds? That's not good."

Jimmie tossed the cork into the trash, then helped finish cleaning up the broken glass. As they began to leave the house, Jack went on out to rally the kids while Jimmie went upstairs to get together some of Irene's things. All of the kids would be staying at their grandparents tonight. Knowing what Irene liked and needed, he quickly managed to get a bag together. As he headed back down the hall, he stopped at the closed door on the left and knocked.

"Jamie, we're heading out. I'm taking the kids over to Dane's parent's."

He waited, but didn't get a response back.

"Jamie?" He tried the doorknob and the door opened. He took a step inside and instantly saw that the room was empty. Just then Jack came pounding up the stairs calling for him.

"Jimmie, she's gone." Jack said before he ever made it to the landing. Well, that explained the empty room. Jimmie stepped back out just as Jack rounded the corner. "She took the car?"

"The kids saw her slip around back."

They hurried down the stairs. "Where would she go?" Jimmie asked, not expecting a response. No one could guess what Jamie had in her head.

The kids were waiting for them at the pickup with their back packs on. Jimmie didn't want the kids to suffer for the sake of Jamie's poor judgment, so as promised he took them to Mosley's for ice cream. Jack made a couple calls and put out some feelers in case anyone around town saw Jamie.

Jimmie tried to keep his face void of worry as he sat in the booth, listening to the kids tell him about school and their friends, but all the while in the back of his mind he was cussing out his sister. Dane's parents showed up ten minutes after Jimmie had called. When they arrived, the kids forgot all about their uncles and only had eyes for their grandparents, so Jimmie and Jack slipped out and climbed back in the pickup.

"We gonna go looking for her?"

Jimmie nodded. "We'll do a pass around town. But if she doesn't want to be found, we won't find her."

Chapter Nine

"Last night was a lot of fun." Lock said when she had appeared from her bedroom that morning. "Do you guys get together like that a lot?"

Sly sat in the middle of the living room floor, a black box that looked like a internet modem in one hand, pliers in the other. "Yep. Well, as much as we can. We basically see each other every day anyway, so it's nice to have something to do that doesn't involve work."

Lock took a seat on the couch, glancing at the instruction manual crumpled up in a ball in the middle of the coffee table as she spoke, "Must be nice having such a close group of friends."

"Yep. Hand me that screw there."

She picked up the tiny screw and held it out for Sly to take. He dropped the pliers and replaced them with a screwdriver and twisted the screw in place. Then he held up the box pleased with himself, "There!"

Then he rose and took the box over to the corner by his desk and plugged a phone jack into the back. A blinking green light announced Sly's effort wasn't in vain. He clapped his hands in victory and walked back to clean up his mess. Lock grabbed a magazine and flipped through the glossy pages, not even seeing what she was looking at, just perusing absently.

Sly grabbed the TV remote from the coffee table as he passed and hit play on the program that had been paused. Up on the TV that hung from the chimney, a man Lock didn't recognize continued speaking, standing on a brightly lit stage,

two bullets

speaking in a strange accent. After just a few words, she realized it was a ministry program and the man speaking was a preacher. Sly disappeared into the kitchen to fix a snack, while Lock kept looking through the outfitters magazine, listening with only half an ear to the man on TV.

"The world will tell you that you have to stay in the place you are. But that's not what Jesus says. He came to give us all new life! It doesn't matter where you're from, the mistakes you've made; everyone has a chance to accept the free gift. But you have to realize that it's a gift. Amen?"

"Who is this guy, Sly?" Lock called.

Sly's voice filtered in from the other room, "He's a pastor from overseas. Real good guy with an amazing understanding of Grace. You like him?"

Lock wasn't sure yet, eyes now up on the screen, the forgotten magazine having gone limp in her hands. "He certainly has a way of speaking."

Sly laughed, knowing what she meant. "He's fluent in Greek and Hebrew and who knows what else. He brings up points in the Bible that absolutely blow your mind. And it's all right there for you to go back and look at yourself."

"Are you sure you aren't just getting sucked in to another ploy to make false promises and then ask for money?"

Sly stepped up to the archway and paused, peering in at the TV. "Why? Do you think he's wrong?"

"Well, I don't know. But you know how these TV evangelists work..."

"Yeah, there's a few bad apples, but this guy is the real deal."

"But how do you know?"

Sly shrugged as he sat in the recliner with half a sandwich piled high with everything but the kitchen sink.

two bullets

"You have to just listen to what he says, and compare it to what you see for yourself in the Bible. You rightly divide the Word. No one's perfect, but there hasn't been one thing I've heard this guy say that I don't agree with. And I'm pretty set in my ways."

Lock sat there facing forward, now completely taken with the man on the screen and listening with all her attention. When the program ended, the TV screen turned to blue, a pop up option asking if they wanted to watch another episode. Sly touched a button on the remote and the screen blinked, returning to normal programming.

"You're not going to watch another one?" Lock asked, looking at him in surprise.

Sly glanced over, "You want to?"

So as not to give away her interest, Lock just shrugged, leaning further back into the couch. "I don't care."

Sly hid a smile, then clicked through the play-list and hit play on another message and it started up.

Something about this particular pastor was intriguing to Lock. She had never heard someone speak so plainly about things of the Bible, and make it so deep. She'd been out of practice when it came to studying the Bible, but the man kept saying that God was love. She knew that was true, but something about the way this man was saying it was like Lock was hearing it for the first time.

"*God isn't dealing with you based on your sins. If you believe in the finished work of the cross; the sacrifice that Jesus made on your behalf, then He deals with you based on Jesus. And Jesus is perfect. When He looks at you, God doesn't see what you've done, He doesn't see your failures; He sees Jesus. And He's pleased. Do you know what that means? God is pleased with you.*"

Despite her instinct to argue with the man, Lock felt a

sudden wave of peace rush through her like cool water. But seriously, could it really be so simple? She didn't think of herself as a bad person, but she'd made mistakes. A lot of them. How could God look at her and be pleased with what He saw?

"Now you might say, Pastor, how can this be? I'm a failure, I'm a lost cause, I've made mistakes. There's no way God can love me now. But you see, you're thinking it's all about you. You're thinking it's about your goodness. Your perfection. But you're not perfect. No body is, y'all I'm not, your friends aren't. No one is except Jesus. And you have to come to this place where you let this word get inside of you and you realize, 'I am not perfect. I can't do this on my own.' And when you do that, that's repentance. You're turning your mind from yourself, and you are able to see that it's God who makes you righteous. It's the blood of Jesus."

He had answered her question even before she'd finished the thought, and it made her pull up in surprise. But she was taking in his words like a dry sponge desperate for water. Over and over, this man spoke words that made Lock feel like he was talking to her, and it was doing something inside of her that she couldn't explain.

After half an hour, the program ended, and this time, Sly went ahead and pushed play again on the next one. Now Lock was hooked, desperate to hear what this man was going to say next. Sly got up periodically and left the room to do other things, but Lock stayed where she sat, aware that the lies she had believed for so long were being squelched. Maybe there was still hope for her after all.

Two hours came and went and Lock hadn't moved from her spot on the couch. Her head was spinning with all this new knowledge working its way through her brain.

two bullets

Collecting the shattered pieces of her heart with a love that many know, but few can explain.

"God doesn't leave you in your sin. He meets you where you are and says, I love you. That's what he wants you to know; he loves you. He always has. Even when you wanted nothing to do with him, even when you put him on the back burner, Jesus says, 'I love you.'"

Lock paused the program and called to where Sly was in the other room, "Sly, I need to talk to you!"

Lock was ready. She was done living in the empty shell of a life she'd found herself in. She wanted to be her old self again; the person she had all but left in the dust. Sly sat with her and poured into her for the rest of that rainy Saturday morning, reminding her of all the things she had forgotten in her search to experience life on the wild side. He opened up his Bible and read her scriptures. In doing so, he was calling her back to what she used to know, reminding her of who she was in Christ.

"Christianity isn't about memorizing scripture or being a professor of theology," he said, "it's about a personal relationship with Jesus Christ".

In showing her scriptures, he was reminding her of what that relationship was supposed to look like.

Sly could see with his own eyes a change in Lock's countenance as they talked. She leaned over his shoulder eagerly as he read, soaking up every word. This was the first time he felt like he had his real niece back, and he shivered with excitement, praying he would be able to speak clearly and not make anything confusing. He'd prayed for this day to come for a long time now, and didn't want to ruin it by pushing too hard. He let Lock set the pace and ask the questions she wanted answered. He watched her come alive that afternoon, and Sly prayed that this was just the beginning.

two bullets

Chapter Ten

I had become concerned about my partner, and was suspicious that he had started taking drugs. There were subtle clues, but I couldn't believe it. Ever since he had come back from an undercover assignment, he had been different.

One night I followed Danson, carefully mind you, to a seedy part of town that was known for being rich with drugs and cheap hookers. I watched my partner go inside and then I snuck in through a side door. I wasn't planning on confronting him, I just wanted to see for myself what he was up to.

The abandoned warehouse was empty and dirty. By the light of a grungy light bulb hanging from a string, I saw my partner shake hands with a man in a nice suit, then hand him a rolled up yellow envelope. The man in the suit handed him a small case, similar to what diabetes meds are kept in.

My heart broke, knowing what I was witnessing. I hurried to turn and leave so as to get out of there before I was caught. But as I slipped out the side door, a man on guard blindsided me and caught me. He drug me back inside and threw me down in the middle of the floor in front of Danson and the other man.

"It seems we have a rat problem." The man announced to the others.

Eyes glaring up into Danson's, wide with shock at the sight of me, I said, "Cincinnati PD; you're all under arrest."

I was obviously in no position to make an arrest, and everyone just laughed.

"You know her?" The man in the suit asked Danson, and my partner quickly shook his head. "I've never seen her before."

"Good," Mr. Suit said, then handed Danson his gun. "Then this shouldn't be a problem. Clean it up."

I made Danson look me in the eye as he held up the gun and pointed it at me. There was pity in his eyes, and I begged with my own for him not to do it.

"Is this the choice you're willing to live with?" I asked him. Our history buzzed between us in unspoken words. Partners for three years, working side by side to clean up the streets of Cincinnati and keep the peace. Three years of friendship, and this is what it came down to.

Mr. Suit spoke when Danson hesitated to pull the trigger. "If you let her live, life as you know it is over. She'll tell everyone your secret and you'll be a disgrace to the badge. You'll be arrested and they'll throw away the key. You have to shoot her."

"There's got to be another way," Danson snapped. "I'm a cop, I can't shoot another one."

"They don't serve narcotics behind bars." Mr. Suit reminded him.

That was when Danson chose his addiction over me. That was When he traded his freedom for my life.

✳   ✳   ✳   ✳

two bullets

Lock was sprinting, running flat out as fast as she could, her body screaming its resistance and her lungs burning, but she couldn't stop. She was pushing through the dark along the back trail in the field behind Sly's house under a blankets of stars, the beam from her flashlight bouncing along the dirt and grass ahead.

There was something freeing about plunging head long into pitch dark nothingness without knowing what was up ahead. She was smothered by the voidless night, and it awoke in her every ounce of self determination she had left. Her heavy breathing filled her ears, but it couldn't overshadow the voices in her head.

Another night terror had woken her, leaving her in a cold sweat and her heart thumping out of her chest. She'd crawled out of bed, the digital clock reading one-thirty in the morning. Slipping from her room, she searched until she found a flashlight hanging next to the front door and took it, then quietly stole out into the night. Ignoring the warnings from her body, the images of Danson holding her at gunpoint pushed her to go beyond her physical limitations. She remembered the sound of the gun firing and her body hitting the floor and she visibly winced, hunching her shoulders as she continued charging down the worn-out trail.

Danson hadn't even had the decency to come over and check on her before leaving the warehouse, not even as she cried out for help. He'd left her behind, her life slowly slipping away as her blood darkened the floor under her.

Tears now streamed down her cheeks, freely sobbing as she stumbled through the dark.

"*I'm sorry.*" Those were the words she wished so desperately to hear, but knew they'd never come.

Danson's denial, his pained expression behind the

muzzle of the gun followed Lock, nipping at her heels. Then she suddenly let out a cry of pure emotion and yanked her body to a stop mid stride, drawing her arm back, then like a shot put, released and threw the flashlight as hard and as far as she could away from her. She watched it go with clenched fists, her own scream echoing in the empty night around her, shoulders and chest heaving, out of breath. The beam of light swooshed up through the dark, end over end as it careened across the sky like a drunk shooting star, arching at the very top and then began its free fall straight down. A soft thud finally came to her ears as the flashlight landed out in the knee-high grass, the beam of light absorbed into the black blades of grass.

She dropped to her knees where she'd stopped, completely broken. "Jesus," she sobbed into the darkness enveloping her. "Please help me. If you really love me, I need to know now. Please, let me know."

She'd been partnered with Shane Danson after her probation had ended, six months after joining the department. He'd seen something in her, he said, and an instant connection between the two of them was born. They were complete opposites, which made their coworkers surprised at the pairing. Danson was a rough, fifteen year vet of the Cincinnati PD, with little to say and a hard exterior. There had been something about the exuberant, untainted female rookie that caused him to soften, to see the world a little differently. Lock was naive, seeing good in everyone, and though she had a natural knack for the job, Danson took it upon himself to make her the best.

But in the end, it hadn't been enough. Danson had a secret that not even the goodness in Lock could fix.

As the night wore on, under a cloudless, star filled sky,

Lock rode the emotional tidal waves as they came, going from confusion to anger, back to confusion, then suddenly felt embarrassed at being so stupid to trust so easily. She had to let herself deal with this new found grief and sense of loss. Like a death in the family, she had to say good-bye to the Danson she thought she knew. She had to say good-bye to the person she had been when she was around him. The person he had helped to cultivate.

All of that was gone now. Buried in the past.

Their partnership and friendship that had no equal was now worthless in the face of addiction and betrayal. Like a movie, she could see in her mind all those times on emergency calls when she and Danson had been each others back up. Day in and day out they had gone out into the city, unsure of what awaited them, and only had each other to depend on. They had laughed together, shared secrets, and made memories. All of those moments had bonded them, brought them so close together that no words could accurately describe it.

But again, all of that was gone.

Lock cried until she had nothing more to give. Then, she wiped her face, her sobbing having dissipated and now all she could hear was the empty night around her. She stomped through the grass to where the flashlight had fallen and picked it up. Her eyes were swollen and her nose ran, but no more tears fell. She stumbled across the rocky, uneven ground back to the worn path running along the edge of the field. She turned herself towards home and started to walk.

Chin up, beautiful, Danson used to tell her. He'd always hated to see her sad or upset. *The worst is over. No more tears.*

"Okay, Danson," she said now with a sniff. "No more tears."

Chin up, back straight, she set her jaw and fixed her

mind on what she knew. Grief, and playing the victim wouldn't change anything. She should have died, but here she was. She was alive.

And she would make it count for something.

Having returned to the house and now back inside, Lock replaced the flashlight where she'd found it next to the front door. There. Everything was back to the way it was to begin with. No big deal. Like her break down had never happened.

She crept quietly past Sly's bedroom door and retreated into her own room, shutting the door softly behind her. She quickly undressed and slipped back under the cold covers, using the last bit of strength she had to pull the covers up to her chin. She didn't even bother to adjust the numerous pillows she used for support around her.

She was asleep the moment her head hit the pillow.

Sly wasn't sure what had woken him at first. He had gotten home after a long day of counseling sessions and mounds of paperwork for the sheriff's department, then crawled into bed, not even bothering to change out of his nice clothes. By the glow of the clock across the room on his dresser, he saw that it was not even 2am yet. He'd only been asleep a couple hours. He lay there in the dark, listening to the sounds of the house, wondering if there had actually been anything that woke him. Then, he heard the loose floorboard in the kitchen squeak with a footstep, and the front door open and close a few seconds later.

Lock?

Had she gone outside?

He rolled out of bed and went out into the living room, standing in the dark as he listened. Then he saw the glow of the flashlight bouncing outside and he walked fast to the french doors at the back of the house and peered out through the curtains. He saw Lock's shadow running past, the light from the flashlight casting long beams of light across the back yard as she headed towards the back valley.

As a teenager, Lock would go running at all hours of the night if she couldn't sleep. She apparently had kept up the practice. Something must have been weighing heavy on her and she needed to clear her head.

"Lord, you've got to help her." He prayed, letting the curtains fall back into place.

He knew that despite Lock's return to her faith just a few hours earlier, there was still a lot that she was having to deal with. Praying for her had become a nightly thing for him over the past couple of years. He would wake up in the dead of the night with a pain in his stomach and Lock on his mind. He would get up, turn on a lamp in the living room, grab his Bible, and pace as he prayed. Sometimes for hours at a time. He wouldn't stop until he felt a release and peace wash over him.

Sly knew his niece better than anyone, and he had been able to tell, almost down to the minute, when she had walked away from her faith. It wasn't simply the fact that she had chosen to put God on the back burner and let sin steal her away that bothered him; everyone has their struggles. Life on earth isn't easy, and everyone at one time or another gets a little lost. What bothered him was what Lock's choices were doing to her and getting her involved in. She had stopped fighting the temptations and had allowed herself to be pulled into the rough, difficult world she lived in.

Ever since she was ten years old, Lock had declared that one day she would be a police officer. It was the only thing she had ever wanted to to, and it fit her. She had a toughness about her that came just as easily as laughter and kindness. She'd always had a desire to see the bullies lose and the little guy win.　　　When she had been in high-school, Lock had challenged the two main bullies in her freshmen class to a fight that would determine the rest of the school year. If she won, the two boys had to leave the nerds and the goths alone; if she lost, then she would pay the full amount of everyone's lunch money for the rest of the semester to the bullies.

But Lock had no intention of losing.

Sly had been there on the sidelines in the garage, making sure neither side got too violent once the fight started. As it turned out, after Lock kicked the first kid square in the chest and knocked the wind out of him, the second boy quickly bowed out of the fight and gave up before ever stepping foot in the ring. Lock had won, and the entire school had been freed from the oppressive bullies for the rest of the school year.

That's who Lock was. She wasn't afraid to stand up for what she believed in, and fight like hell to protect it. Even for nerds and geeks and outcasts in her school that she barely knew. She just wanted to protect them because no one else cared to do anything about it.

But as stubborn as Lock was, there was one chink in her armor; she hated not being liked. After she had gone to college, and then started her first year as a rookie at the CPD,

Sly had seen the fruit of what the big bad world had done to her; the world that made fun of you for having principles and demanded you try new things before you pass judgment. Lock had started out well and stood her ground for awhile, but then....she stopped fighting back. She had learned that to make friends, one had to compromise. Sly knew what it was like, having experienced a lot of the same pressures and taunting when he'd been in college. Lock didn't like being made fun of and being alienated for her faith. She wanted friends. And she was willing to make compromises here and there just so that she had some. She had a soft heart and thin skin, and a desire to be accepted. By the time Lock had teamed up with Danson, her resolve had weakened and she was tired of being the good girl all the time.

The way Lock talked about him, the man was a confident, cocky vet who drilled into her that she wasn't in Kansas anymore. Sometimes one had to cross the line to see results. On and off the job.

"You should see us out there on the street, Sly!" Lock would gush, "it's like we've been partners forever. And he knows things. If I stick with him, I'll make detective in no time!"

Officer Danson was a weathered, popular jock, and Lock, the lowly, awkward freshmen. He paid attention to her, feeding her lines that puffed up her head and gave her false hope. He'd encouraged her to try new things, push moral boundaries, and she'd chosen not to question any of it.

"You just don't understand what it's like, Sly. I'm not a little kid anymore."

Lock had started drinking to drive out the ghosts from hard nights on the beat. Her language had become foul, and she no longer sought to see both sides of an argument. She no

two bullets

longer saw broken people as victims; they were all possible suspects that she didn't have time to deal with.

Then, when Sly had confronted her and told her she no longer sounded or acted like a Christian, Lock had told him to go to hell and hung up the phone. It had broken his heart.

Only now, it wasn't just her seeing the light and returning to her Heavenly Father's loving arms that Sly had to pray for. It was for Lock's broken and betrayed heart. She had lost all of her friends, the ones she had compromised so dearly for. Danson had turned on her and committed the ultimate betrayal, pulling the proverbial rug out from under her entire world. For that, Sly wished he could exchange a few words with Officer Danson and inflict the same pain on him that he caused Lock.

"Lord, she's Yours. Remind her of that. Somehow You've got to show her that only You can give her what she needs. Help her find her way back, and then give her the strength to stand in it. You complete her. You have her back. Somehow God, show her that. Be her strong tower in the midst of this storm. And when it all blows over, I pray that she can stand tall and shine forth Your Light, Your love, Your Grace. In Jesus' Name, Amen."

"Lock," Sly began before either of them had taken a bite of breakfast, "are you okay?"

She sat across from him at the dining table, crowded

into the tiny nook between the kitchen and living room. At the probing question, her thoughts flashed to her run through the back forty last night. She cleared her throat, eyes down on her unbuttered toast. "No. Not really."

"I heard you go out last night, something on your mind?"

She stabbed a clump of eggs with her fork and plopped them into her mouth. "What isn't on my mind?"

Sly held up a hand, "Okay, that was a bad way to ask the question." He continued to eye her, the tip of his tongue rubbing a back molar. Lock kept her head down, eyes concentrated on her plate as she pushed around her food with her fork, seeing them without really seeing them. Then she sighed, dropping her fork as she looked around the room.

"I just don't get it. Yesterday was so good for me! I feel like I finally got it, you know? Then last night it's like the hammer dropped and just obliterated everything. I just wanted to feel okay for half a second..."

"That's what the enemy does, Lock. He comes after a breakthrough and knocks us back to our knees and makes us question everything. He reminds us of our wrongs and makes us think there's no actual hope."

Lock rolled her eyes as she bobbed her head, "He certainly did that." Then she spoke in barely a whisper, "I feel like I'm a crazy person."

"You're definitely not crazy."

Lock heard him and nodded. But she was too caught up in her own head to really let the words sink in. She didn't like this conversation; she didn't like how it made her feel. She just wanted to go back to bed and start the day over. She glanced up over Sly's head at the clock hanging above the sink. "You should probably get to work. It's almost eleven."

two bullets

Lock was avoiding him, and he knew it. Sly sighed, "Lock..."

Immediately, she pushed back from the table and stood as she said, "I'm going to go shower. I'll text with you later." The she turned and left the room, leaving Sly sitting alone in the empty room, listening to the distant ticking of the clock.

Sly finally shook his head, staring after the trail of smoke Lock had left behind in her hasty get away. "Just hang in there, Lock. It will get better."

Chapter Eleven

Wednesday

Jimmie and Bass were on lunch, sitting together at the bar of Mosley's Diner, both men looking at their phones as they waited for their food. Bass was checking the stats on his favorite sports team back home, not liking what he was seeing when the sound of Jimmie cursing under his breath pulled him back to reality. He turned his head. "You alright?"

"It's been three days and still no one has heard from Jamie." Jimmie dropped his phone with a clatter to the counter and groaned, rubbing a hand over his face.

Bass clicked off his own phone and the screen went black, turning his full attention to his friend. "Still nothing, huh?"

Jimmie just shook his head and reached for his glass.

"I don't even know what to think anymore," he said, after the waitress had brought them their food. "Is it awful of me to hope she's never comes back?"

Bass kept his attention on the salt he was shaking onto his hash browns as he considered the question. "Well, you have to protect the kids. That's priority number one."

"But she's my sister," Jimmie protested. "Shouldn't I be out there scouring the hills for her?" Bass had never heard Jimmie sound so desperate. He was talking out of both sides of his mouth, saying he wished his sister wouldn't come home, then immediately arguing with his friend when Bass agreed with him.

Bass shrugged his shoulders, keeping his attention on

his food as he said quietly, "Jimmie, you tell me what you want me to say and I'll say it."

"Tell me I'm not a horrible brother for letting things get this bad. That in the end this isn't my fault."

Bass could do that, especially since it was the truth. He looked at his partner straight in the eye. "You're not a horrible brother. And it's not your fault things have gotten the way they are. Jamie is sick. All the love in the world you could possibly give to her still wouldn't change the fact that she has decided to sleep with her demons. I know you, Jim, and you've done the best you can."

Jimmie's head drooped softly over his plate, defeat relaxing his shoulders, and he nodded. Then he straightened and cleared his throat. He didn't say anything, and neither did Bass. They didn't have to. They ate their food in silence then, watching the fish in the large fish tank behind the counter swim in lazy trails.

The bell over the entrance jingled behind them, announcing a new patron's entry.

"Hey, Bon," a waitress behind the counter called with a wave.

"Howdy, Miss Emma," the vagabond in a droopy hat called back with a toothless grin. Recognizing the hoarse voice, Bass spun around on his stool, cheek full with a bite of chicken fried steak. "Hey, Bon!"

"Deputy," Bon nodded, shuffling from the entrance. He nodded at Jimmie who had also turned around, "Deputy number two."

"Bon," Jimmie said, returning the nod.

Ribbon "Bon" Shifter was a character with no equal, with lips that flapped like wind-sails when he talked on account of his nearly empty gums. He was a Barrier Ridge

two bullets

man, born and raised, and had seen the town grow from just a few shacks and a bar into the booming lumber town it had been for the last fifty years or so. He had been an important man back in the day, or so went the legend, but the bottle had taken control of him sometime back, and now was rarely ever seen sober except on Sunday's. Seeing as how today was Wednesday, his clothes reeked of liquor and his eyes had a glaze to them, but he walked a straight line and talked without a slur.

"Beautiful day out there," Bon said, tipping his hat with a knobby finger.

Bass looked out the nearest window to see it pouring down rain and lightening flashing across the black sky. He nodded. "Gorgeous..."

"What happened, Bon," Jimmie asked in good fun, "they kick you out of the pub early today?"

"Just making the rounds, Deputy-number-two; no reason to get all smart with me. I'm still your elder."

Jimmie glanced over at Bass and chuckled.

"What *are* you doing out in this weather, Bon?" Bass asked, hiding a smirk.

"Oh, just making the rounds, ya know." the man replied in a cheerful, high and scratchy voice. "Stopped in to see old Humphrey at the barber shop, didn't have time to stay for a cut though," He winked and gave his hat a nudge, revealing the strands of wild, white hair poking out over his ears. A days worth of stubble grew on his double chin.

"Then, I wandered over that way, and then back that way..." The man swung his arms around, looking like the Scarecrow from The Wizard of Oz trying to give directions. Town drunk or not, the man had a way of making even the hardest soul smile at least once.

two bullets

"Oh!" Bon suddenly exclaimed and reached his hand into the back pocket of his pants, pulling out a small note card. He read it, squinting as he brought it all the way up to the end of his nose. "Uh-huh, that's it." He dropped his hand with the card and exclaimed, "I came in here to see you!"

Honestly surprised, Bass asked with wide eyes, "You had to write that down?"

"Wha..?" The man gaped at him as if he didn't understand, then looked down at his hand. He jumped as if he'd never seen the card before. Then he stuffed the paper back into his pocket as he said, "Oh that. That's nothing, just my grocery list."

Jimmie mumbled something into his coffee about there only being alcohol on the list, but Bon didn't pay him any mind. "T's wanted to tell you I talked to my brother BoDine today. He lives over in Beckworth, ya know. Funniest thing, I reckon."

The man stopped talking, folded his lips in between his gums, and with eyes green as emeralds, looked back and forth between Bass and Jimmie. Eyes rounded, Bass slowly nodded his head, hoping to encourage the man to finish what he was saying and explain. But Bon just stood there, hands thrust into his tattered suit coat pockets, blinking long and hard between glances.

"...and what did Bo say?" Bass finally said, trying very hard not to laugh in the poor man's face.

Blink. "What did Bo say about what?"

"Well he called you, right?" Jimmie asked, his irritation with life showing in the lines of his furrowed brow as he turned on the stool.

"He did! But how did you know that?"

Jimmie gave up, throwing up his hands as he spun

two bullets

back to the counter, "I quit."

Bon suddenly let out a cackle, laughing a good belly laugh at his own joke, "I'm just messing with you, Jimmie-Ol'-girl. I've still got three beers before I'm that bad."

"Bon," Bass called, bringing the man back to task, "what was it you wanted to tell us about Bo?"

"He knows where you can find those bikers ye been looking for," the man said matter-of-factly. Now he had their attention. Jimmie shared a look with Bass as he slowly spun himself back around to face the drunk. "You might have wanted to lead with that."

"Well, I was starting to, but then you had to go asking all your distracting questions, trying to confuse me."

Bass held up a hand before Jimmie could dole out a retort. "Go on, Bon," he nodded, "tell us the rest."

"Well, it would seem that there has been a lot of traffic coming and going out of that Pure Nations compound just outside Beckworth. Ya follow?"

"It's taking me a few wrong turns, Bon, but I'm following."

"Now Bo doesn't know much; poor kid got dropped on his head when he was a pup, but the way he tells it, there's been some unusual looking characters staying out there. Now, you know that those racist White Heads only let their kinds of people up there; everyone else gets shot on sight. You gotta have a card and the blood of a goat in the shape of a V across your chest-"

Bon kept going while Jimmie leaned over to Bass and mumbled, "If he's right, we're going to have to go out there."

"I know." Bass whispered back. The last time law enforcement had dared confronting the leader of the local White Society group, bullets had flown for the sake of

two bullets

"trespassing," never mind the warrant being issued. If members of the Demon Troop were hiding out there, another visit could easily result in the same welcome.

"-and it's basically all about that there that we know," Bon finished.

"How many bikers did you say?" Jimmie asked.

"Oooh, quite a few"

Jimmie looked at Bass. "It could be them. There were five bikes on that footage at the gas station, heading west."

Bass nodded in agreement. Jimmie turned around to the bar, pulling out his wallet to pay the bill, and to have them throw on a steak dinner for Bon in payment for his help.

Bass stood and grabbed his coat from the stool next to him.

"You've been a big help today, Bon." Bass said as he angled for the entrance. "Dinner's on us. Let Bo know we appreciate his loyalty. Keep this to yourself, you hear me? Not a word to anyone."

Jimmie walked by Bon then, stopping to fix the poorly tied tie hanging crooked from the old man's neck. He straightened it as he said, "You're a good man, Bon. Don't ever stop being you."

Then he clamped a hand on both the man's arms and nodded good-bye before stepping away. He caught up with Bass who was standing outside, holding the door open as he waited.

"Bon Shifter." Bass said, completely amazed that the first lead they had in days came from the town drunk purely by chance. He pulled out his keys as they started for the squad car.

"God bless Bon," Jimmie replied with a grin, then like two kids let out of school early, they took off running across

two bullets

the parking lot, exhilarating excitement surging through them.

The small community of Beckworth was over the mountain and through the woods, and a good twenty minute drive west of Barrier Ridge. Beckworth was a ranching community, while Barrier Ridge was a lumber town. With mutual respect and honor, both townships kept to their own space and followed the rules, knowing that each one was doing its own thing for their respective communities.

All the years of logging in the eastern slopes of the Chelan mountains had forced much of the wildlife out to both the north and west, where roads became scarce and man had yet to defile. This meant that while wildlife was scarce around Barrier Ridge, the fur trade was booming in Beckworth.

Barrier Ridge's lumber mill was one of the last of its kind, but had somehow managed to stay afloat during the Mountain Pine Beetle infestation of '98. Beckworth had opened its arms to the many unemployed Barrier Ridge mill workers until logging picked back up, creating a lasting bond between the two towns.

Ten miles just short of Beckworth's town limits, a gravel road branched off the main highway and followed a snaking river up and around and deeper into the mountain folds, pressing in deeper and deeper into the Yukon Forest. Harkin Mountain loomed ahead, rising up like a great creature from the sea of lower mountain ranges and surrounding forests.

Around a sharp turn on the narrow road, with a steep cliff on the right and a rock face on the left, a road appeared out of nowhere just where the rock face ended and a sloping hill of trees began. Bass slowed the car and took the turn, seeing the handmade sign bent backward next to the road:

The Order of the Pure Church.
Two Miles Ahead.
Only Whites Allowed.
All Others Will Be Hung By The Neck Until Dead.

"Well doesn't that just make you feel all warm and fuzzy on the inside," Jimmie said, slipping on a pair of black wool gloves and a matching skull cap. Bass was nodding his agreement of distaste when he saw the color of things Jimmie was putting on.

"Black? Really? You didn't have anything white? Are you trying to get us shot on sight?"

"It's all you had in your duffel bag. You don't like it, be more prepared next time we go cruising into white pride territory."

It was so dark for the dark clouds and the dense forest around them that Bass had to turn on the headlights. After going over one more hill, there came a turn in the road. Bass took the turn, but suddenly in front of the car rose a tall gate blocking the road. It came up so fast around the corner that Bass had to slam on the brakes. Both men were thrust forward, then slammed back into their seats, the nose of the car only a few inches short of the gate.

"There's a gate there," Jimmie groaned, rubbing his neck.

Bass twisted in his seat to look out behind them, then back at the white gate. "I didn't even see it. I thought it was the road." He shifted into reverse and rolled the car back a little and stopped.

"You thought the road was white and shiny?" Jimmie teased as Bass put the car in park.

"It was a short corner! I thought maybe they got snow up here or something." Bass opened his door and stepped out, Jimmie following from the other side.

"I'm just saying, maybe I should drive back down. There might be potholes that you think are oil stains or something."

On his side of the car, Bass stood with his hands on his hips, thoughtfully looking up at the tops of the trees. He listened carefully to the silence around them, taking in every smell and everything he saw with analytical prowess. He looked back down at the gate in front of him, biting his lip.

"You know," he said, "you sound more and more like Jack every day. What is it with you guys having to be so cynical all the time?"

"Jack is cynical; I'm a realist."

"Same thing."

"It's how I know you've got a thing for Sly's niece. The cute blonde one."

Bass gave no obvious reaction, looking at the gate's heavy-duty chain hanging from the top and looping down through a gnarly barbed-wire fence grown over by a common hawthorn. He took a step forward, touching it with his hand as he said, "And tell me how either of those two things have anything to do with the other?"

Jimmie stood in front of the car, leaning back on the hood. "Because I know you. I know how you work. I mean, I don't blame you; she's hot. I'm just saying, something has changed since she's come around."

"With me?"

"With everyone. It's like she cast a spell over everyone. I don't know what it is exactly, but there's been a shift in the universe."

The lock on the gate was locked up tight, with rust working its way up the prongs and had leached onto the chain itself. This gate hadn't been unlocked for some time, which meant either he had taken a wrong turn, or there was another entrance into the compound.

"Does any of this look familiar to you?" Bass asked, turning around, his back to the sheet metal gate, staring back down the road behind the car.

Jimmie stepped away from the car to turn and follow Bass's gaze. "Um...maybe?"

Bass's eyes narrowed. "Something's wrong. This gate hasn't been opened in awhile, and with all your rambling going on, we should have ten White Heads pointing their pitchforks at us by now."

"Well maybe you took a wrong turn somewhere."

"Maybe," Bass replied, slowly taking a step or two forward, eyes now on the dense forest surrounding them.

"Or maybe they moved on out of here."

"Yeah," Bass said absently. He ran his eyes up and down the forest's edge but saw nothing lurking in the shadows and turned back towards the car. "Or maybe Bon Shifter set us up."

"You mean Bo."

"Either one."

"But that's impossible, right? I mean, we know the Pure Nation chapter is up here. It has been since I was a kid.

We just saw the sign for it."

"I know," Bass replied, chewing on the inside of his cheek. He turned to lean the front of his body against the car, hands laying out on the roof. His head was on a swivel. Something didn't feel right.

Jimmie then moved to copy Bass's stance, leaning against the car with his fingers laced, arms resting on the roof. His head was turned away from Bass, looking over towards the gate. When he spoke it was so faint that Bass almost missed it.

"Over my right shoulder. Thirty paces out and up."

Bass didn't move his eyes right away to the spot. He looked over his own shoulder behind him, then up, then over, then around, and along the way found the spot Jimmie had called out. Bass didn't see anything until he moved slightly to the left, then he caught the reflection of something like metal or glass about halfway up a tree.

He pulled his left arm back to rest his temple against his fist, letting his right hand lazily drift down from the hood and rest on his side arm. "Sniper?" He mumbled.

Jimmie shrugged. "It's not where I'd be, but it'll do in a pinch."

"Can biker's even climb trees?" Bass asked.

"Bass," Jimmie scoffed in dismay, his tone drawing Bass's eyes up from the peeling paint on the roof. Jimmie tilted his head, "Come on now; that's racist."

Bass just smiled. "You see anything else out there?"

Jimmie shook his head ever so slightly. "Nah. He's alone."

"On the count of three, then?"

Jimmie sniffed. "Takes too long."

As if set on a spring, both men pulled their guns and cleared their holsters, aiming together for that spot in the trees.

two bullets

"Barrier Ridge County Sheriff," Jimmie called out good and loud, his voice thundering. "Show yourself!"

Footsteps crunched in the underbrush, and like an army of ghosts, tree after tree bore a man stepping out of hiding. There were eight men all together, each brandishing their weapons like clubs, a few brave enough to actually hold the weapon on the two deputies.

"He's alone, huh?" Bass murmured.

"Yeah... I could have been off by a few."

Chapter Twelve

They were out-manned and out-gunned, but Bass and Jimmie didn't waver. They kept their guns trained on the men dressed in camouflage, standing before them like practice targets lined up along the forest edge. There was not a full head of hair in the bunch; all of them bore shaved heads, though most of them wore hats for the cold spring weather. They all stared at the two deputies like a bunch of back-woods hillbillies who'd never seen city folk. Bass wouldn't have guessed any of them to be over thirty years of age.

The Gate Keepers. The Watchers of the Gate. Whatever they called themselves, they were definitely not friendly, and wanted nothing to do with newcomers.

Bass could hear his pulse beating in his ears. His gun sat heavy in his hand, but he dare not drop it. Not yet.

No one spoke. No threats were hurled across battle lines. No ultimatums were given. It was just a good, old fashioned stare down.

Then, from the direction of the gate came a loud whirring sound, like that of an engine. Bass knew better than to look, but then came a loud, metallic crash and the whirring changed. Then the middle half of the gate began to lift up off the ground and then rotate over like a garage door.

It was a hidden door, within a door. Clever.

An army jeep, low to the ground with no roof or windshield, came buzzing up and slipped easily enough under the horizontal piece of gate and pulled off to the side.

"Gentlemen," a man in a dress shirt and pleated pants

called, stepping out of the passenger side, "State your business. Quickly now, before my men tire of looking at you."

"Sheriff's Department. We'd like to have a word," Jimmie called over his shoulder, not ready to turn his attention away from the wall of men.

"I can see that, son, by your car. Now, what do two Zionist Imperialists have reason for coming up here and disrupting our prayer service?"

Bass spoke now. "We mean no disrespect Sir, we just have questions is all. There was a shooting a week ago in Barrier Ridge. We have reason to believe some of the men responsible may be taking refuge up here."

"And how did you come across that notion?"

Bass flashed the man a smile, "It's a small town, Mister. Hard to keep secrets around here."

This humored the man and he smiled, dropping his head. Then he lifted his hand up over his head and waved.

"Fall back. They mean us no harm," he called, and his men back at the forest obeyed, slipping back out the same way they had come through the trees.

Bass and Jimmie both lowered their guns slowly. Bass went ahead and holstered his weapon as he turned around to offer his hand to the leader, "Deputy Bastion Jones."

The older man shook his hand. "Reverend Lee Banks," he said flatly. "This doesn't mean we're friends, deputy." He had close cropped gray hair, and silver wire glasses over gray eyes. Even the man's skin appeared gray.

Jimmie stepped up then, his gun back in his holster and also shook reverend's hand. "Lieutenant Reeves. Nice gate."

Lee smirked. "Thank you. We like it."

"Must be hard to get your tanks in through there

though." Jimmie said, purposefully trying to get a rise out of the man.

"Like I said earlier, Mr. Banks;" Bass went on, "we're here looking for a particular group of men. They're bikers from out of Reno. We don't have anything on you or your group, we'd just like to look around."

Lee's eyes narrowed at him. "And I assume my word on the matter that we are not harboring a band of outlaw bikers won't mean much to you."

"We prefer to do our own fact checking." Jimmie said with an encouraging nod.

Lee sighed. "Well, on any other day I might be persuaded otherwise, but like I told you earlier, we are in the middle of a special service. I don't have the time or the men to show you around."

"That's fine," Jimmie assured him, "we can take care of ourselves."

Banks smiled, fully aware of what Jimmie was trying to do. "No members of the Z.O.G. will be allowed to traipse around behind these walls. You have my word on that, Deputy."

Just then a radio squelched from the hip of Lee's driver, still sitting in the running jeep, and he held it to his ear. Then he jumped from the vehicle, hurrying up to his boss, "Mr. Banks, it's Rochelle... she's taken a turn."

Banks gave the young kid in camo green a hard look, but the kid only nodded, obviously feeling terrible for the news he was passing along. Banks recovered from his shock before turning back to face Bass and Jimmie. "I'm sorry but I need to get back to my people. You know your way out?"

"What's wrong?" Bass asked, stepping after the retreating religious leader.

"It's family." The Reverend called back, waving the

deputy off. "It doesn't concern you."

"Mister, we're deputy's. It's our job to help people." Jimmie said, standing in front of the Jeep now with his hand on the green hood. "I have some medical experience, if that counts for anything."

Were Reverend Banks not dealing with the pain of possibly losing his only child, he might have thought that maybe the only reason the deputies were offering to help was so they could do some sneaking around.

But, Banks wasn't thinking straight now, or "Johnny-On-The-Spot", and in a move that surprised his driver, he nodded. "Okay, but you stay where I can see you. If you can help her, then maybe I'll let you look around."

"Reverend!" The driver exclaimed in horror. As far as Bass knew, no law enforcement officers had ever stepped foot onto the compound with a welcome. Banks held up his hand to silence the driver and nodded to Jimmie and Bass. They wasted no time and hurried back to their car before Banks came to his senses.

The renowned "Pure Nation Compound" was nothing more than threadbare tents, and rickety old shacks held together by duct-tape, looking like a mix between a junkyard and a campground. American made vehicle parts, new and old, lay strewn about and in piles in the open spaces that weren't taken up by tents or cabins. The only nice and new looking thing in the place was a large shop, made entirely out of sheet metal and painted red. Blood red; a coincidence that Bass didn't think was unintentional. He wondered why the members of the group didn't all just move into the shop, especially in this rainy weather. It would easily hold them all; twenty families or so.

He parked on the left side of the building in the grass

next to Bank's jeep, and they hurried out to follow the reverend inside. In a surprising twist, the inside of the shop was painted entirely black. Black walls, black ceiling, even the concrete floor was painted a glossy black. The deputies didn't have time to dwell on the strange interior design, but it was shocking. String lights hung on ever seal in the place, outlining the walls and roof and floor. Four large florescent lights hung down from the ceiling. It brightened the room, but with no windows it still felt like a cave.

At the far back of the building, a crowd of people stood gathered around. With the entrance of their leader, all heads turned around to watch him pass by. When they saw the two deputies following along behind, they stopped and stared.

As they neared the crowd, a man with broad shoulders and a receding hairline stepped forward. "You brought the Z.O.G. here? I thought you said we weren't ever to bring in outside help."

"Extenuating circumstances, Paul. They're alright for now." Banks assured the man.

For now. Bass and Jimmie both shared a quick glance. They had to be on their best behavior now.

Reverend Banks made his way through the parting crowd to what looked like a low stage built at the end of the room. The deputies now could see a sleeping bag laying on a pallet on the stage. A young girl, maybe seven or eight, lay inside, the bag zipped up to her chin. Her eyes were closed and she shivered, sweat glistening off her tiny forehead.

A woman stepped forward out of the crowd, eyes red from crying and she clutched the reverend tightly as she wailed, "She won't wake up! My poor baby! Lee, what are we going to d-o-o-o?" She collapsed into the man's arms and sobbed, smothering her face into his chest. He patted her back and turned to Bass, jerking his head for them to go on to the girl.

Bass nodded and slipped around the grieving couple and hurried up the shallow two steps onto the stage and knelt beside the girl. Something crunched under his boots, and he realized there were pine needles and salt sifted around the bed like a halo.

He reached out and touched the girl's head. She was burning up with a fever.

"How long has she been like this?" He asked, hand on the girl's chest over the sleeping bag as he looked over his shoulder at the leader.

"She got the fever last night. But she's been ill for three days."

"What's her name?" Jimmie asked, his voice low, now kneeling on the other side from Bass.

"Rochelle."

"What are you thinkin', partner?" Bass asked only loud enough for Jimmie to hear. Jimmie thoughtfully shook his head, prying the girls eyelids open to see her eyes.

"It could be a lot of things," he replied, then he said in a louder voice up to Lee, "she needs a doctor. And I mean yesterday. Why haven't you taken her?"

Lee started to shake his head, but the man named Paul stepped in then, having followed them through the crowd. "There's a black man working at the hospital. He'll kill her if he gets the chance. Men like that shouldn't be doctors. Ain't smart enough. The government gives them a free pass, even though they fail the medical boards."

Bass scoffed, a guttural clearing of his throat. "You ever gone to medical school, Paul? Ever taken the exams?"

The man pulled up at this, but shook his head.

146

"Then don't talk about what you don't know." Then to Lee, "She needs antibiotics. Her body's trying to fight off something, but she can't do it on her own."

The woman still clinging to him wailed loudly now, and Lee held her tighter, biting his lip, but shook his head. "She stays here. If God sees fit to take my little girl, that's his business. But she won't die in some sterile hospital."

"Sterile is the key word there," Bass growled over his shoulder. His patience was gone, replaced with contempt for these people who were basically killing their child for the sake of their misguided beliefs. "You said earlier this was a worship service. You all are here praying for her I assume? If you believe God has made her sick, then why bother praying for her at all?"

Lee had no reply. Bass looked from him to the crowd surrounding them, but they all averted their gaze from his, worry and fear etched on every face. Then a woman with a mouse brown pony tail and a tattered sweatshirt stepped forward from her spot at the front of the crowd. "It's her leg."

Paul, who was standing right next to her, suddenly spun around and back handed the woman with a mighty smack. "He didn't ask you, woman. Step back and shut up!"

"Hey!" Bass barked as he rose to his feet, ready to face off with the man. Paul stayed where he was, arm still on it's way down from the follow through, his head snapping back around at Bass's call. Bass gave him a warning look, then with a much softer impression, he looked to the short lady and bobbed his head. "I'm asking you. What about her leg?"

The woman's eyes flitted nervously from up at Paul and back to Bass, shoulders hunched with her hands thrust down into the sweatshirt pocket. She wanted to speak, but Paul's correction still stung and she shook her head.

"Bass." Jimmie called in an even tone. Bass turned around, about to speak, but then stopped. Jimmie had unzipped the sleeping bag all the way down and had flipped it open to reveal the little girl's legs. The outer side of the girl's left calf was nearly black. Bass thought it a shadow at first, but then came the stench. His stomach turned. Gangrene. The infection ran from the knee all the way down to the ankle, and was working it's way across the top of her foot. His heart sank and broke all at the same time.

"How could you let it get this bad?" He demanded to those behind him, but no one answered. Then the woman with the pony-tail found a bit of courage.

"She fell off her bike and broke her leg. We didn't notice the infection until two days ago."

Scenarios ran through Bass's mind in the same amount of time it took him to take in two breaths. Lee Banks was never going to agree to them taking the girl to the hospital. It was out of the question. He could make an executive decision and sweep the girl up and take her to the car, but every man, and possibly woman, in the building was armed. They'd never make it to the door alive.

The other option was to just turn around and leave. But in reality, that wasn't actually an option.

As bad as the rot in that leg was, the only logical answer would be to cut it off. But Bass didn't have the stomach for it, and neither would Jimmie, no matter how logical a decision.

There was a fourth option, but it was risky for many different reasons.

Bass turned around before he could talk himself out of it, and looked Lee dead in the eye. "You don't know me, but I have to ask you for a favor. Can you trust me?"

two bullets

The man frowned, pulled between wanting to save his daughter, and wanting to save face in front of his people and god. Bass didn't give him time to answer. "I need everyone to leave. Now. Get out, except for you and your wife. You're the parents, correct?"

Lee nodded slowly. Bass turned to the crowd and addressed them as a whole, "Everyone out, right now! Go out side and let us help Rochelle."

Chapter Thirteen

No one moved. No one even blinked. Bass felt ridiculous with his hands up in the air like Moses parting the Red Sea. He dropped his hands and looked at Lee. "If you want her to live, you'll do what I say."

A second passed. Then three seconds. Then twenty. Lee finally sighed and nodded. "Leave us."

Hesitantly, the crowd began to move, slowly at first, then all at once, backing away and pushing for the door.

Bass turned and rushed back down to take a knee next to the girl. Jimmie rocked back on his heels, still crouched on the other side of the dying girl.

"What exactly do you have up your sleeve, Deputy?"

Bass's body had taken on an unintentional shiver. Who did he think he was? He touched his hand once again to the girl's forehead, and she moaned.

"We're going to pray, Jimmie. We are going to pray to *our* God, and He's going to heal this little girl." The idea had pressed upon him every second he sat with the girl. He was no prophet, but he knew when God was talking to him.

Shock and a little bit of fear shot through Jimmie, leaking out onto the expression on his face. He gaped across at his friend. But then, his faith was activated inside of him, and he was on-board. He didn't know if he had the great faith required to make the worst stage of gangrene he had ever seen disappear, but he had gone through the same scenarios in his mind as Bass had, and he knew they were out of choices.

"Alright, Bass," Jimmie finally said, "I'm with you."

two bullets

Bass nodded, boldness rising in him. "Go out to the car and get in my tactical bag. In the front pocket there's a small New Testament. Get it."

Jimmie was up and gone before Bass had finished, running for the side door they had come through. Bass didn't even turn around to look behind him at Lee and his wife. His eyes were on Rochelle, and he began to gently stroke back her damp hair, closing his eyes as he murmured, "Okay God, it's your turn. You love this little girl, even if her parent's are stupid. We need a miracle. Your Word says that we will lay hands on the sick and they will recover." Bass stopped and cleared his throat nervously. He opened his eyes and gazed down at the young, innocent face in front of him.

Would this work?

If it didn't, Lee Banks would certainly hang him and Jimmie.

"Oh God in Heaven, what have I gotten myself into?"

These are my people, Son. They're lost, just like you were once. I have given you all authority on heaven and earth. Rochelle will live, and it will be a testimony to her family. I brought you here at this time, on this day, to do My will.

Bass had never before heard the Lord speak so clearly to him in the way he was now. It was like a voice in his head, and he knew it wasn't his own thoughts. It wasn't up to Bass to perform the healing; he was just an instrument, and this revelation brought some peace.

Jimmie had returned to the shop with the small Bible and showed it Bass with a wave. "I got it."

Bass nodded, turning on his heels to scoot closer to the putrid leg. "Just start reading. Anything you can think of on healing. The gospels when Jesus went around healing people. Just read."

He had taken off his coat, then peeled off his warm layers down to his undershirt, and pulled it off, instantly shivering as cold air passed over his exposed skin. He slipped back on the two long-sleeved shirts, but didn't take time to adjust them. With his boots he scraped away the pine needles underfoot as he got in as close as his nose would let him, ripping his t-shirt into strips. He laid them each out in turn over the rotting flesh, lips moving in a silent prayer. When the white strips covered the leg from the knee down, he moved back up and took the girl's small, warm hand into his own and cupped it.

"Sweetie, just listen to my voice. You have been lied to. There is a God in heaven who loves you. Not because of the color of your skin, but because you are His child. His will is for you to live, not to die." Then he once again closed his eyes and still holding her hand, reached with the other and laid it on her forehead, muttering in words not found in the English language. Jimmie was reading quietly, unable to think of any particular scriptures and had just started reading where the book opened. He was reading the story of Jesus cleansing a leper, and Bass nodded. "Jesus, you healed a man who's body was riddled with leprosy. You restored his rotting flesh with fresh, clean skin. Thank you that nothing is too big for you, and no sickness is too great."

He ignored the leg now, and didn't look under the t-shirt bandages. Either God was going to heal her or not. Stealing peeks wouldn't change that.

The sound of shoes scraping concrete came from behind Bass, and then Lee's voice broke through. "Oh my god. What is that?"

Bass could feel it too. It was like the entire shop around them was buzzing with electricity. He looked over at Jimmie, who had stopped reading. Matching grins broke out across their faces. Bass turned his head to peer over his shoulder as he said to Lee, "That's the power of God, Lee. The real kind, not the kind you try to conjure up with pine needles and sea salt."

"Make it stop!" Lee cried.

"Shut up, man," Jimmie growled, "don't you see? This is the real God. He's here, and He's healing your daughter." Then he dropped his voice and leaned in close to whisper at Bass, "Are you kidding me right now? Have you ever seen anything like this?!"

Bass grinned, giddy as a child at what was happening in front of his own eyes.

Where two or more are gathered, there I am in their midst, came the scripture, recalled to Bass's memory. This wasn't anything of his own doing. This wasn't magic, or conjuring spirits; this was Jesus. This was what true faith and walking in it was like. This is what being a Christian was all about, but only a few had ever experienced it.

Hillary, Lee's wife suddenly began to weep openly, falling to her knees next to her husband, overwhelmed by the warm, comforting presence of the living, breathing, true God. All of them that lived here, because of Lee and his twisting of the Bible to fit his racist propaganda, had only ever known God to be something like that of a sword wielding King high up in heaven, who demanded blood and vengeance. For years they had been under this oppression, the same they had brought on to Barrier Ridge all those years ago. After that traveling evangelist had come through and brought the real Gospel to the people, Lee Banks and the remaining members of his group had retreated to the hills, no longer having any control on the will of the people. This was a mini version of the great revival, and the irony wasn't lost on Bass.

Bass was nearly in tears himself, but he kept on praying, talking to Rochelle and keeping her burning hand in his cold one. Jimmie stopped reading, his curiosity getting the better of him and he set the book aside as he leaned over and pulled back a corner of what was left of Bass's t-shirt. He sucked air.

"Bass!" he hissed, "look!"

Bass was suddenly afraid to look, but he knew he had to. He shifted his weight and leaned over to see. What had once been melting, rotting flesh, was now a dark shade of brown. The texture of the skin was still mangled and pitted, but there was definitely a change. Assurance rushed through him. "It's healing," he said. "It's working!"

The temperature of Rochelle's skin was still warm, but not burning to the touch. Her breathing was less haggard and she seemed to have relaxed a little, though her eyes remained closed.

"What do we do?" Jimmie asked.

"Yeah, God," Bass whispered, "what do we do?"

Tell her to wake up.

"Rochelle?" Bass said gently, leaning his entire upper body over the girl, staring hard down into her face as his hands hovered around her head. "Wake up, honey. Come on. Let me see what color those beautiful eyes are. In the name of Jesus, wake up!"

two bullets

The girl sucked in a sputtering breath, her lips parting slightly as she breathed in. How close had she been to death? Hours? Minutes? They may never know.

"Atta' girl. Come on. Wake up. Open your eyes."

Her eyelids suddenly popped open, her eyes rolling back down from out of her head, revealing bright blue eyes, clear and open. She gasped.

"Hey, sweetie."

"Mama?" She asked in a thin, frail voice.

"Oh my god!!" Hillary cried and rushed forward, nearly pushing Bass out of her way as she laid herself over Rochelle and pulled her up in a hard embrace.

Leaving them to have their moment, Bass stood and moved down to the girl's lower half to look at her legs. Slowly, with unsure hands, he once again pulled away the strips of fabric. From the knee down to her foot, her skin was now flaky, gray like ash, and he carefully flicked away a few pieces. A black line like a vein still remained, set deep into the mangled flesh, but Bass was sure that even as he watched, it began to fade.

"That's right," he said, "you just keep fading."

Lock thought that with Sly gone to work and the house all to herself that she would feel content and relaxed. But a shadow had passed over her soul ever since she'd woke up and she couldn't seem to shake it.

two bullets

It was hard when Sly was around. Her uncle meant well, but she was still getting used to them getting along again, and she'd forgotten just how intuitive he was.

And positive.

And upbeat.

Last night had brought yet another nightmare, identical to the one the night before. A replay scene for scene of the shooting. She had thought that since a run the first time had helped clear her head, she'd try it again, despite the pouring rain. She was regretting it now. She'd pushed her body to it's limit and it was telling her in dramatic fashion. After spending an hour or so in the bathtub, she stepped out onto the rug and slowly dried herself off. She stepped into the sweatpants and immediately was hit with a sharp pain inching it's way through her belly and she gasped.

After a moment, she could see again and she finished pulling on the pants. Irritation washed over her then. She was mad at her life, mad at her own weak mind, frustrated that after all her spiritual progress, she still felt like a worthless pile of garbage. Traces of the nightmare still trailed through her mind, always right there to draw her back in when she thought she was fine. It was a constant reminder as to why she was here.

She grumbled and fought with the shirt she was trying to pull over her head with one hand. Her body ached and protested with every movement; her payment for going out and running when she knew full well that she was in no state to do such a thing. The fading, healing scars were false advertising and made her think she was much more healthy than she really was.

Once again blinding pain shot through her. She suddenly became very dizzy and nauseous, rushing to the toilet just in time. Weak and overcome in shivers, she numbly climbed her way back up to the sink and gulped down a handful of water.

Light-headed and feeling like every ounce of blood had rushed to her head, she dropped back down onto the floor, unable to keep herself on her feet. If she could get herself to the couch, she could snuggle under a blanket and give in to the exhaustion that weighed down her eyelids. She crawled up onto all fours and started making her way out of the bathroom into the hall. But soon she could no longer hold herself up, and the soft carpet under her called her down into it's weave. She laid her head down and the soft carpet accepted her as one of it's own and she closed her eyes, letting the pain overtake her.

*　　*　　*　　*

Bass didn't want to go home. After returning from the compound and telling the sheriff all that they had experienced, Cassidy gave him and Jimmie the rest of the evening off, telling them to go home and decompress. But as Bass stepped outside with Jimmie and waved good-bye, the thought of going home to an empty house with nothing to do just didn't sound inviting.

Putting the key in the ignition and turning on the radio, Bass didn't think about his next move very thoroughly, he just put the Ford in drive and pulled out of the parking lot. Sly's vehicle was parked in front of the church as Bass drove by, and he knew Lock was probably alone at the house, climbing the walls with nothing to do. Maybe she would like some company.

two bullets

He stopped at Mosley's diner and grabbed some food for the both of them, hoping Lock would be okay with him ordering for her.

Turning onto Sly's road, Bass drove up the drive he had driven a hundred times, only this time feeling rather nervous. He liked Lock. A lot. He had a few reservations, such as where she stood when it came to her faith, and if she would be sticking around town once she was healed up. But though she tried to put up a good front, he could see through it and see the woman she was. And he liked what he saw. She was tentative about letting anyone in close, and Bass felt a strong desire to be there for her and prove her doubts wrong.

Climbing from his pickup, he grabbed the plastic bags containing the food and walked up to the front door. Usually he just walked right in, but he paused and gave the door a knock with the toe of his boot, his hands full with the drink carrier and bags. When no one answered, he managed to turn the doorknob and push the door open.

"Lock?" He called, stepping into the kitchen. He set the food and drink down on the island, glancing in to the empty living room. He called for Lock again, but there was still no answer. Maybe he had been wrong and she was in town with Sly.

Just then, Judy came sauntering up around the corner of the hallway and looked up at him, tail wagging.

"Hey girl. Where's Lock?"

She sniffed and turned away, disappearing in a hurry and curious, Bass moved to follow. When he stepped into the living room, his head was already turned to look up the hall in search of Judy. She stood over a black form laying in the middle of the floor, sniffing and pawing before stepping back to look back at Bass.

two bullets

Realization struck Bass like lightning.

"Lock!"

two bullets

Chapter Fourteen

Bass rushed up the narrow hall and slid down next to Lock. On her stomach, she laid in the bathroom light. Her arms lay up on either side of her head, her hair a mess and covering her face. He shook her shoulders, gently at first, then harder when there was no response. "Wake up, Lock. Come on, girl, wake up."

He brushed back the tossed strands of hair from her face, feeling the warmth of her skin under his fingers. Her eyes were closed and she seemed to be asleep, her breathing shallow, but breathing none the less. The lurch in his stomach eased, but concern still strained the muscles in his face.

"Lock?" He whispered.

Behind her closed lids, her eyes shifted, then she blinked, slowly drawn to consciousness.

"Daddy?"

Bass didn't realize he was holding his breath until he heard her small voice, and he quickly took in a lungful of air. "No, it's Bass."

"Am I okay?" She asked, not quite with it yet.

"You will be," he said gently. "Do you remember what happened? Did you faint?"

She curled the fingers in front of her face into a fist, closing her eyes as she whimpered softly. She was confused and still not fully awake.

Bass quickly but carefully rolled her over to her back, slipping his arms under her shoulders and knees and lifted her up. Pliable and weak, she molded into his hold as he stood and

two bullets

he quickly carried her into her bedroom. He leaned over the bed and eased her down softly, her head resting on the pillow. Shivers rattled her frail body.

Bass sat next to her on the edge of the bed, his fingers gently moving the matted strands of hair from her damp forehead. Her head turned towards him slowly as her eyes opened into slits, seeing him for the first time. He smiled, his heartbeat slowly returning to a normal pattern as the initial fear of seeing her so helpless eased.

"Hey stranger," she rasped, a smile curling the edges of her mouth.

"Hey kid."

She slowly adjusted her head against the pillows, clearing her dry throat before licking her lips. "Well, that was fun."

Her attempt at humor eased the tension and Bass chuckled softly. Her shivers continued as the shock wore off, and Bass felt comfortable leaving her to go to the kitchen. While the water for tea heated in the microwave, he texted Sly, though he wasn't sure what to tell him. The microwave beeped and he finally worked out a quick text to tell Sly he had found Lock passed out on the floor, but she seemed to be okay, and to call when he could.

Then Bass put in the teabag and dunked it a couple times, then let the string hang over the side as he took the cup back to the bedroom. Lock was fully awake now. She had managed to perch herself up on the pillows and was sitting up when he came in.

"Here," he said, placing the cup in her hands.

She gave him a shy smile, eyes on the cup as her fingers numbly wrapped around the handle. "Thanks."

Dozens of questions flashed through Bass's mind as he

sat next to her, but none of them seemed appropriate at the moment, so he said nothing and they both sat there in the silence. Though no one spoke for awhile, there seemed to be a wordless conversation buzzing through the room, and the usual awkwardness of a moment such as this was no where to be found.

Lock kept her eyes on her cup while Bass kept his eyes on her. She felt the gaze, and knew she owed him some sort of explanation. What words could she start with that would make sense?

Then revelation hit her and she looked up him sharply, "Wait a minute, what are you doing here?"

"Cassidy gave me the rest of the day off. I figured you were climbing the walls so I thought I'd stop in to see how you were."

A smile flirted with the corners of her mouth. "Surprise!" she said with a laugh.

Bass smiled as she slowly took a sip of tea. Then she spoke, her voice once again strong. "I went for a run this morning."

"Oh?"

She laughed, nodding as she turned to set the cup on the nightstand just out of reach, and Bass bridged the gap and set the cup down for her.

"That's good. You must be feeling better."

"It was more desperation than anything. I had a bad dream and needed to clear my head. Guess I thought I was Superwoman or something. But, I guess I over did it. I was getting dressed in the bathroom and got sick."

She sighed and laid her head back against the headboard. "I tried getting myself out to the couch, but it seemed so far away and the carpet just looked so inviting."

"It's a nice bed in a pinch," he agreed, and Lock opened her eyes at him and they shared a smile.

"So," she said, absently adjusting her blanket over her chest, "how was your day?"

Bass looked down at his hands and dug his thumbnail across his palm. "Well, we thought we had a lead on Heinous, but it turned out to be nothing. We went up to a White Society compound out in the woods, and ended up praying for the leader's little girl."

"Wow! That's pretty awesome." She said, genuinely excited. Then, "I didn't know you had those kind of groups up here."

She reached for her tea and Bass was quick to get it for her. As he handed it to her waiting hand he said, "They've been around for awhile. It was before my time, but I guess they were quite a big deal back in the day until the townspeople ran them out. Barrier Ridge was a different place back then, I hear."

Lock's eyes widened as she remembered the conversation with Sly. "Oh that's right! Sly told me about that."

Bass nodded. "Yeah, it was a pretty big deal at the time. We've had a few dealings with them here and there, but they're pretty untouchable when it comes to the law. The FBI used to watch them like hawks, but they gave up on them and bestowed the trouble to local law enforcement. The group abandoned their drug dealing and mainly they just keep to their compound, making animal sacrifices and experimenting with dark stuff."

"But they let you pray for their daughter? That's something!"

"Yeah," he nodded, "it was definitely a God thing."

He didn't go into any more detail and Lock saw no reason to push it, except to keep the conversation on something other than her embarrassing nap in the hallway. She glanced to his uniform shirt and jeans, a gun holster secured to his hip, looking every bit the part of a cowboy deputy. He wasn't wearing a hat today, and his dirty blonde hair hung down his neck in soft waves, the top ruffled and swept out of his eyes. A light five o'clock shadow graced his strong jaw and gave him a scruffy look that fit him well, somehow making his eyes brighter and more intense.

"So tell me about these nightmares," he said suddenly and it jolted Lock back to reality. She shrugged off the question, concentrating on the cup in her hands. "It's not a big deal. Just comes with the territory."

Bass slowly leaned over her legs, supporting himself on his hand next to her left calf. "Well they were a big enough deal to send you out running before you were ready."

Lock looked sharply into his face. Didn't he know you don't just ask a person to talk about their trauma so openly? She looked back down and shrugged again, but he wasn't going anywhere, or giving up. He bunched his shoulders casually, saying in the most gentle but forceful way possible, "Tell me about it. What got to you?"

Lock found a focal point on the holster of his gun and stared at it, pursing and unpursing her lips awkwardly. What would it hurt to talk about it? She wanted to talk. She needed to release the built up tension in her mind. But, it was scary to open up like that, exposing so much of her inner pain with a stranger. She'd never been good at secrets, so even though part of her wanted to be secretive and carry the pain on her own, her need for emotional connection and to actually talk about what happened in full disclosure outweighed her pride.

"Did Sly tell you why I came here?"

"Because your partner shot you. Right?"

two bullets

164

She adjusted herself on the pillows, dipping her head. "That's part of it. Something happened...well actually a lot of somethings happened. But a couple days after surgery, I woke up in the middle of the night. I thought the room was empty. It was dark and quiet. But then I got that feeling like I wasn't alone. I'm still not sure if it was a dream or not but it freaked me out. I suddenly realized someone was sitting in the chair in the corner. They were hidden in shadow and all I could see was the guy's tie.

"I said, 'who are you?' And then in this deep voice, he said, "It doesn't matter who I am, Lock. I know who you are and that's all that matters. It's time for you to get out of town. Leave, and never come back. Or the next bullet won't miss.'"

Lock shuddered slightly at the memory.

"Did you tell anyone?"

"No. I honestly thought it was a dream. I guess I went back to sleep because the next time I opened my eyes, it was daytime and my parents were there. About a week later my parents found a note on my bed that said the next time I wouldn't be so lucky, and they'd see me at the funeral." Lock shook her head and cleared her throat. "The next day I was on a plane to here."

Still leaning over her legs, Bass reached to touch her knee over the covers and rubbed, a sympathetic frown darkening his face.

"They don't want me back," she said, glancing up at him. "All my friends...they jumped ship as soon as they thought I was a dirty cop. And Danson is still out there, working for the department like nothing happened. Like he didn't shoot me. What am I suppose to do with that? How am I suppose to just move on from all that?"

Bass said nothing, his eyes low as he thought for a

two bullets

minute, still rubbing her leg. Then slowly he rose his lower half off the bed, and moved himself up next to her, stretching out his leg as he came to sit next to her. Staying on top of the covers, he sat up against the headboard as he eased his arm under her head and tugged her in close. He encircled her as she rested her head on his chest, his chin resting on the top of her head.

"I can tell you one thing," he murmured, eyes fixed at the wall across from him, "you're not alone. Not anymore."

*　　*　　*　　*

After a while, Lock moved out into the living room and sat on the couch. Bass apparently had no intentions of going anywhere. He heated up the cups of soup that had come with their meals, willing to get her anything she needed so she could continue resting on the couch. She felt bad to be such a burden, but Bass was adamant that she relax and enjoy being pampered. All of which he said with an amused and gentle expression.

When she needed to go to the restroom, he helped her off the couch, but she assured him she could manage the walk to the bathroom alone. Closing the door behind her, she caught sight of her blotchy skin and unruly hair that had dried while she slept, and she gasped. She hadn't even thought about her appearance while she talked with Bass, and now embarrassment rushed over her as she quickly combed back the curls and put them into a pony-tail.

When she opened the door to return to the living

room, she could hear whistling and moving around coming from the kitchen. Her heart nearly burst out of her chest. He reminded her a lot of Sly. He always seemed to be smiling, but there was something about the way that he carried himself that spoke volumes of his self confidence and strength. There was no going back now; she had fallen hard. Without trying, or looking, she had found someone who cared about her well-being, and wasn't scared off by her past. Or her messy hair.

She had woken up that morning feeling once again lost and broken, but God had known exactly what she needed, and had even made sure to bring someone to the house to pick her up off the floor and carry her to safety.

As she took her place on the couch once again, she heard Bass's phone ring and he stepped outside to take it. Turning on the TV, she cued up her favorite show, an old Steve McQueen series that always made her feel better. As the theme song blasted through the surround sound speakers, Judy hopped down from the couch and retreated to the much more quiet area of Sly's bedroom.

When Bass opened the door and stepped back in, Lock looked up and he grinned at her.

"Soup's on!"

"Yaye!"

She turned down the volume on her program and adjusted herself as Bass brought in the soup and the rest of their food. Handing her the cup of hot soup, he arranged the drink carrier and food containers, took his seat next to her on the couch.

"What are we watchin'?"

"An old TV show from the '60s."

Eyes up at the TV, his brow furrowing. "Rawhide?"

"No, Wanted: Dead or Alive. Do you know who Steve

McQueen is?"

He shook his head.

Lock got excited at this. She could talk all day about the man and his movies, which she went on to do. After ten minutes, head resting back on the couch, he looked over at her with an amused grin. "Well at least you aren't a super-fan or something."

She blushed. Then she changed the subject. "This is a silly question, but do you have westerns in Australia?"

He nodded, balancing his bowl of soup against his chest. "Yeah, we've got everything there. Though for my house personally, it was more cartoon films and musicals."

"Oh yeah? How come?"

"I have twelve brothers and sisters-"

"Twelve?!"

"Yep, and I'm the middle one. The best way to keep ankle biters distracted is anything loud and with lots of color."

Lock closed her eyes, shaking her head perplexed, "I'm sorry; I'm still stuck on the whole twelve siblings thing."

"Why? What's your family like?"

"Oh, well I'm the oldest of one..." Lock said, chest bubbling with a laugh as she waited for Bass to get her joke.

He did, cheeks wrinkling as he grinned. "So you're the youngest and the eldest!"

She nodded emphatically, adjusting her feet perched on the edge of the table. "Yep. So with that comes a lot of being spoiled, and knowing nothing about having a big family."

"But you had Sly though, right?"

"Well, yeah, but there was only two of us fighting over the TV remote, not twelve."

"Oh, it's not that bad. If you don't want someone to

change the channel, you just toss it into a kangaroo's pouch as she goes running by." Bass mimicked the motion he was inferring with a fake throw, but he was having too much fun and broke into laughter before he even finished the sentence. Lock promptly smacked his arm, trying not to laugh but finally ended up snorting despite her effort.

"Oh, come on! That was a good joke!" He exclaimed.

Lock threw her head back laughing. It felt good to laugh again.

When they had both quieted down, Lock said, "So what's your favorite musical then?"

"Hm," Bass's brow furrowed deeply as he thought hard on the answer. "That's a hard one."

"Please don't say Moulin Rouge!"

"Um, no," he chuckled, then, "Probably 'An American in Paris, or 'The Sound Of Music.'"

"I love The Sound Of Music!!"

He nodded. "It gave me false hopes of becoming a Navy Captain and falling for the nanny."

"Don't forget all those children."

They took turns going through the list and trying to remember all of the names of the Von Trapp children, happily laughing at each other as they went.

Lock tried to remember the last time she had had this much fun sober, and at peace in the presence of another person. The last time she'd had friends come over to her apartment in Cincinnati it had been a birthday party for Danson. She had gone all out for the event, decorating her modest studio apartment and cooking a feast for the guest of honor. Every one from their department had been invited, and had arrived for the occasion in dressy clothes, ready for a good time. Lock remembered standing in her kitchen looking out at all the familiar faces, but feeling like a stranger. Those people only knew the side of herself that she'd let them see. The side she'd created so as to fit in.

Now that she thought about it, it had all seemed empty and meaningless. Empty conversation, empty laughter, empty relationships.

When her own birthday had come around a month later, she had been greeted with a card signed by a few people hanging on her locker in the women's bathroom, and a text from Danson. She had hoped that everyone would want to at least go out to dinner or something that night, but nothing had been planned and everyone had other engagements. When Lock had gotten off work that night, she had returned home to a dark apartment, and ate cold pizza and drank flat pop alone.

At the time she'd tried to brush it off as no big deal, but it had hurt. She'd smoked an entire pack of cigarettes by herself sitting on her deck, listening to the wafting sounds of laughter and music coming from an apartment above her. At least someone was enjoying her birthday.

Now that she was thinking about it, she realized that the only time her friends ever got together was to go to the bar, or because Lock had made the plans and rallied the troops. It was ironic now, she thought, that she was sitting next to a man she had just met, who was treating her better than she had been treated by anyone since high school.

"Do you like to dance?" Lock blurted, turning excitedly towards Bass.

He grew serious. "I'll have you know I have more soul in my little finger than anyone you've ever met."

She giggled. "I love dancing, but no one ever wants to do it with me. When I was little, my mom worked nights a lot, so Dad and Sly would put on this old 'Soul Train' sampler cassette. I think they did it just to wear me out before bed, " she laughed, "but those are some of my favorite moments."

"Dean Martin or Frank Sinatra?"

"What do you mean?"

He leaned in now as he whispered, "Don't tell Sly, but I know he's got a vinyl collection that could use some dusting off."

Eyes filled with wonder, Lock answered. "Dean Martin."

With that, Bass nodded and pushed himself off the couch. He walked across the room to a shelf set up against the side of the fireplace and cleared off the antique round table. Lock wasn't sure what to do, but she put her empty soup bowl to the side and moved herself to the edge of the couch, watching Bass peer through all the vinyl spines until he found the one he wanted.

"Here we go. This one's brilliant." He glanced at Lock as he set the record onto the table and moved the needle. "You aren't even ready for what's about to happen."

Dean's voice began crooning in a slow, echoing voice as backup singers crooned behind him, and Bass started swaying a little with the rhythm. Then in an excited dash across the room, he grabbed Lock's hand, pulling her up to her feet as she giggled with delight. He gave the coffee table a shove out of the way and grabbed her hand as he began singing the words to her in a half serious, half silly voice as he scrunched up his face, howling along with Dean.

Still holding his hand, she slowly spun herself in a circle before returning to his arms. They began to sway around the room as he continued singing, trumpets blaring over the crackling of the needle riding the vinyl.

Bass was thoughtful, and made sure not to move too

quick, but Lock wasn't feeling any more pain. She was the closest she had ever been to the man who had sat down with her in the ER. He'd helped her forget her panic attack then, and he was making her forget everything else now.

They danced in the living room as rain pattered against the windows. As thunder rumbled in the distance, Lock's nightmares became just a distant memory.

Chapter Fifteen
Thursday

Bass wiped his brow and set down the drill. Pulling off his work gloves, he tossed them to the side of the makeshift table. It was a perfect spring day, the sun high in the sky and not a rain cloud in sight. Birds were chirping high up in the leaves of the trees. There were distant plops and splashes as fish played out in the cold lake. Out here away from town on the opposite side of Gibson Lake, Bass had found himself a little slice of heaven. For the past year he had been working in his spare time to make the run down cabin a place to call home.

Standing in the road in front of his garage, Bass gave his work of the new garage door a long, hard look. His eyes were on the freshly fixed hinges, but his mind was somewhere else. This seemed to be the normal with him lately.

He grabbed up his bottle of Coke and started over to the side yard where Jimmie and Jack sat around the fire pit. They were all taking a much needed few hours off, leaving the town under the care of the reserve deputies and the sheriff. If you looked hard you could see signs of town, miles away on the other side of the lake. The towering black mountains that backed the edges of Barrier Ridge rose through a veil of low, wispy clouds. Bass never got used to the sight, and didn't want to. This was heaven on earth out here.

Jimmie Reeves was in the midst of telling Jack Stone about what had happened out at the White Society compound. They sat in metal lawn chairs, the cushion seats worn down from whoever had owned them before. A low burning fire crackled inside the bricks of the fire pit as Bass walked up and swiped Jack's feet out of the chair he was using as a footrest.

"Looks good, buddy." Jack said with a nod towards the saw horse table as he adjusted in his seat.

"Thanks. I appreciate the help." Bass said sarcastically.

Jack threw his hands up. "Hey, I'm just here to help with the manly stuff. When it's time to put the door on the hinges, then I'm all yours."

"The place is finally looking like a house, Bass." Jimmie said from the other side of the fire, looking over his shoulder at the single story log cabin. Bass agreed, slouching low in his seat as he propped his boots up on the bricks of the fire ring. It was about time for those boots to come off.

The work in progress cabin sat on a twelve acre lot, tucked in the shadow of the large mountain on the north end of Gibson Lake. It sat just a few paces back from the water's edge, and had a killer night view of town. It was perfect for a country boy like Bass who'd grown up working for Australian cattle companies. He'd bought the place from an old man who was looking to get rid of it for a steal of a deal. Having spent all his savings on the land, it had taken up until about a year ago before he'd saved enough money to start renovating the cabin.

"If you get married someday, you might have to build some additions," Jimmie added.

"Why? It's better than the bedroll and six other guys nearby, camped out around a fire," Bass said, eyes staring into the glowing coals at the bottom of the pit as he reminisced about the old days.

"So. Have you talked to Lock lately?" Jimmie was trying to hide a coy smile as he took a drink. Bass slowly moved his eyes up to look at him.

"And what's that suppose to mean, brother?"

Jimmie held up his hands in defense. "It's just a question."

Jack Stone leaned forward in his seat. "He's asking if you've stopped being an idiot and asked her to marry you yet?"

Bass promptly lifted his leg and kicked the arm of Jack's chair, sending Jack and his chair rocking and rolling over onto two legs. In doing so, he bought himself a couple extra moments to come up with an answer.

Jack was laughing as he got himself and his chair back on steady ground. "I'll take that as a big fat no."

Marriage? It was too soon to consider that. Lock had been in town what, a week?

A chuckle came from Jimmie's side of the fire. He was shaking his head as he leaned forward over his knees, holding his bottle close to his chest. "So what's your deal, Bass?"

"She just got here, ya know? I mean, she has a lot going on. I don't want to push anything. Besides, I barely know her."

"Is that why you go out to see her every chance you get?" Jack asked, giving Bass a knowing smirk.

Bass held up a finger. "Once." Then he sighed, "Come on guys, even if I am interested, she's probably going back to Cincinnati in the end anyway."

Jimmie's right eyebrow arched. "*If* you're interested?"

"You seriously think she's going to want to go back?" Jack asked. "Especially after meeting us?!"

"Did she tell you that?" Jimmie asked, to which Bass shrugged. "Well, she hasn't said anything about staying."

The sight of Lock laughing in his arms as they danced around her living room came to him like a warm ray of sunshine. Had he thought about asking her to stay? Of course he had. But she was lost and still trying to find answers. How could he throw his hat in the ring while she was in the middle of the worst time of her life?

"Well," Jack said with a sniff, bending back his foot to prop on the fire pit. "It's like I always say. If a girl can hold her own in a fire fight, then she's marriage material."

Bass snorted, "When have you said that?"

"You're right," Jack replied flatly, taking a drink from his soda bottle. "Why would she want to stay here?"

"Yeah," Jimmie said, catching on, "what does Washington have that Ohio doesn't?"

"Mountains." Jack answered with a one shoulder shrug. "Fresh air. Peace of mind. Us."

Bass had to laugh and shook his head. They were good. And rather persuasive. They knew him well enough to know that even if he didn't admit it, the thing he wanted most in this world was Lock. They knew it, and they approved. And their approval went a long way for Bass. Bringing a woman into their group required someone who could fit in, and that they all liked. Someone who understood and appreciated the strain and pressure of their hectic schedules. If things worked out with Lock, she would be the first woman ever to join their all boys club. Jimmie had dated a few women here and there, but it was never serious, and never lasted long enough to create a new routine. And Jack had vowed that he was never getting married. Ever.

Bass himself wasn't the type to run out and chase down ever girl he saw in hopes that she would turn out to be "The One." Sure, he'd dated a few women in the past, but they had all turned out to be wrong for him in different ways. His older brother Hugo told him he was too picky and that he needed to just pick someone and then make it work....this advice was possibly why Hugo had been divorced twice.

Bass was confident that when the right girl came along, he would know and he wouldn't have to just "make it work." He wasn't looking for, or expecting, flashing signs or no effort on his part, but he was expecting the puzzle pieces to at least fit. He'd never sat down and wrote out a list of the things he wanted, but if he had, he was pretty sure Lock would fulfill all of the requirements.

Except for the fact that she was only visiting.

"I don't know," he said with a sigh.

"We also have the Seahawks," Jack said. "Who, by the way, are having a great season." He lifted his drink in a salute and took a swig.

From his side of the fire, Jimmie became serious. He leaned forward in his seat again, peering hard at Bass. "I've never known you to be scared of anything–"

"And I'm not now! I'm just trying to be thoughtful and considerate of her position!"

Jimmie held up a hand. "Okay fine. There are some risks. But I think you're thinking about this a little too hard. Lock's a big girl, and if she isn't ready for something serious, I'm sure she'll tell you. Everyone knows that you guys have a connection–"

"–Seriously, *everyone.*" Jack added with an emphatic nod, looking almost annoyed by the notion.

"–and," Jimmie continued, "a girl like Lock only comes along once in a blue moon. And if God says, "get it!" then you better get on your feet and go running after her."

Bass nodded thoughtfully, but still was on the fence.

"I don't even know for sure if she's a believer or not. You know what Sly's said about all of that. Not to mention she's running for her life from a partner that wants her dead."

"Yeah, running right into your arms of love," Jimmie teased.

Bass groaned.

"Have you prayed about it?" Jack asked.

Jimmie and Bass stopped and stared at him. Jack was a Christian, but he wasn't exactly known for his deep, spiritual ways.

He shrugged at their stares. "I'm just saying, if there's ever a moment to pray for an answer, this seems as good as any."

Bass looked over at Jimmie, brows raised, and Jimmie returned the look. Leave it to Jack to be the voice of reason. If Jack was suggesting praying for wisdom, Bass knew he'd better do it.

The three friends spent the rest of the afternoon talking and praying and finding out what God had to say about all of this. If Bass was going to make a move and actually take a chance with Lock, he was going to need all the help he could get.

two bullets

Chapter Sixteen

Sunday

Butterflies danced in Lock's stomach all the way into town. Friday Bass had called and asked her to hang out with him after church. Just the two of them. She knew she shouldn't be as anxious as she was, but this was Bass Jones! The sheriff's deputy with enough swagger and charm to make any girl swoon with just one absent smile. And he'd asked *her* out!

They'd been talking on the phone the last few days. And every time, his thoughtfulness and patience astounded her. He made her want to be happy again. He'd shown her in the short time they'd spent together that life could be good. That there could be peace amidst the chaos. He'd shown her that there are still good, decent people left in the world, something she had practically given up hope for.

Aside from her father, and Sly, Bass was the only man she had ever met who could be kind, patient, and endearing, while also having no problem getting his hands dirty and doing whatever it took to protect someone else. He was tough, and he didn't have to prove it.

Lock tried not to be obvious about how excited she was, but Sly could read her like a book. He didn't broach the topic specifically as they headed to church, but he did mention that he liked her outfit. She had chosen to wear a dress that morning, something she almost never did, and he knew it had to do more with Bass than just dressing up for church. And it made him smile.

It was good to see Lock actually excited about

something, and just a little out of her element. The fact that a bit of a sparkle had returned to her dark green eyes was a blessing all its own.

All through service, Lock was a nervous, distracted mess. She tried to follow along in her Bible as Sly preached a wonderful sermon on the death and resurrection of Jesus, but Bass was sitting next to her. They sat together, along with Jimmie, Jack, and Cassidy on the very back row, and she kept finding herself thinking about him rather than the sermon.

It finally got to the point where Lock was annoying herself, and she had to give her emotions a talking to. *Seriously kid, just relax. You're a grown woman who used to chase bad guys around for a living, not some thirteen year girl who knows nothing about boys. You're hanging out with the man, not going to prom. Just relax.*

She asked for some heavenly help, took a quiet, deep breath, and turned her attention back on to the sermon. She was even able to keep her poise when Bass leaned over and nudged her, asking what verse Sly was in.

After service, the two of them slipped out of the back row and were the first outside, met by a glorious day with warm sunshine. Bass held open the door of his pickup and she stepped up, pulling the skirt of her dress around her legs. He drove them south through town, then around to the east side of Gibson Lake to a diner that sat on the front edge of a park. The neatly manicured grass ran down a slight incline to the rocky shores of the crystal blue water, tall trees creating a canopy of shade.

Mosley's Diner was like taking a step back in time. Outside it was shaped like a large barn, painted red with white trim. On either side of the front door were wooden barrels turned into planters with red, purple and yellow flowers waving gently in the breeze, as if welcoming the patrons to come on in.

Inside, there was a long counter where customers could sit and watch the staff make the ice cream delights in front of a large aquarium built into the wall. Booths ran parallel to this, curving around the end of the room like an "L," just like all those roadside diners you see in the movies. To the right of the door and towards the back was a separate lounging room. Lock could see that it was decorated in western style with warm colors. Stuffed animal heads hung in between the floor to ceiling book shelves that encased the space. There was also a large spiral staircase that ran up to the second floor where there was a stone fireplace and walls of board games for those cozy winter days.

Working behind the counter, Lock was surprised to see Aria, the paramedic with purple hair who had helped her after the hospital shooting. Lock waved as Bass led her down the aisle to a booth in the lower part of the "L" shape. Aria's face lit up in genuine delight as she waved and called back, "Hey girl!"

"You know her?" Bass asked as he took a seat, his back to the hall that led into the kitchen.

"Yeah," Lock replied, removing her light jacket before taking the side of the booth across from him.

She glanced around at the patrons sitting in the other booths, and she noticed that her and Bass were the main attraction. She straightened a little and looked at Bass, who was happily reaching for the menus tucked up at the back of the table behind the salt and pepper shakers and silver napkin dispenser.

"Do you bring your dates here very often?" she teased, taking the menu he offered. When he looked at her with questioning eyes, she suppressed a grin, then gave a barely noticeable jerk of her head towards the rest of the room. "They seem to think you're pretty interesting."

Bass glanced around. "Oh. They're not looking at me," he said, smiling as he looked back at her. She blushed and quickly hid her face behind the menu.

Aria arrived at their table, delivering two glasses of water and straws.

"Hey guys," she said, careful not to tip over the glasses as she dealt them out. When her task was complete, she straightened up and pulled a pen and pad from the front pocket of her apron.

"How's that side doin'?" she asked and Lock nodded. "Oh, much better. Healing up just like you said it would."

Aria smiled, her eyes wide with enthusiasm. "That's great! Love that dress by the way. Are we ready to order?"

The options were limitless. Everything from Italian sodas to bacon flavored soft serve ice cream filled the dessert page. Lock went the safe route and ordered a chocolate milk shake and a plate of fries, while Bass ordered a pistachio ice cream and walnut Sunday. He assured Lock it tasted better than it sounded.

"You got it, guys," Aria chirped, clicking her pen closed. She turned to walk back towards the kitchen, but paused when she was behind Bass's line of sight and turned. With an excited grin, she winked at Lock and gave her the thumbs up, miming her approval. Lock dipped her head, hiding a smile so as not to give herself away.

"So, how are you feeling?" Bass asked. He let his hands rest on top of the table, interlacing his fingers together. He wore a light blue denim button down shirt over a white t-shirt. There was a gold ring on his right ring finger, and the

two bullets

dark blue face of the watch he wore on his left wrist seemed to bring the whole outfit together. His thick hair was combed back from his face, and it appeared that he might have gotten a haircut recently. Lock approved, though she wouldn't say so out loud.

"Much better," she smiled, bobbing her head to ward off any concern. "And I don't know if I told you, but I really appreciate all the trouble you went through...you know..with me."

Bass scoffed, lifting a hand to wave her off. "Nah, it's no trouble at all."

Lock smiled as she looked to the left out the window at the canopy of trees hovering over a small gazebo that overlooked the water. "So, I think you need to tell me more about how a navy brat became a fisherman turned deputy sheriff."

Bass chuckled, leaning back from the table, resting against the back of the booth. "You want to just jump into that, huh?"

Lock knew she had struck gold, seeing him grow uneasy with the spotlight on him. She smiled sweetly, holding out her hands, palms up. "We're here to get to know each other, right?"

Bass groaned a little, knowing he was caught. He leaned over toward the window, settling his elbow up on the sill.

"Alright," he said, "but on one condition; you have to tell me how you became a cop. Deal?"

"Absolutely," she said. She leaned forward over the table in anticipation.

He started by telling her about growing up in the Australian Outback. He'd worked on a cattle ranch most of his life, growing up on the back of a horse, learning how to defend what was his and seeing what hard work produced. His face lit up as he told a story about rustlers getting into the herd one night and taking what they could under the cover of night. Bass and two of his friends had taken off, tracking down the rustlers for days, and then after exchanging a few broken noses, he and his friends returned to their camp with all of the stolen cattle, safe and sound. Lock loved the way his accent got thicker when he talked about the old days.

"I think that's what I miss most," he went on, brow wrinkling thoughtfully as he ran a thumb down the side of his glass of water, "everyday was different. It was man against himself out there. The rules were simple, and when someone wanted to break 'em, they knew they were playing with fire."

Lock smiled, completely understanding. He fed on the chase and the adventure, not much different than herself. Another thing they had in common.

He continued. "When my father ended up moving us all here to the states when I was eighteen, everything I knew, and what I was good at, was taken away. Me and my brothers set out on our travels to explore our father's home land and see what opportunities awaited us. I think I was looking for something to give me that good old feeling again. I did every kind of job you can think of, staying a few months here and there, saving up enough money until it was on to the next town. The next job. Then Hugo got he and I a job working on a fishing boat." He shrugged at this. "It was just another job. I was horrible at it-" he chuckled, "-but I loved it. I loved the open sea. It reminded me of home. Gave me a chance to catch my breath and find a piece of myself again. Then I hurt my hand."

He stopped to look at his hand, just long enough to

brush over the scar on his palm with the tips of his fingers. "I suddenly found myself without a job, no purpose, and as dramatic as it sounds, no reason to live. At the time I thought my life was over. Years of constantly moving around ended with me not having a place where I felt that I belonged. I knew how to do a lot of things, but it wasn't enough. My identity was in what I could do on my own, and being the best at all of it.

"Honestly, Cassidy saved my life. Because of him, I picked up a Bible for the first time and read it. I had nothing but time, so I just read. And that's when I realized I was putting my identity in myself and what I could do on my own. And since I'm not perfect, I fail. And since I fail, my identity as I saw it was a lie. I accepted Jesus as my savior in my bedroom, and felt like God was telling me to accept Cass's job offer and moved down here. That was three years ago, give or take."

It wasn't lost on Lock that the same three years that had caused Bass to find himself, had been the same three years in which she had lost herself. He was laying himself out plainly for her to see, and she was touched by his honesty, but she suddenly found her own story inadequate.

"And now I'm here." he said with a wide grin, brightening the mood. His blue eyes searched hers as he said, "and I'm starting to think it was all worth it."

Well, now he was just getting cheesy, Lock thought. She playfully rolled her eyes at him and laughed. He smiled, but didn't drop his gaze from hers until he was sure he had made his point clear. Then he reached for his water and took a drink.

Aria returned with their orders, apologizing for the wait. When she had left them again and they were settling back into the comfort of it being just the two of them, Bass took a bite of his Sunday, then motioned towards Lock. "It's your turn to spill, Love."

Lock picked up a fry and shook her head. "But I like talking about you! Your story would make a great movie! You should move to Hollywood and try to sell it to some high rolling director."

Bass laughed at this. "No one wants to hear my story. They'd probably screw it up anyway."

"Well, you've got the looks for it, anyway," Lock said, taking a sip of her water.

It was the first time she had attempted anything flirtatious, and for Bass it had been worth the wait. Taking a bite of green ice cream, he watched the cute blonde across from him realize what she had just said and try to quickly move on. Her maturity and poise overshadowed the fact that she was six years younger than him. He liked seeing the genuine awe and giddiness peek through, showing a softer side to her usual serious demeanor. Her eyes held a deep knowledge of life, showing the weathered woman and police officer that she was, revealing more about her life than words ever could. She very well may only be twenty-four, but she'd lived through enough to give her a unique outlook on life. It made him think that he wasn't anywhere near her league.

"Tell me how you found yourself in Cincinnati," he said.

"I never wanted to do anything else except be a cop. I mean, not necessarily in Cincinnati, but I always wanted to work in a large city. I went to college but that was mostly just to make my parents happy. I kept myself busy with classes until I was twenty-one, then I applied to the academy. I was one of the lucky ones who caught the eye of a recruiter, and by the time I graduated, there was a position waiting for me in the exact precinct that I wanted."

"Let me guess," Bass said with his eyes thoughtfully narrowed at her, "the roughest part of town possible?"

She laughed. "You got it. My very first call was a drive-by shooting. I ended up working overtime that night, and got sent to the morgue to watch the body until someone came to I.D. it. My training officer wanted to keep me out of the way since this was a really big case for the area. That's also the night I got written up..."

Bass's eyes widened with amazement. "And what did you do to get into trouble so quickly?"

Lock laughed, pausing to take a drink of her shake, then said, "While I was at the morgue, an officer came down to see his girlfriend, the medical examiner at the time. He saw me sitting on a stool in the corner. I think he was just showing off for his girlfriend, but he approached me and asked what I was doing there when all the excitement was upstairs. I guess he could tell I was bored out of my mind. I explained that I was waiting for the family to come ID the body, to which he scoffed and told me they wouldn't be there until the morning. Then he asked me if I wanted to be a *real* cop. I was a naive rookie who should have known better, but I ended up saying yes. We left and I rode around with him the rest of the night, looking for the shooters from the drive-by. When my TO found out that I had left my post, he was furious. He and the officer got into it then, the officer telling my TO that I deserved to be treated like a cop, not a ride-along."

Lock thoughtfully looked down at the table between them, momentarily distracted by the memory. "Anyway, I got in trouble, but my TO made sure that he never left me alone again. We actually ended up getting along and I made it through my probation without anymore write-ups."

"And the other guy?" Bass asked as he ran his finger

two bullets

along the inside of his empty dish, "What happened with him?"

Lock took a drink of water, eyes low as she set the glass down. "We became partners six weeks later when my probation was over."

Bass was confused at first at what he was seeing in Lock's sudden uneasiness, but then it suddenly dawned on him that the man she spoke of was her ex-partner. The one who had shot her not that long ago. The man who wanted her dead. She couldn't talk about her past as a cop without talking about her ex-partner.

Bass was seeing the various shades of Lock on display in front of him. She was fun and cheeky with a whole lot of spirit, but she carried heavy weights in her heart like rocks, the scars evident in the flitting of her eyes, unable to meet his gaze as the pain of what she'd been through leaked through.

"I'm sorry, Lock. I shouldn't have brought it up."

She looked up into his eyes, and with each second that skittered by, he was able to ground her. Pull her out of the turmoil, the swirling tornado of emotions and bring her back to reality. Bass didn't know it, but Lock was very aware of the peace drifting through her. Her muscles unclenched and she was able to release the breath she had been holding.

"No," she said, suddenly shaking her head and with it the dust of the past, "No, it's okay. It's just weird to talk about it all." She laughed nervously, uncrossing and recrossing her legs under the table.

"We can change the subject if you want." Bass assured her. She sat there for a moment, thoughtfully biting her lip as she stared at her fingers, picking at the polish on her thumb.

"To be honest, I just don't know how to do this whole thing."

"Do what?"

two bullets

"I don't want to scare you off."

He frowned, shaking his head. "Nothing you say will make me run away."

Lock was skeptical at this. "I'm a mess! Everybody knows it. I woke up this morning, put on a dress, did my hair, and for the first time in a long time was actually excited about what was to come."

She paused and rolled her eyes at her self, turning to look out the window as she said, "But no amount of make-up, hairspray, or a pretty dress can cover up the truth."

She manged to meet his eye, tears now glistening in her eyes and she smiled apologetically.

Bass was angry. He was angry at the fact that Lock had been hurt so bad that even the act of feeling emotions was something she felt that she needed to apologize for. Her partner had taken a bright, happy, perfect young woman and turned her into a tortured soul. She thought it was her fault that bad things happened to her, and that because of that, Bass wouldn't want her when he saw the raw truth. Well, maybe some guys were that shallow, but not him.

"You didn't ruin anything." he said with a soft smile, "And you're not a mess. You're getting better. That takes time. You don't need to apologize to me, or anyone else for having feelings. And, I'm sorry if I made you feel pressured in any way to be a certain way. I like you, Lock." his eyes narrowed. "And there's nothing you can do to change that."

She smiled and gave a short laugh, but she nodded.

Bass took a moment to look out through the window as the tension of the moment ebbed away. Then he said. "We prayed for you a lot when you were in the hospital, you know."

"You did?" she asked, completely surprised at this, eyes wide at him.

two bullets

He nodded. "It was really hard on Sly to be here and not with you. He did come see you for about a week I guess it was, but you were still unconscious and he had to come back to work."

"Sly came to see me?" Lock asked, her voice low in disbelief.

His brow wrinkled as he frowned. "You didn't know?"

She quickly shook her head, "No one ever told me!"

Way to go Bass, drop a bomb after you just put her back together.

He coughed into his hand, clearing his throat. "Yeah. Well, I mean, you guys weren't on very good terms at the time. I'm sure he didn't tell you because he didn't want to guilt you in to feeling anything that you wouldn't otherwise."

Lock knew he was probably right. "Well, that's true." Then with a smile, said, "Thanks for telling me. I had no idea. All this time I thought...well it doesn't matter what I thought." She looked him straight in the eye and said honestly, "It means a lot."

The moment was suddenly interrupted by a taunting call from across the diner; "Well hey there, Lover Boy!"

two bullets

Chapter Seventeen

Jack Stone walked towards their booth with a wide grin plastered on his face. Jimmie Reeves trailed along behind him. Lock quickly cleared her throat and looked away, slipping a strand of hair back behind her ear. She glanced over at Bass. He sat with one arm on the table, the other thrown across the top of the booth. He was scowling at his friends.

"What are you two doing here?"

"Well," Jack said, coming to bend over the table, planting his hands down on the space between them. "We were just in the area and thought we'd stop in. Saw your truck out front and wanted to say Hi."

"No you didn't." Bass said with a smirk, shaking his head incredulously.

Jack straightened up and turned, motioning for Lock to move over. She laughed and slid over towards the window, dragging her glass of water and still hot plate of fries with her. Across from them, Jimmie crowded in next to Bass, the table descended upon by mischievous grins.

"So, you two here alone?" Jack asked, arching his eyebrow over at Lock. She nodded with wide, innocent eyes, then offered him her left over shake. It was melted into soup, but still cold.

Jack took it, pleased. "Don't mind if I do. Want some, Jim?"

"Oh, I'd love some." Jimmie reached out and took the cup, using the unused spoon inside to draw out a taste.

"I'm sorry, do you two need something?" Bass asked,

two bullets

giving both friends equal opportunity with the dirty look he shot. Then he quickly flashed Lock an apologetic wince. She grinned. She was rather enjoying it all.

"Keep your knickers on there, Aussie," Jack said with a frown, holding up his palm as he reached for the shake Jimmie had set down. "We just wanted to make sure you weren't taking advantage of Cincinnati over here." He took a long slurp of the last bit of shake, then set the cup down with a clunk at the end of the table.

"Figured we'd offer you an alternative to Bonehead over here," Jimmie added, addressing Lock as he thumbed sideways at Bass.

"Seriously?" Bass exclaimed, "Where's the loyalty?"

"Hey, you're the one who ditched us for a date." Jack challenged. Then he leaned over towards towards Lock and said in a low voice, "Has he called you "Sheila" yet?"

Bass was about to say something, but bit his lip and shook his head, leaning over into the windowsill, resting his head on his fist in defeat. Jack turned his entire body now to face Lock, flipping his braid back over his shoulder before crowding Lock with his arm up over the back of the booth behind her.

"See, Jimmie and I are old news now to Bass. It's okay, don't worry about it. We can be put on the back burner to be picked up later. We understand, but as his best friends, it's our job to make sure you are worth being left out in the cold for. He hangs out with you now, and he'll want to hang out with you all the time. And we are left to eat dirt."

"Jack..." Bass growled, shooting him a warning look. Lock thought it was sweet.

She was about to defend herself to Jack, when all of a sudden all three of the deputies cell phones suddenly rang. The playful banter was put on hold as they pulled out their phones and looked at the message, One by one, their happy faces grew serious.

"Are you seeing this?" Jimmie asked, edging closer to Bass to see if his phone said something different.

Bass nodded grimly. "Yeah, I see it."

Jack immediately turned away and pushed himself out of the booth to stand, Jimmie following suit from the other side.

"What is it?" Lock asked as Bass pushed off the window ledge and scooted out.

"Lock, I'm sorry but something's come up."

"Is it bad?" She asked, grabbing her coat and started to follow. Bass hesitated, trying to figure out how to be a cop and answer the call, and at the same time not just ditch his date.

"You coming, Bass?" Jimmie called, already halfway to the door. Bass nodded at him emphatically, then looked back at Lock, his mouth open to speak.

"Can I come with?" she interrupted, hoping to ease the conflict. He looked back over at the others. They nodded, if for no other reason but to get this over with and leave. Bass turned back to Lock and jerked his head towards the door. "Come on."

Inside the pickup, Bass flipped a switch on the dashboard, turning on the blue and red lights built in to the grill as he sped to keep up with Jimmie and Jack as they left the parking lot.

"So what is it?" Lock asked, tightening her seat belt as Bass took a tight corner.

"Neighbors just called in that they heard what sounded like a gunshot from the house next door."

"Any way it could just be a prank or misunderstanding?"

two bullets

"That'd be nice," Bass sighed, but shook his head, sucking on his teeth. "Vester has been going through a rough patch lately... his girlfriend left him a couple weeks back and took their daughter with her. We've been worried that the depression would take over."

"He's a friend?"

He glanced over at her, nodding. "Yeah," he said softly. That was the downside of being a cop in a small town; knowing everyone and having to be there for the bad stuff.

Lock frowned sympathetically and reached across the cab to touch his arm, giving him a reassuring squeeze. He blew out a breath of pent up anxiety, then moved his arm to take Lock's hand into his own. He lifted the back of her hand up to his mouth and kissed it.

When they arrived at the house, curious neighbors had drifted out of their homes and out into the street. An ambulance was already there waiting, its lights silently flashing.

A neighbor waved from the street as Bass pulled in behind Jimmie and Jack. "His truck's home," he called as the officers ran towards the house, Lock scrambling to keep up.

"Anyone else inside?" Jimmie called, running across the yard.

"He didn't have any visitors that I saw."

"Get everyone back across the street," he shouted over his shoulder. On the porch, Bass was already at the door, pounding on it hard with the side of his fist. Jack and Jimmie moved along the porch in either direction, trying to see in through the curtained windows, all of them calling out for the man inside. With no answer to their calls, Bass wiggled the doorknob, but it was locked.

"I'll check the back door." Jack said, and bounded off

the porch past Lock and disappeared around the side.

Bass pulled out his cell phone. "I'll call him."

"Call the house." Jimmie said, moving back to stand with Bass. He glanced back over his shoulder at the street. A few seconds passed and then came the all too real sound of a ringing phone inside.

"Don't do this..." Bass pleaded, stepping back, looking up to the second floor window that was dark.

Every heart skipped a beat as the front door shuddered and opened inward, but it was Jack in the door, his face revealing what everyone feared. Lock's heart dropped.

"No..." Bass said quietly, pulling the phone down. The Indian somberly shook his head and stepped back. Bass hurried in past him, disappearing inside the home. Jimmie was quick to follow, and Jack gave Lock a parting look before turning to follow his friends much more slowly. He had left the door open, so Lock slowly let herself in, pushing the door open a little farther before crossing the threshold.

The smell of gunpowder still hung thick in the air. The living room opened up to the right and Lock came to a stop in the small entry area, seeing where Bass was crouched down on the floor. Jimmie stood nearby with a hand on his hip while he ran the other through his hair. Jack was pacing, trying not to look but unable to stop stealing glances.

Past them, Lock saw the deceased sitting in the recliner facing them, a shotgun laying where it had fallen at his feet. She'd seen her share of bodies, but still her stomach churned at the sight. She quickly looked away, her heart breaking for the men who were having to see their friend like that. She bit her lip, eyes blinking rapidly as if it would remove the image from her head.

As she turned back to the open door, she caught sight

of the bystanders outside who were waiting for word, inching their way closer to the house. She reached out and quietly pushed the door shut.

Suicide.

The word hung in the air like a ghost. Lock tried to stay out of the way as the house filled with volunteer officers, volunteer fire fighters, and the funeral home director/medical examiner who looked too old to be driving anymore. No one spoke unless they had to, out of respect for the situation. When they did speak, it was in hushed tones.

A sheet had been placed over what was left of Vester Carhart's body out of respect, if not for modesty, until his body could be removed. Blood and tissue samples were taken for verification of identity, but it was obvious to everyone in the room that this was Vester. A high school class mate of Jimmie and Jack's, and a friend of Bass's.

Most of the people filling the house carried disturbed looks and ghostly faces as they were forced to do their jobs, and Lock felt inappropriately out of place. She had been to many crime scenes similar to this one, but had never had any kind of connection to the person, or the others working around her.

Sheriff Cassidy soon arrived on the scene, a strange look passing over his face when he saw Lock standing off to the side just inside the front door. She merely nodded and dropped her gaze from him, unsure of what to say.

Jack, obviously the one with the stronger stomach, oversaw the examination of the body and talked with the paramedics and ME, while Jimmie and Bass stood behind the chair in the kitchen doorway talking to Cassidy. The mingling of voices was a low rumble, a somewhat haunting sound echoing off the walls. Lock stuck to her place on the wall in the outer hallway, watching as grim faces came and went through the front door. There was an unspoken sense of understanding and they returned her acknowledging nods.

Lock found herself constantly looking for Bass, as if he was a safe point in the room of crisis. Now was not the time or place, but she couldn't help but notice how the shadows in the dim house projected onto his strong, tanned neck. And how the way he stood brought him to his full height, establishing his leadership among all those around him. She shouldn't be noticing, shouldn't feel the attraction, but she did.

For the most part, she was able to separate herself from the grisly scene around her. She didn't know the man who was dead. He was just another poor soul who'd given up. She'd become accustomed to crime scenes over the years, having seen everything from burned bodies to mutilated body parts rotted with time. But what did get to her was the sight of her new friends emotionally strained. Despite the loss of a friend, they were forced to do their jobs while Vester's body sat a few feet away, a silent ghost watching their every move.

Bass finished talking to Cassidy and turned to leave, passing by the recliner and stepped around the shotgun laying on the floor. It looked as if the weight of the world was on his shoulders. Lock wanted desperately to run to meet him and throw her arms around him and comfort him, but she contained herself. She stayed in her spot near the front door, arms folded behind her back against the wall.

When he looked up, he caught her eye, and she winced a smile. Despite his pain, he managed a weak smile in return and started in her direction. As he stepped into the tiled entry way, he held out his arms and Lock quickly pushed off the wall, standing on her tip-toes to wrap her arms around his neck.

At first Bass was stiff as a board and reserved in her arms, but then he melted into her, his resolve weakened as he hugged her back so tightly she couldn't breathe. Her healing wounds cried out, but she ignored them.

They stood like that for a good minute, unspoken words passed between them, comfort and empathy saying what words couldn't.

"Thanks for stickin' around," he whispered.

"I'm so sorry, Bass." she said.

His hand tightened on her back, but he didn't reply. Then when they finally pulled apart, he gently kissed her forehead.

"Some first date, huh?" He rasped, his voice void of humor, despite the effort.

"I called Sly," she said, stepping back. "He's on his way."

Bass nodded, looking back over his shoulder into the living room. Lock followed his gaze to where Jack and a group of five or so others were gathering around the recliner, poised to lift what was left of the mangled body onto the tarp now lying flat on the carpet. Lock gave Bass's back a quick rub and said, "Maybe we should wait outside?"

He turned his head to look down at her and nodded, but said, "You go on."

As if to reassure her, he reached back to touch her leg

and patted it, jerking his head to the door. But she didn't move. She stood with him, watching in silence as the body was placed in a black body bag, then lifted onto a metal gurney. As the gurney was wheeled towards them, Lock hurried to open the door. She pulled it open and stepped back, giving Jack and the others space to pass by and roll the gurney out onto the front porch.

Outside, the sun was hidden by clouds, the nice day replaced by a wet, chilly afternoon. The flashing lights of all the emergency vehicles parked in the driveway lit up the yard, seeming almost comforting in their familiarity, and eery all at the same time.

The crowd of curious neighbors had seemed to have doubled across the street. They stood behind the large, orange cones that had been set up in the road, yellow police tape strung between them. It wasn't raining, but precipitation hung heavy in the air, and there was a light smell of a wood fire somewhere down the street.

There was a collective gasp from the waiting crowd as the gurney was moved onto the porch and carried down the steps. A few wails ascended into the air as the answer to the question appeared; local man Vester Carhart was dead.

Bass stepped away to talk to Cassidy back in the living room, and Lock stood watching the scene outside from the doorway. Seeing the faces of the bystanders and wondering how they knew Vester.

As the men wheeled the gurney down the sidewalk to the waiting funeral van, Lock saw her uncle stepping to the side for the gurney to pass, then begin climbing the stairs.

"Hey," Lock said, walking out to meet him.

"Hey," he said as they exchanged a quick hug. "Vester killed himself," he said thoughtfully, shaking his head as they pulled away. "I can't believe it."

Then Sly nodded towards the door, eyes peering inside, "How are they?"

Lock just shook her head. "They're taking it pretty hard."

He went on inside, and Lock stayed on the porch, walking to the railing and glanced out at the scene playing out in the yard. Shock and dismay continued to ripple through the gathered crowd, the sounds of grief and disbelief filling the air.

She turned around and leaned back on the railing, then bent her leg to reach her high heeled shoe and took it off, first the left, then the right. Sly eventually reappeared in the doorway, walking out with Cassidy, Jimmie, and Bass in tow. Lock heard Cassidy say that Vester's parents had been called and were on their way to the police station. Jimmie and Bass both agreed that they wanted to be there when the news was given.

Jack returned from helping with the gurney, quietly climbing the stairs of the porch. Cassidy turned from the group to him, saying, "Jack, you coming with us to talk to Vester's parents?"

Jack shook his head as he walked past, moving to the wall next to the door. He crossed his arms over his chest, his back straight, baseball cap pulled low over his eyes. Jimmie said something about Jack needing to be there, but the Indian wouldn't budge.

"I'm staying here. Keep an eye on everything," he announced flatly.

"You don't need to, Jack," Cassidy told him. "Brad and Kyle can handle it by themselves."

"I said I'm staying." Jack snapped.

"I'll stay too," Lock offered. Sly glanced back at her as

she approached the circle.

"You sure?"

She nodded. Her concern was centered on Jack. The man had been there for her after the hospital shooting. She owed him. He put on a good front, but it was obvious he was hurting.

Sly left the porch first, followed by Jimmie and then Bass. As Bass passed, he reached out his hand and found her's. They shared a quick squeeze, a silent gesture of reassurance.

Cassidy walked over to Jack, getting right in his face and said something too quiet for Lock to hear, but she could tell the deputy was being corrected. Jack stayed squared off with his boss, turning his head a little to the side and nodded, jaw clenched tight. Then Cassidy turned to walk off and replacing his cowboy hat on his head. He nodded to Lock as he went down the stairs.

Now it was just Lock and Jack standing there on the porch under the light. She quickly tried to come up with something to say. Before she could think of something Jack dropped his arms and turned, stomping back into the house. Then the door slammed shut, leaving Lock awkwardly standing alone on the porch.

Not exactly what she'd had in mind when she offered to stay behind.

two bullets

Chapter Eighteen

She ended up waiting for Jack for an hour on the steps of Vester's house, doing nothing but staring into the empty yard while people came and went out of the house. A number of vehicles had pulled away by now, leaving only two squad cars with their lights still flashing, the orange cones still set up down the middle of the road in an arch, blocking off the one side of the road. The onlooking neighbors had since moved along, returning to their own homes, leaving the street deserted.

Part of Lock regretted not going with the others to the station, but then she thought about what was happening there; parents learning that their son not only was dead, but that he had taken his own life. Sitting here in the cold was ten times better than standing off to the side like an unwanted fly on the wall listening to a family grieve.

Emotional instances had always made her uneasy, not because she didn't have compassion, but because she had a lot of compassion. It was so hard to see others in pain and be unable to do anything about it except watch their hearts break. She had learned early on in her job that it was much easier to stay in the background and remain separated from the trauma. Maybe that's why Jack hadn't wanted to go either.

Finally, she heard men's voices talking behind her as they came out of the house. They talked for a minute, then three officers walked down the steps around Lock, mumbling good-bye to her and headed out into the yard. She watched as they gathered up the cones from the street and stacked them in

two bullets

the back of one of the squad cars.

Jack shut off the porch light and locked up the house. Lock stayed sitting on the top step, and soon felt Jack step down and take a seat next to her. He sniffed. His legs were too long, and he kept his hands in his pockets as he leaned forward over his bent knees like a man who had sat in a kid size chair. Both of them kept their eyes out on the empty street.

After a few moments of silence, Jack asked, "Do you think they're done?"

She knew he was talking about the others at the station. "I don't know. Maybe."

"We'll give 'em a few more minutes," Jack decided, uncurling himself to stretch his legs down the descending steps. He lifted his hand in a wave as the two final squad cars pulled away.

"How are you holding up?" Lock asked, turning her head to look at the man. He wore a denim jacket, layered over the unbutton dress shirt and t-shirt he'd worn to church. He black hair was smoothed back into a tight braid, now hanging over his shoulder.

He had been the one to find the body, and then help with the clean up. No matter how tough a person was, Lock knew that had to be a heavy weight to bear.

Jack sniffed again because of the cold, flattening his already thin lips into a frown, "Fine."

"You don't have to be, you know," she said gently.

"Yeah, well I don't have to not be either," he countered briskly. His eyes were intense, resentment darkening his features.

Lock was stunned and looked away. "I'm sorry, I just thought you could use a friend..."

"If you're waiting for me to break down in tears or

something, you can stop holding your breath."

Lock was hurt. She'd expected him to appreciate her emotional support. They were friends, weren't they?

"I didn't even really like the guy. He was kind of a jerk," Jack said.

Then the two of you should have been great friends, she thought bitterly. Then out loud she said, "You don't mean that."

"Like heck I don't."

"But you just were in there-"

"It's the job, Lock. You know that as well as I do. I'm trying to prove my worth to the sheriff and get myself on the department full time. I'll do what ever I have to to not have to guard bed wetters and sick people at the hospital anymore."

Lock was stunned silent. How could he be so cold and heartless? Didn't he have any sense of tact or respect? Now she really wished she'd gone on with the others to the station.

Jack eventually stood and plodded slowly down the steps. Once at the bottom, he turned around in front of her, holding out his hand to help her up. It was an out of character gesture for the attitude he was harboring, but sitting so long in the cold had stiffened her joints and she could use all the help she could get. She took his hand and pulled herself up, feeling awkward as they started down the sidewalk to the street.

"The sheriff's station's only a few blocks away," Jack said, "You're not going to collapse or anything, are you?"

Lock snorted. "No, Jack, I won't. But thank you for your concern."

He shrugged. They walked up to the end of the block, crossed to the other side and turned right, heading north towards downtown. Jack suddenly pointed at the house they were walking past. "That's the house that Jimmie and I grew up in."

"You grew up together?" She asked, surprised.

"Yeah. It was us and his sister, and a couple other kids on this block, including Ves. We'd set up in the middle of the street and play hockey or basketball until our parents called us home for dinner."

Lock smiled at the thought. She'd never thought of Jack as a little kid before.

"How did you end up living with Jimmie's family?"

"What?" He asked, looking at her in disbelief as he asked dryly, "You didn't know I was actually white?"

She shrugged, letting out a confused chuckle.

He smirked. "The Reeves took me in when I was twelve."

"I thought tribes didn't like their kids going to white people?"

"They don't. Mine was a "unique" case," Jack said, his fingers making the quotation marks in the air, and left it at that.

"Oh." She relaxed a bit, relieved that Jack seemed to have eased up a little bit.

After a couple more steps, he said, "That house across the street was where the sheriff lived."

"I bet that kept you all in check, having the sheriff right there."

Jack chuckled for the first time, obviously remembering something as he looked at the house. "Oh he tried, but we were pretty wild. There was one time during the holidays that Ves climbed up over that fence carrying a Santa garden gnome, you know one of those ones where the pants are pulled down so it's mooning everyone? Ves shimmied up the back porch and onto the roof, and super glued it to the shingles. In the morning, we watched the sheriff come out and look up, and all he saw was Santa's butt glaring down at him."

Jack was all out laughing now as he recounted the story about his friend. He got his breath, and smiled at the house across the street as they kept walking. "We spent Christmas day re-roofing the porch because the Santa had pulled up the shingles when Sheriff Walsh took it down."

Lock grinned. Then Jack shook his head and cursed. It was finally hitting him that his childhood friend was gone. Maybe Tin Man actually had a heart.

"Sounds like Ves had his moments, huh?" Lock asked quietly.

Jack sniffed, and this time it wasn't from the cold. But his voice was gruff as he shrugged, "I guess."

They cut through an alley and some dark back parking lots to get to the side street running next to the Sheriff's station. When they got around to the front facing main street, they saw a few vehicles parked along the curb, and Jack instantly slowed his gate. "Let's wait out here."

"Are Vester's parents still here?" Lock asked and he nodded.

"Are you sure you don't want to go in?"

Jack seemed less angry as he just shook his head. Lock understood then that it wasn't that he didn't care, it was because he did. And he didn't know how to handle it.

She followed him to the back of Bass's pickup parked in front of the station. He reached over the tail-gate and pulled a handle, the gate giving way and folding down. He hopped up and took a seat and Lock followed. Sitting side by side once again, their legs swung over the side as they settled in to wait.

Jack reached into his pocket and pulled out a pack of gum, offering it over to her to take a piece. She took a stick wrapped in foil and unfolded it to reveal the red gum, folding it over and popped it in her mouth.

"So how was your date going before we showed up."
Jack asked as he took out a piece for himself.

Lock pursed her lips at this, hiding a smile as she
looked across the road, "It was pretty fun."

"Bass was a gentleman?" Jack asked, seriously.

"Define gentleman."

"Let's put it this way, was he anything like me?"

"Absolutely not."

He nodded. "Then he was a gentleman."

Jack was warming up to her now. Putting her hurt
feelings aside, she saw how different he was from his friends.
She didn't think of Jimmie or Bass as soft or emotional, but put
them up next to Stonewall Jackson here, and they were
crybabies. It made her wonder how they had all become such a
close group. The differences in personalities was striking.

Jack was difficult and an independent thinker, not in
the least worried about what others thought. He was a bully,
cynical, and crass, all due to what was probably a rough
childhood. He was the last kind of person she imagined herself
spending an evening with. But despite all of these traits, there
was a human side to Jack, which if you told him that, he would
probably take it as an insult.

"Being friends with you isn't easy."

"You might be surprised to hear that I've heard that
before," Jack said, eyes shifting low in her direction. She
smiled, keeping her eyes ahead of her across the street.

Jack's head tilted to the side, and without looking at
her, he asked, "You believe in God right?"

"I do."

"Do you really think there's an afterlife? Like heaven
and hell? And don't give me the church's politically correct

two bullets

answer. I want your opinion."

Thinking, Lock took a deep breath, watching her legs swing underneath her. "Well, I guess if I believe in God and what the Bible says, then yes, I believe there is an afterlife."

"Do you think we all end up in the same place?"

She had to laugh at this, "I'm the last person to be giving the faith and hope talk. I'm just now figuring it all out myself."

Jack turned to look at her, his brow furrowed. "Why?"

Bunching up her lips, she tilted her head back to look up at the dark sky. "I don't know. I've made a lot of stupid choices over the years. Coming here has only made me realize just how much of a mess I've made of everything."

"Hey," Jack said shortly, "we're talking about me here, not you. Just tell me what you think happens after we die."

She slowly dropped her head back down, bringing herself back to earth. "If we put our faith in Jesus and believe he died for us, then we go to heaven. If we don't accept the free gift and live for ourselves, then I believe that we go to hell. There's only two options." The sound of her own voice saying those same words she had heard in church all her life surprised her. She still knew it all, even if she'd tried to forget.

Jack grumbled at this, shoulders hunched as he played with the gum wrapper in his hands. "I was afraid you'd say that."

Lock eyed him curiously. She'd just assumed that because he was close with Sly, and went to church and bible studies that he was a Christian. But by his genuine disappointment with her answer to his question, it appeared that he was still on the fence when it came to faith.

It had been her own idea to stay back with him, but she was starting to get the feeling that maybe God had wanted

two bullets

it to be this way. But whether it was for Jack or herself, she wasn't sure.

"Are you thinking about Ves?" she asked. Jack straightened, reaching down to scratch his leg as he joked, "Oh, he's definitely in hell. No doubt."

Lock snorted, "Oh, come on."

He just shrugged. "It's okay. I'll see him again someday. But I'm gonna ask for a bunk *way way* way on the other side of the camp..."

Lock had to giggle at his expressiveness, but asked honestly, "And that doesn't bother you?"

"In the end, we are who we are. We have to pay the piper."

"Come on now, you've spent time with Sly. You know it doesn't have to be that way. Right?"

Jack mulled that over, scratching at his chest as his mouth hung open with an unspoken answer.

She was waiting for an answer when the sound of the station doors opening behind them startled her and she peered back over her shoulder to look. A group had stepped outside, and a couple whom Lock assumed were Vester's parents were shaking hands and giving hugs to Sly and the deputies. She turned back around to Jack, who seemed content to stare down at his hands, fingers working on folding his gum wrapper into a square.

"You should go say something to them." She suggested carefully, nudging him with her shoulder.

"They don't want to hear what I have to say," he mumbled.

She leaned in closer, whispering, "I bet they'd like to talk to you though. Just keep it brief and shallow..."

He balked and turned to look her directly in the face.

"And say what? 'Your son was a coward and gave up on the chance of ever getting his daughter back because of a little bump in the road?'"

"Well, I wouldn't say it quite like that..."

He suddenly hopped down off the tailgate and turned to face her, leaning in a little too closely as he snapped, "Anna left Ves because he was a drunk and an abuser. His parents knew it and they did nothing, leaving Anna to handle it alone. They don't deserve my sympathy and Vester sure doesn't deserve my tears."

Then he straightened and started to walk away, glancing around the truck back towards the others on the sidewalk. Lock watched him go, sitting in the middle of the awkward silence that thickened the evening air. No way those on the sidewalk hadn't heard Jack's little speech, but if what he had said was true, maybe that wasn't such a bad thing.

two bullets

Chapter Nineteen

Tuesday

Sly's job and the multiple hats he wore caused him to carry a heavy weight of responsibilities in the days following Vester's suicide. He was busy in town with counseling sessions, not to mention keeping up with pastoral duties and meetings when he could find the time.

When he would eventually come home, it was usually very late at night, and all he wanted to do was eat and hang out watching TV. With all of the demands placed on him, it was hard for him to relax and decompress, so Lock did her best to make his time at home peaceful. She cleaned the kitchen and living room, did the laundry and tried to have dinner ready for whenever Sly would trudge in. It was a rough couple of days, but despite it all, Sly still managed a smile.

What he didn't know was that Lock had begun to entertain the idea of going back to Cincinnati. She wasn't sure when it happened, or why. It didn't have anything to do with the recent stress. She'd enjoyed her time of recuperation and the healing Barrier Ridge had offered. But talking with Bass at the diner and telling him stories from the good old days had spurred a deep sense of hope in her. She wanted so badly to have those days on the street back. She wanted her old life back.

It wouldn't be easy; she was still tainted with Danson's accusations, and no department would ever consider her application if she didn't get things straightened out. That would require doing her own investigating, and confronting Danson, neither of which excited her. And there was the whole fact that Danson, or whoever had left the note, wanted her dead.

But leaving would mean leaving Bass. She was torn between the past and what seemed to be happening in her present. But it was because of what had happened since arriving that she felt the courage to go back. She wasn't the same broken girl who'd left under the cover of night just a couple weeks ago.

Tuesday night after Sly went for bed, Lock stayed up late watching TV, journaling and texting with Bass. He was working through the trauma of losing his friend, but he seemed to be handling it all rather well. As she was typing a reply text to him, she received a notification of a new email. It was from Jimmie.

"I wanted to apologize for how everything went down Sunday. Interrupting your date was Jack's idea. Lol But I'm glad you were there at Vester's. It was good having you around even though everything was crazy... I know Bass appreciated your support."

"Thanks," she wrote back, "and don't worry about it. You guys obviously care a lot for Bass and I enjoyed the interruption. :) In regards to Vester...I didn't do much. I felt like a tag-along. I can't imagine what you guys are going through."

She got a reply a few minutes later. "You weren't a tag-along. You were right where you needed to be. I hope you stick around...we could use more Lock in our lives."

We could use more Lock in our lives. Her heart soared as she read that.

She thought about Jack Stone then, and the many sides of him that she'd had a front row seat to. He could be kind and patient one minute, but other times he was over dramatic and

two bullets

blunt. Apparently being his friend took a little bit more work. Did he think having her around was a good thing?

A recent phone conversation with her mom came to mind. Kerri Locksley had suggested that Lock talk to Cassidy and see if he'd be interested in hiring her. This wasn't the first time that idea had been suggested. "God, are you trying to tell me something?"

She'd made a lot of decisions in the recent past based on what *she* wanted and what *she* thought was best, not caring about what was right or wrong. Maybe it was time to find out what God wanted. Her wanting to go back to Cincinnati- was that just her pride talking?

She needed some alone time to pray about all of this. She slipped on a pair of rain boots and one of Sly's sweatshirts and took her questions outside. Dusk had settled over the countryside, everything shrouded in gray shadows. She wouldn't be running tonight- she'd be seeking, searching for truth in the connect-the-dots pattern above her in the sky.

She walked across the front yard towards the barn and corrals across the road. By the glow of the motion censored light on the barn, she made her way to the right of the barn where a large corral sat.

As she neared, Sly's black stallion quietly neighed and turned to trudge toward her, his hooves plodding in rhythmic steps. She held out her hand through the bars and offered him the apple she had brought. Stetson's hairy lips found the apple and quickly nibbled it off her palm. She felt his nose with her fingertips and followed it up to his forehead and gave him a good scratch. Stetson finished chewing the apple and then stepped forward with a shudder in his flanks. Pushing against the corral, he dipped his head down to the pocket of her sweatshirt.

"Sorry bud, I don't have any more."

She ran her hands down his long nose and around, under his chin. She imagined what his eyes looked like in the light; lines and craters looking like that of a dry desert at night with flecks of blue. He offered a soft neigh, then snorted in her ear and she pushed him away, giggling as she wiped at her face.

She stepped to the side and pulled herself up onto the fence. Taking a seat on the top, she quietly watched the stallion's tail swish in the bright aura of light.

The peace and quiet of the night enveloped her like a warm blanket, and suddenly her worries and frustrations didn't seem so stressful. She let out a long sigh, rubbing her hands together as she tilted her head back and looked up into the clear, star filled sky.

"Ok God," she breathed, "I need your help. I'm a little out of sorts tonight. So much is going on and I can't seem to find steady ground. I know You love me. I know that You brought me here and have been working in me. But something's missing." She dropped her head down to her chest and stared through the dark at her hands. "What am I missing?"

No answer came, but she stayed quiet. Lightning flashed on the horizon in front of her and thunder rumbled. The sound comforted her.

She took a steadying breath, clasping her hands between her knees. "Things have been really great," she continued. "You brought me to a great group of people, and I can really see myself staying here. But you know my heart. I want to be a city cop."

Why? She stopped mid-prayer and thought about that for awhile. Why Cincinnati? Why that city? Why not Barrier

Ridge?

In her head, she knew it was because of the excitement and activity that came from the city. She loved the familiar buzz of electricity as she went out on patrol in her division night after night.

But Danson wouldn't be there. Hadn't that been what made the job complete? Could she really go back, try to find a new partner, and move on with her life?

She shifted and climbed down from her perch into the corral. Patting Stetson, she turned and began to walk around the outer edge of the pen, her shoes crushing the soft dirt clods into pancakes. She heard heavy footfall coming from behind her and with a glance back, saw Stetson slowly following after her. She smiled and kept walking. She led the way all the way around the pen, back to where they started and then started on a second pass. She kept walking like that for awhile, pacing around the pen with her company not far behind. Walking and praying. Praying and walking.

She was on her sixth round when she was hit with a revelation that both startled her.

She needed to forgive Danson.

"How?" she said, still walking, "How can I forgive him after what he did?"

But the answer came to her before she even said the words; forgiving Danson didn't let him off the hook, it let *her* off the hook. She'd heard that in many-a sermon growing up. But it was a lot harder to actually do it after a betrayal such as this.

Her mind strayed back to the night of the shooting. As always, she replayed it from beginning to end. But for some reason, tonight was different. She was seeing it all from a different angle. Maybe it was where she was; outside in the

two bullets

dark rather then in her bed. Whatever the cause, in Lock's mind she turned her attention off Danson holding the gun on her. Then she shifted her attention to the man in the suit. The one who'd given Danson the gun.

She'd never thought about him much before. He was always a distant shadow at the edge of her mind. The snake in a suit that whispered encouragement into Danson's ear. He was the one who had given Danson the ultimatum that caused Danson in the end to pull the trigger. She recalled little about the man's appearance. He had short hair, right? Maybe a hat? He was older, and white. Not the typical idea of a drug dealer down on Hard Row.

For the sake of argument, Lock wondered what the man would have done if Danson hadn't actually pulled the trigger. What if he had defied the man in the suit, and said no. Would the man have killed Danson instead? Would Lock have been shot anyway to keep her quiet? This realization gave her pause. Mr. Suit wouldn't have hesitated to kill her.

She replayed the scene again with her new view point; Danson had shot her from where he stood, a good twenty yards away. A reasonable distance that they had practiced countless times at the range. And Danson had never missed the bulls-eye, even when Lock had tried to distract him in good fun. Natural ability and years of practice made him an expert shot. One of the best in the department. And yet, when he had shot her in the warehouse, he hadn't aimed for her head, or her heart. She had been in civilian clothes; no bullet proof vest.

He hadn't gone for the kill shot he was trained to take. If he had, he would have ended everything right then and there. But instead, his shots had hit her in the shoulder and side. Neither placement on its own fatal. Had it not been for the fact that she had laid bleeding for such a long time without

two bullets

medical attention, she probably wouldn't have been knocking on death's door. The doctor at the hospital had told her parents that it had been the blood loss that nearly killed her, not the shots themselves. Lock had just always chocked it all up to luck.

She stopped walking. Stetson stopped with her, dropping his nose to nuzzle the dirt. Overwhelmed, she slowly rubbed her hands over face.

Could it be possible that Danson had intentionally shot her in the places he knew wouldn't kill her? He had the skill to do so. She was a good shot in her own right, and she realized that yes, it was a very good possibility.

She'd never looked at it this way before. She'd been so blinded by her pain and anger at Danson's betrayal that she'd never looked at it any other way.

He shot her, pure and simple. But had that been merely for show? To make the man in the suit think that Danson was on his side? To actually *save* Lock's life?

In contrast, if the man in the suit had been the one shooting, Lock would for sure be dead. He wouldn't have messed around, and would have blown a hole through her head without giving it a second thought. He couldn't let her walk away, not after she'd seen his face and knew what he looked like.

There was no possible scenario where she would have left that warehouse alive, except for Danson wounding her.

Returning to the spot she had climbed down into the pen, she numbly climbed back up the the bars and dropped down outside into the grass. She couldn't go there, could she? Could she even consider the possibility that her being shot had actually been an act of mercy? It didn't negate that fact that he still had lied about the whole situation and threw her reputation out the window. Or the note! There was that. But maybe, just maybe...

Lock dropped her head into her hands. "Oh Danson, what did you do?"

Up until now, it had all been black and white; Danson had put his drug addiction ahead of their partnership. He had betrayed her. Became a stranger to her.

But what if she'd been wrong? And if it were true, did it change anything? She had still been betrayed and left for dead. Her friends had abandoned her. Her world had been shattered.

But at least you aren't dead. Possibly thanks to Danson.

"Oh Lord," she whispered into her hands, "help me."

Slowly, in her minds eye, she saw an image of a barbed-wire fence appear in front of her. Each strand of gnarly wire had been put up as a protective barrier to isolate her. It was a prison, secured by nails and wooden posts. Danson's name was on one of those nails. Actually his name was on more than one of the figurative nails securing the barbwire on her "fence." His handiwork showed in the stringing of the wire, the pounding of the stakes firmly into the cold ground. He'd earned her trust, then like a piece of string, had broken it, taking her captive to fear and grief and hate.

Regret was carved into the next nail. Guilt and fear shared the prongs of the next. And on it went. Lock's own name even had its own personal place on the fence. Yes, even she had a part to play in all of this. She'd forsaken her faith and true self. Built up walls to protect herself from the damage she had caused by living the life she wanted, and in turn, had moved herself out of God's protection.

"God, I'm sorry for what I've done," she whispered.

two bullets

Once again she saw that fence in her mind. Only now, a faceless man walked up to it, a pair of wire cutters in his hand. He placed it against the top wire and squeezed, the barbed wire snapping and falling away. It was like a balloon popping and Lock felt her breath catch in her chest as if she was physically connected to the wire.

One by one, that hand that wasn't her own worked its way down the strands of wire, cutting them each away until all that was left was a hole, a jagged gate between the erect posts. Then the hand lifted and reached out for her, and a voice filled her head,

"Give me your burden. Let me carry the weight. I have loved you, despite you turning away from me. I never left you. You can be free from your prison of pain and self condemnation, but it's up to you. You can forgive and be free. You can either follow me, or you can stay where you are. See? I've made a way of escape. The names on the fence don't matter. Why it was put up doesn't matter. I'm bigger than all of it. Let me show you what my love and forgiveness can do."

Love rushed over her like the warm sunshine at midday, despite it being the middle of the night. She was tired of living in this murky water. Half in, half out but never really free. The only Person who had never let her down was standing in front of her, living on the inside of her, asking her to take a leap of faith and leave the past behind.

"But God, I lived like a sinner. I'm tainted. How could you ever love me after I turned so far away from You?"

"Your sin is no greater than another. I don't love you because of what you have or haven't done; I love you because you are My child."

He didn't hold her mistakes, or her rejection of Him against her. He was inviting her to come back into His protective embrace of Love. To give her a fresh start at life.

She suddenly saw herself reach out for that hand, and felt her mental legs step forward. And then just like that, she was on the other side of the fence in an open field that smelled of newness and freedom. She was wrapped in the loving arms of the One who had created her.

The heavy weight she'd been carrying for so long seemed to just roll off her shoulders, and new life coursed like fire through her veins.

She was free.

Chapter Twenty
<u>Wednesday</u>

It was four-fifteen in the morning when Lock's cell phone rang, waking her from the best sleep she'd gotten in weeks. It was Bass, and he had news.

The Demon Troop biker gang was back and staying the night at the Order of The Pure Church compound. Lee Banks had gotten a hold of Bass, and told him that if they wanted to catch and arrest the bikers, they needed to come early while everyone was asleep.

All of the department's searching with no clues came down to this small window of opportunity, thanks to a man who had seen the light and who's conscience had gotten the best of him.

The raid was set to go down just after six that morning.

"You were there at the beginning. Want to see this thing through?"

Lock was instantly wide awake and scrambled out from under the covers, hurrying to dress and get into town as soon as possible. She barely even noticed that she didn't feel a single prick of physical pain or tightness the whole time.

✱   ✱   ✱   ✱

Bass absently packed up the arsenal set out in front of him into a duffel bag. It was still dark outside, the sun still a

two bullets

few hours from rising. He was wearing the same black shirt he'd been wearing yesterday, not having had the chance to change. He'd been up most of the night with Jimmie and the sheriff on the phone with Canyon City SWAT, going over their plan of attack to make sure everything was ready to go for the raid.

As he stood over the table and packed his bag, Bass let his mind wander a little. Since losing Vester, life had seemed to become much more fragile and finite. He grieved for his friend, replaying their last conversation over and over in his mind. They hadn't been best friends, but in a small town like Barrier Ridge, friends are few but important.

Knowing that the man had never given his life to Jesus hit Bass hard. He would never have the chance again to talk to Vester about Jesus. He wished that he would have tried harder. Or that in his darkest hour, Vester would have reached out for help.

But a talk with Sly helped him realize that Ves had made his choice, and no one could have stopped him. His demons had caught up with him, and he'd made it known for a long time that he had no interest in God. Bass couldn't carry the guilt for that.

Nevertheless, death is never easy. It was hard knowing they'd never see each other again.

Ves's death also made Bass realize just how truly precious life was, and that there was no time to take it for granted.

His eyes flashed to the plain gold ring he wore on his right pinky. The band caught the light as he fingered it with his thumb. It had been his grandfather's. Major Lochlin Jones had bought it while he was on furlough during the second world war, and had sent it home to his girlfriend with a letter, asking if she was crazy enough to marry a man she barely knew. A man who may never come home. Months later he had received a letter back with a paper ring and a note that simply said, "Yes. I'm crazy."

Bass's grandfather had given him the gold band a few years back, making him promise to only give it to a girl who was just as crazy as his grandmother had been. Someone with grace and integrity and a whole lot of spunk.

Bass slipped his gun into its holster as Jimmie leaned around the door, bracing against the door jam. "Lock's here. Ready to go?"

He quickly nodded and picked up his duffel bag. It was time to go to work.

They had Ezra Crane's official statement and verbal recognition of one of the biker's thanks to Jack's video from the hospital. The department had also received the results from the Canyon City crime lab of the evidence collected at the campsite where Ezra had been beaten. The DNA results proved the identity of Ezra's attackers, and that they had been camped near Ezra's campsite.

Today, Bass, Jimmie, Lock and Cassidy, with the help of Canyon City SWAT and a handful of Beckworth officers, would be issuing arrest warrants, and hopefully be able to finally close the case on Ezra's assault. The thought of finally arresting Heinous spurred everyone on like a fire had been lit under them.

There were a total of five vehicles leaving Barrier Ridge enroute to the White Society church compound. Slipping out of town through the dark, the convoy headed west. Since Lee Banks was Bass and Jimmie's informant, the two of them would be taking the lead on the raid.

Their pickup was followed by Sheriff Cassidy and

SWAT Leader Max McClane, followed by a squad car carrying four more reserve deputies. The fourth and fifth vehicles were blacked out SUV's full of Canyon City SWAT officers, armed to the teeth and wearing black tactical gear.

They were only looking to pick up five men, but by the end of the day, if the Demon Troop and the white supremacy group wanted to fight back, things could get ugly.

The car ride from Barrier Ridge to Beckworth was quiet and somber. Those who believed in God were getting right with their Maker, while the rest were internally envisioning what was to come and preparing themselves for battle. All in all, every man knew they may not be returning home to their families tonight. Lock sat in the back seat behind Jimmie, watching out the window as they sped through the early morning haze of dawn, praying under her breath, once again feeling the rush of adrenaline and excitement. It was intoxicating and her hands trembled nervously.

Over the radio, Jimmie called out a ten minute warning. Dropping the radio into the cup holder, he said, "Any regrets?" Next to him, Bass held a shotgun loaded with bean-bag rounds propped between his legs.

"Maybe one or two. You?"

Jimmie gave a hearty sigh as he sank further back into his seat. "After what's been going on in my personal life the last few days, I'd say I could write a book on regrets."

"Still no word on Jamie?"

Jimmie bit the inside of his cheek as he shook his head. "Not even after what happened with Ves."

"Well, I mean she's done this before. She always comes back eventually. She's probably in Seattle or somewhere with friends.

Jimmie just nodded. "That's life right? Out of my

two bullets

hands. I guess I've got five miles to clear my head."

Bass reached over and patted Jimmie hard on the chest. "Let's just live through today, and then we can worry about what happens next. If it makes you feel any better, those kids are going to turn out okay with an uncle like you."

"Thanks, brother." Jimmie said, and the two shared a knowing look across the cab. Jimmie turned his attention back to the road, adjusting his grip on the steering wheel, then let out another sigh, "Just live through today, right?"

Bass nodded, then he twisted in his seat to look back at Lock. She stared out her window, chin resting in her hand.

"How you feeling, Cincinnati?"

She pulled away from the window to look at him as she nodded, "Ready to go."

Jimmie glanced in the review mirror at her. "What about you? Any regrets you'd like to share?"

She smiled. "Actually, no. I'm ready to kick some butt!"

If she died today, it would be with a clear conscience and a clean heart. Seeing those two men sitting in front of her, she couldn't think of anyone else she'd rather storm the gates of hell with.

"Alright then." Jimmie nodded, returning his eyes to the road as he began to slow for the coming turn. "Let's go have some fun."

Bass lifted his hand and reached back towards Lock with a closed fist and she bumped it.

"See you on the other side."

two bullets

Just short of the final corner before the compound's main gate, Jimmie slipped out of the pickup into the darkness, Bass moving over to take the wheel. Working quietly through the trees, Jimmie made his way around to where he knew the sniper guarding the gate would be hiding. The man never knew what hit him.

At the gate, someone used bolt cutters to snap the rusted lock. It took five SWAT officers to push it open. With everyone back in their vehicles, the convoy was ready to move. Bass looked anxiously out into the inky blackness. "Come on, Jimmie, where are you?"

As he moved the gear shift into drive, Lock spotted a flash of light out the right window. "There he is!"

Jimmie's dark form appeared from the black forest with the handcuffed lookout. He walked the prisoner to the paddy wagon on loan from Beckworth that had just joined the group. Then Jimmie hurried up the line of cars and slipped back in with Bass and Lock.

"What took you so long, Lieutenant" Bass chided, easing the pickup forward, "Did you stop for coffee?"

"Well, Deputy, there's this thing you do when you arrest a person called 'mirandizing.' It takes a delicate touch."

"Which is a way to say you're getting old and you got tired."

"I can still beat you in the four minute mile."

"That's still yet to be proven."

Jimmie grinned. "It's a date then."

They surged on into the camp like a crashing wave. The officers spilled out from the vehicles like ghosts, covering the site with silent precision. SWAT began sweeping through the cabins and tents like spirits wearing Kevlar. Cassidy showed the arrest warrants to the bewildered guards.

two bullets

Lock stuck with the sheriff and helped to secure all the weapons, keeping the residents quiet as the rest of the officers moved to take the large shop building. Had there been even whispers of cops coming to raid the compound, the place would have been a ghost town by the time the department arrived. But as it was, everyone was there. The only person who wasn't surprised was Lee Banks, though he pretended very well.

Bass and Jimmie led the attack on the shop. Each took a group of men and entered through the two doors on opposites sides of the building. Four flash-bang grenades were tossed in, sending bikers and White Pawns Of The Order scrambling like rats caught in a spot light, blindly running for the exits, only to find that every way of escape was blocked. Fists thrown in desperation caused a brawl to break out amidst the calls for surrender.

On opposite sides of the painted black room Jimmie and Bass fought the desperate men. It was one great big sea of wildly thrown punches and take down maneuvers. At one point, Jimmie saved Bass' and another police officer's life by shooting a rushing man wielding a machete. Bass returned the favor by shooting a man in the leg who had a gun aimed at Jimmie's head from behind. Jimmie gave his friend a thankful nod before getting the handcuffs on the man he had down on the ground.

Suddenly, over the deafening roar in the hall, the shout came that someone had slipped through and was making a break for it out the back. Without hesitating, Bass holstered his weapon and took off running, sprinting around long dining tables and leaping fallen chairs to get to the swinging back door.

Outside, he saw the man in jeans running for the woods. Bass kicked it into high gear, leaving the meeting hall

two bullets

behind. He followed the fleeing biker into the trees, hurdling bushes and sidestepping fallen logs as he charged ahead, arms pumping in rhythm with his heart, eyes never leaving his target.

The trees began to clear as they came up to the edge of a swamp. Bass saw the man slow and leap to his left, glancing over his shoulder to see how close he was being followed. Bass changed up his angle and started running for where the man was going to be, cutting the distance in half.

When he was about ten feet away, Bass lunged and took a flying leap through the air, timing it just right to crash into the man. The pair went flying sideways and splashed into the murky, cold water. The man under Bass screamed his surrender, thrashing and clawing to keep his head above water.

Bass got his feet under him and grabbed the back of the man's shirt, pulling him up out of the water, then spun him around and forced him down onto his stomach on the soggy bank, slapping on the cuffs.

"You, my good sir, are under arrest."

Jimmie and a SWAT officer came running up and helped Bass get the biker up onto his feet.
Jimmie stepped over and slapped Bass's back.

"You good?"

Bass was bent over, hands perched on his knees as he gasped for air. "Please tell me he's one of the ones we're after."

"Buddy, you hit jackpot!" Jimmie praised. Bass relaxed and hung his head, chuckling as he shook with adrenaline.

Chapter Twenty-One

As they returned to the main yard of the compound, the sight of bikers and skinheads alike spread out across the grass was striking. The members of the Demon Troop were in their own area, while the men of the Order sat in groups across the yard.

Sheriff Cassidy and Lock had been busy dealing with the larger Order groups, keeping them contained until every one was organized and processed. As Bass and Jimmie returned with Flynn Bauer and put him into a group with his buddies, Cassidy and Lock made their way through the sea of people towards them.

With his own eyes, the sheriff confirmed his men were okay. Jimmie had a cut above his eye from being clipped by an elbow, while Bass was soaked from his tumble in the lake, and had a gash on his arm from a shard of glass. After being checked out by paramedics, it was determined that the piece of glass was still in Bass's arm, and he would have to go to the hospital to get it removed and receive a tetanus shot.

Sargent Kyle Cobblestein, and Officer Mark Schultz had been injured, but none of their wounds were life threatening. Four White Society henchmen were going to the hospital with various injuries, and five members of the Demon Troop were going to jail. All in all, it was a job well done.

"Smoke 'em if you got 'em." Cassidy announced to everyone within earshot. "If you have phone calls to make, step aside two at a time. No one goes anywhere alone."

Jimmie stepped away with Lock to call Jack. The

two bullets

sullen man who was still bitter about not getting to be on the raid.

Bass took a turn guarding one of the Pure Order groups. The ten men sat cross-legged in the grass.

Lock was watching Jimmie's back as he talked on the phone. Across the road, one of the detainees in Bass's group called out.

"I want my phone call."

Bass looked over the heads of the men to Archer Banks, Lee Bank's brother.

"You're not under arrest," Bass said. "Just sit tight."

The man would probably go free and return to his "good work" of traveling around to racial festivals, or selling drugs, but for now, he was under investigation and Bass had the upper hand.

"If I'm not under arrest, then why am I in handcuffs? You Jew loving pigs ever even heard of the Bill of Rights?"

"You think the Jews are running the government, but you still worry about your rights under the constitution? That's gotta get confusing." Bass said and turned away.

"What about a cigarette?" Archer called. "You got one of those?"

Bass was short on patience. "Please, stop talking."

The man Bass had been talking to had caught Lock's attention. He seemed familiar, but she couldn't place him. There were a lot of faces around the area, and it was a little overwhelming. Maybe she had just seen him earlier absently and his appearance had stuck in her head.

Jimmie finished on the phone and gestured they could leave. They walked across the gravel road to where Bass stood.

"Everything okay over here?" Jimmie asked.

two bullets

"Oh, just brilliant." Bass replied. He grinned at Lock.

Someone shouted her name over the commotion. She turned to see an officer coming near with the coat she'd thrown off. She smiled thankfully and took it from him as he passed. She slipped it on and crossed her arms, hunching her shoulders against the cold. Her eyes went to the group of men sitting in front of her, the man who had been pestering Bass catching her eye. She was shocked to see him staring at her and quickly dropped her gaze.

Jimmie was looking at Bass's injured arm. "You really should get that looked at."

"I'm up next for a ride into town. I was just giving Hughes a break."

Jimmie stepped back and turned to Lock. "So how's it feel being back in the middle of all this?"

She smiled happily, "It was just what the doctor ordered."

"You did good."

"I agree." Cassidy said, stepping up to join their circle. His eyes were on Lock. "There's a spot on my team if you want to make it official."

"Really? You want me around all the time?" She smirked, and he nodded seriously.

"The sooner the better."

Three times. Three times the suggestion of working for the department had come up. And this time, straight from the sheriff himself. *Ok God. I get it.*

She had the bug again, and she enjoyed the feeling of having a gun in a holster on her hip again. There was just something about being around all these cops that reminded her of being a recruit at the police academy, and being excited about the future.

two bullets

"Hey, pig!" Lee's brother called again from his seat. His glasses were crooked on his nose. His nice shirt was wrinkled. His close cropped hair looked out of place in this sea of bald heads and army fatigues. "How about my phone call?"

Jimmie and Bass turned and answered in unison, "Shut up!"

Lock rode into town with Bass and Jimmie in the ambulance. She was supposed to have gone in for a check up with Dr. Martin days ago but hadn't made it. She'd have herself checked out, which meant she got to spend some more time with Jimmie and Bass.

They were placed in a private exam area off the ER, blue curtains sectioning off each bed station. After the nurse left, Bass pushed back the curtain and sat on the edge of his bed. Across from him, Lock mirrored him, her legs swinging just short of touching the floor. Jimmie sat on a short stool on wheels between them. Like kids staying up past their bed time, they talked as they waited for the doctor.

The door opened and they turned to see Jack enter the "private" room, carrying a clipboard in his hands.

"Nice to see you all alive and chatty," he said. Sulking, he dropped into a chair in front of a medicine cabinet. He swung his feet up and perched them on a small desk against the wall and situated his clipboard on his legs.

"Aww, is someone feeling left out?" Bass teased in a

mocking voice.

"Well yeah! I was there too at the beginning, ya know, not just Lock. But I see you took the girl and left the Injun. A low-blow, guys."

"Oh calm down, Jack," Jimmie laughed. "You had to work, remember? You were given the chance to come but you decided to stay here."

"Well, I won't make that mistake again," Jack said, drawing a straight line across the paper in front of him and let his hand swing out dramatically into the air.

Jimmie rolled his eyes at the others and they all laughed.

Twenty minutes later, Dr. Martin came in, a blue surgical cap atop his head, his white lab coat swishing as he walked. "Who's first?"

Lock looked at Bass questioningly, but he held out his arms. "Ladies first."

The doctor put on a pair of latex gloves, and without so much as a look in Jack's direction, said, "Stone, get your feet off my desk."

Jack quickly took his legs down, then waited until the doctor began to exam Lock then put his feet back up.

Dr. Martin moving on to check her range of motion and the incision sites that were now merely a dull pink scar.

"Well," he said when he was finally done, "You seem to be healing up just fine, despite missing your check-ups. Ween yourself off your pain killers as much as possible, and you'll find that hot baths are your best friend. You doing your exercises in the morning?"

"Actually yes. Think I'll need physical therapy?"

The man frowned, wagging his head. "For most people in your case, I would say yes. But you seemed to have regained your muscle, and the tissue has healed up nicely."

Lock hadn't expected this and looked excitedly from him to her friends. They smiled and gave her two thumbs up. Dr. Martin then turned around to Bass, who held out his arm.

"How do you spell, "spontaneously?" Jack asked from his slouch in the rolling chair, feet still up on the desk.

"Just say it happened really fast," Bass replied, watching Dr. Martin take the bandage off his arm. The gash was small, but there was a thin sliver of glass wedged in deep. As the doctor adjusted his glasses on his face and grabbed a pair of tweezers, Lock realized he must be why she thought Archer Banks looked familiar. The men had similar facial structures, and their hair was basically the same.

"I don't want to say it happened fast; I want to say it happened spontaneously." Jack whined.

"Well if you can't spell it, then you shouldn't use it," Jimmie said, "What are you writing anyway?"

He rose from his seat and walked over to Jack, snatching the clipboard out of his hands. His eyebrows went up. "This is a crossword puzzle, Jack!"

Jack snatched the clipboard back from him. "I know that. I got bored writing my report."

Lock laughed, spelling out the word, "S-p-o-n-t-a-n-i-o-u-s-l-y."

"It's 'e-o,' not 'i-o'." The doctor corrected without looking up.

"You sure?"

"Hey, he's right!" Jack said with enthusiasm.

"Well I was close." Lock muttered.

"Keep it wrapped up for a few days and take some antibiotics. You'll be fine." Dr. Martin said to Bass, snapping off his gloves. As he began to walk from them to the door, he

two bullets

passed by Jack and quickly nabbed the clipboard from him and continued walking out of the room into the hall.

"Hey!" Jack cried, rushing to his feet to chase after the doctor. "I'm not done with that yet!"

"You guys want to grab a drink to celebrate?" Jimmie asked as they all began to rise.

"I can't." Lock said, slipping on her coat. "I should probably get home to Sly and tell him about today."

"Yeah, and I'm her ride." Bass said, pretending to be apologetic at Jimmie, but he really was more interested in being with Lock.

Jimmie just eyed them knowingly, but they didn't budge. "Alright. Well, I'll see you later. I probably should get back out there anyway. The town can't protect itself, ya know." He grinned and turned to leave.

*   *   *   *

Bass opened Lock's door and she climbed down. "Want to come in and help me tell Sly about today?"

"A chance to spend more time with you?" Bass said with a smirk. "Definitely."

Lock's face lit up at this and she grinned, turning away towards the house. Judy waited on the path to the porch, tail wagging, tongue hanging out.

"Some guard dog you are," Lock teased, pausing to scratch the wolf's ears.

Another day spent with her, another chance to share his work with her. Bass smiled as he watched her play with the dog. He wasn't sure he'd ever seen her so relaxed and joyful.

The idea of her leaving and going back to Cincinnati nagged at him. It wasn't something he had to think long and hard about; he liked her and suddenly couldn't see his life without her.

She led the way to the front door and let herself in. Sly sat on the couch, rising as Lock announced she was home.

"I've been on pins and needles all day. How'd we do?"

The three stood around the kitchen island as Bass and Lock told Sly all about the day's events. Sly watched as they proudly tag teamed in the story telling. He saw the way they looked at each other. Bass leaned down on the island, while Lock stood, talking with her whole body. When was the last time he'd seen the real Lock before tonight? Had he ever seen Bass look at another person with such pride and interest? They talked about fist fights and chasing bad guys, and yet there was a sweetness between the two of them that filled the room. It was nearly nauseating. They were made for each other.

Sly grinned.

Lock left the room for a moment, and Sly could tell Bass had something he wanted to say. "Out with it, Aussie."

Bass, still leaning on his arms, looked up with innocent stupidity. "What?"

Sly's eyes narrowed as he walked from the island to the sink. "You want to ask me something, don't you?"

Bass rolled over, now supporting himself on his elbow as he faced Sly. "Do I?"

"I'm gonna throw this glass at your head if you keep dodging my questions," Sly said, motioning with the glass he'd taken out of the drainer.

Bass chuckled and dipped his head, absently fingering the gauze wrapped around his forearm. Sly filled the glass from the faucet, then handed it to Bass. He took it, nodding his thanks. Filling his own glass, Sly turned, leaning against the edge of the sink. As he took a drink, his eyes were on Bass.

"I like her, Sly," Bass said, suddenly self conscience.

"I can tell. Everyone can tell. Have you told her?" Sly took another drink.

Bass shrugged. "More or less. Every time I think about saying something, something comes up."

Sly drained his glass, then angled back to put the cup in the empty sink.

Bass couldn't read his friend. He was being subtle, and Bass wasn't good with subtle.

"Do I have your permission to say something? I mean, are you okay with us?"

Sly crossed his arms, then his feet, resting back again into the counter. "She's been through a lot. I don't think she could handle another heartbreak."

Bass nodded, keeping his eyes low. Then he shifted so as to look back over his shoulder. Lock still hadn't returned. He turned and settled back down, then said, "I've never been so sure of anything in my life, Sly. I want to ask her to stay. But I won't if you're not okay with it."

He swallowed hard. He respected his friend and his opinion, and he prayed that he wouldn't have to keep his promise.

"Well," Sly said, pushing himself up and took a step, "if it was any one other than you, I'd chase you out of here with my shotgun. But I haven't seen Lock so giggly since I don't know when. If you choose to talk to her, you have my blessing." Sly's face softened with an amused grin as he held out his hand. Visibly relieved, Bass chuckled and stood, firmly returning the brotherly shake.

two bullets

Sly left the room, and not long after, Lock returned.

"I'm about to head out," Bass said, pausing long enough for Lock to offer to walk him out. Lock walked with him outside, closing the door behind her. Bass lifted his cowboy hat and placed it on his head, working up the courage to say what he'd been working on his head.

"Lock, I know you miss being a cop," he began. "Now that things are getting back to normal, you're probably thinking about heading back to Cincinnati."

She nodded, eyes dropping as she crossed her arms. The thought of the death threat that had been left came to mind. "I'll be honest; I've thought about it."

"And of course it's your choice," Bass went on, "but I have to tell you that I think that it would be a big mistake. You can be just as happy here as you could there. And if you stay, I'd like to think maybe we could, you know, see where all this is going. With you and I. The guys like you, and I know Cassidy would give you a job."

Lock looked up at him sharply. Her breath caught in her chest. He had simply glossed over the mention of the two of them, but Lock hadn't. He wanted her to stay.

The moment was interrupted by Bass's cell phone suddenly going off. Visibly irritated by the interruption, he held up his finger, fishing the phone out of his jeans, a bit distracted as he answered. He listened, then nodded as he promised he would be on his way. He hung up and Lock hurried to recover what ever was left of this moment, "Bass, I-"

He cut her off, and as only he could, speaking in a soft voice that floated on a smile, reassuring as he said, "We're not done talking about this, I promise." Then he leaned down to kiss her cheek and left with one final look before hurrying to

two bullets

the steps.

Lock watched him go. She couldn't let him go. Not like this. She spoke before her mind had a chance to catch up.

"All the single ladies around here are gonna be mad," she called after him as she stepped up to the top of the stairs. She shivered nervously as she wrung her hands in front of her.

Bass stopped, turning around slowly as he nodded thoughtfully, "That is very possible."

She took another step forward, her toes now hanging over the end of the stair. "What about your reputation? They say I'm a dirty cop. What will people think?"

She was teasing, trying to be coy, but she was also giving him a way out. Making sure he remembered just who he was asking to stick around.

She saw the grin spread across his face, hands moving up to rest on his waist on either side of his gun belt. "I could care less about my reputation, Love. I want you, Lock. And I'm okay with whatever comes with you."

Still nervously wringing her hands, Lock shrugged at him, bunching her lips together tightly in a coy smile.

"Well, I *have* been thinking about going back."

She let the words hang in the air for a moment. With her thumbnail she dug into the paint bubbled up on the railing beam next to her.

Bass waited.

She looked at him and with a sly smile, she casually rolled her eyes, "You know. To get my stuff. And then come back..."

Bass didn't need anymore than that. He dropped his hands and started walking back to her, quickly jogging up the steps. He barely slowed down before removing his hat and dipped his head to plant a kiss straight on her lips. She

two bullets

stumbled back a step, but didn't step away as she kissed him back.

When he pulled away, he was grinning, his eyes quickly searching hers.

"Does that mean you'll stay?" He asked. She giggled, then nodded. He ducked back in for one more kiss, this time wrapping his arms around her waist to pick her up, spinning her around while she laughed with glee. The grin he carried on his lips stayed with him the entire drive to town.

Chapter Twenty-Two
Later that evening

Bass pulled in to the parking lot of the abandoned Catholic church and cut the engine. The towering steeple of the stone church cut through the darkening evening, creating a stark void in the otherwise clear sky. The historical building was the main attraction of what the locals called, "Old Town," which was basically just the southern half of Barrier Ridge.

The Heart of Mary's Church had closed down ten years ago and had become merely a passing historical sight for tourists to take selfies with. The locals liked to take midnight strolls through the back garden, albeit a rather creepy place at night, in Bass's opinion.

Lieutenant Jimmie Reeves and a deputy named Kyle Gunther stood in front of a squad car. They were talking with two baby faced teenagers who looked rattled and more or less ready to get the heck out of there.

As Bass approached, Jimmie was in the midst of telling Gunther to put the teens in the back of the squad car and call their parents. As the three walked past him, Bass gave them a quick look over before stopping next to Jimmie. "Quiet night?"

Jimmie snorted. "Not in the least." Then he took a closer look at Bass's face. "Are you smiling?"

Bass just smirked, but kept his friend on topic. "You said something about suspicious noises?"

"You are smiling!" Then the pieces came together, revelation appearing on Jimmie's face. "Oh, that's right, you were with Lock."

two bullets

"You said it was urgent, Jimmie."

Jimmie stared hard at Bass, trying to read what he saw on his friend's face. When he couldn't get him to break, he just nodded and moved on.

"The Hardy Boys over there were apparently hunting around for priceless ancient artifacts for their clubhouse in the back garden when the back door just happened to open on its own."

"So like respectful citizens, they investigated."

"Yep, walked right in and started looking around. That's when this happened." Jimmie pulled out one of the boy's cell phones and hit play on the paused video for Bass. The video wiggled and bumped around as the videoer searched through the dark for something to focus on. The moving screen scurried around, showing dirty floors and old painting tarps strewing the floor, but it was too dark to make out anything very clearly. Then the angle changed up to the front stained glass window, illuminated by the full moon behind it. Then suddenly a dark form passed across the screen, there and gone in a flash and the video ended.

"Did I miss something?" Bass asked as Jimmie took the phone back.

"They say the figure was not one of them. Something ran in front of them and took off up the stairs to the balcony. Then they heard a low wail that was..." Jimmie paused to look at his notes, "'something out of a horror movie. A ghost warning them to leave it alone.'"

Though seasoned and experienced with things that go bump in the night, the hairs on Bass's neck raised a little. But he wasn't one to believe in ghosts. He stepped back a little and looked up at the church towering over them. A flock of birds took flight just then from some nearby trees, taking to the sky as they squawked and called out as they passed by the steeple.

"So someone's in there that shouldn't be." Bass stated flatly.

"Feel like going ghost hunting?" Jimmie asked wryly and Bass just grinned at him.

It grew darker with each passing minute; the mountains to the west hiding what was left of the setting sun. Not wanting to yell across the parking lot to alert whoever was in the church, Jimmie radioed Gunther back at the squad car and told him to secure the boys in the car.

The front doors were securely locked with heavy chains so Jimmie led Bass around to the back entrance, still hanging open like an empty tomb, flanked by waist high statues and out of season bushes. Jimmie pulled out his flashlight and clicked it twice to remind Bass to only use the light in short bursts. They didn't want whoever was still inside to be able to follow their beams and sneak up from behind.

Jimmie entered first, stepping to the side for Bass to come in next to him, shining the flashlight for just a moment in the space before them so they could get their bearings. The entrance opened into a empty back hall where there was a bathroom on one end, and offices on the other.

They quickly cleared these areas before moving on through the last door, which opened up behind the pulpit at the front of the sanctuary. Jimmie worked his way down the right side of the pews while Bass stole quietly across the stage and moved slowly down the middle aisle.

Their flashlights popped on and off in tandem, swinging between the pews. Outside light coming through the stained glass windows that rose up on either side of the large room cast haunting rays of light across the dark chapel. It was eerily quiet in the large room. Bass felt his instincts kick in as his visual senses were limited, pausing every so often to listen, distinguishing the sounds of Jimmie moving just off to his right from any other sound.

Then the sound of pressure on the wooden floor boards up in the balcony echoed through the dark. Both men stopped where they were. They shifted their attention to the back of the room and up at the black hole that was the balcony. They stood still, holding their breath as they listened, their lights finding only emptiness in the balcony.

Then down from the bell tower came a low, wistful wail, almost like someone was singing but wasn't sure of the melody.

Jimmie let out a low, barely audible whistle that only Bass would hear. They quickly hurried to the back pews near the chapel entrance. The singing/moaning continued as they got to the staircase and began to climb. With the aid of the light from outside, they cleared the rows of pews in the balcony, then regrouped at the base of the final staircase that led to the tower. The voice, obviously female, was still going at it, now a little more confidently, from above them.

Standing with their guns pointed above them up the stairs, Jimmie took a deep breath.

"Sheriff's department," he called up into the dark, his voice bouncing off the walls around them. The sudden sound surprised Bass, despite knowing it was coming. The singing instantly cut out like a blown out candle.

"You are trespassing on private property. If you have weapons, lay them down on the ground. Get down on your knees and place your hands behind your head."

No more sounds came from above. Jimmie shared a look with Bass, both nodding. Bass took the lead this time, climbing the steps slowly, one foot over the other as he inched up to the gaping mouth of the open steeple door. There was no way he was going in there without a light. He flicked on his flashlight and kept it low, pausing at the door, leaning into the side wall as he strained to see into the room.

"Hello? Sheriff's Department. We're coming in."

Next to Bass on the top stair, Jimmie stood with his weapon pointed into the room.

"Go!" he hissed.

Bass ducked and slipped in, staying low, sweeping his gun and flashlight around him as he cleared his way through. A row of old pews partially covered by a tarp jutted out into the room, cutting into the space under where the large bell hung high at the center of the room. The paneless windows encircling the room opened the space to the outside air.

Bass and Jimmie each took a side and cleared the area around the ropes hanging from the bell, but it was obvious even before that, that the space was empty. Other than the pews and a broken statue of Mother Mary gathering dust, there was nowhere to hide.

"Umm..."Jimmie said, rather perplexed. He spun around in a circle with his flashlight. "Huh. That's a new one."

Bass walked over to one of the windows and looked out, seeing the vehicles down below in the parking lot. There was no sound or movement suggesting anyone down there had seen anything. He turned his head and was moving to holster his weapon when he caught movement across the tower. He stopped and did a double take.

Outside the window directly across from him, a woman was balancing out there on the peak of the roof of the main sanctuary, slowly walking with her arms out like she was walking a tight rope.

"Uh. Jimmie?"

Jimmie looked and saw Bass pointing towards the window. He turned quickly and crouched for a better view. His eyes widened in amazement.

"Really?"

They both moved to the window. This one had a design of a cross made of re-bar spanning the height, the thin arms reaching out to either side of the concrete window. The space was too small for either one of them to get through, but a small woman on the other hand could have easily been able to slip through.

"What do we do?" Bass asked.

Jimmie just shook his head. "I honestly have no idea. I don't want to startle her and cause her to fall."

"How far is it to the ground?" Bass asked. He pressed his face up to the re-bar to try and see the ground.

"She wouldn't die, but she'd break a few things."

"We don't get paid enough for this job." Bass said, knowing he might have to climb out there. He wasn't afraid of heights, but he wasn't a fan of them either.

"Aww, come on Bass. Where's your sense of duty?" Jimmie teased, only because he was thinking the same thing.

They watched the woman dressed in jeans and a baggy t-shirt continue to slowly inch her way out to the edge of the roof, immediate drops on either side that would send her straight down to the ground with no chance to catch herself.

"She's got a great sense of balance." Bass said, rather impressed, fingers digging into the edge of the concrete window sill.

"Uh-oh." Jimmie said.

"What?" Bass hissed, not daring to look away for fear his gaze was the only thing keeping the woman steady.

"That's...umm. Well that's Jamie."

two bullets

Startled, Bass dared a glance at his friend. "Your sister?!"

Jimmie took in a deep breath. Then nodded, eyes glued to the frail woman's back. Bass's jaw clinched, his words coming out in more of a sigh than a statement, "Crap."

$$*\quad*\quad*\quad*$$

Jimmie strained against the re-bar that inhibited him from going out on the roof. He was watching his best friend since birth walk a fine line between delusion and reality, life and death. He tried calling to Jamie quietly, careful to not speak too loudly for fear she would turn around and lose her footing. But she was in her own world out there on the roof, walking her delusional tight-rope, bathed in moonlight in the same clothes she had been wearing when she'd left her home.

Jimmie couldn't take the time to wonder where she had been all this time. Or how she'd ended up here. Right now, she was there in front of him, one wrong step from sliding off the roof.

Bass had stepped away, quietly talking into his radio, relaying the situation to dispatch first, then calling Pastor Sly Malone on his phone.

"Jamie, concentrate on my voice," Jimmie was saying, pressed up tightly against that confounded re-bar that denied him access to the roof. His arm was stretched out through the window towards his sister. He had no idea what he should be saying to her.

two bullets

He couldn't ask her to turn around; she'd absolutely fall. If he told her to stop, she could also just as easily get off balance and start falling. But he wasn't going anywhere, unable to take his eyes off the shell of the person who had once been a strong, funny, healthy woman. His real sister was in there somewhere, and he would do whatever he could to bring her back.

Bass got off the phone and walked back up to Jimmie, tapping the man's shoulder with a single finger. "Hey," he whispered, and Jimmie's head turned slightly, eyes dropping as he listened. "We need to get something out there to her that she can grab and get a hold of."

Jimmie shook his head. "Anything we get out to her, she's going to have to bend down to get it. It's too risky."

"It's better than nothing. Right now she has nothing to grab for stability. A shift in the wind could throw her for a loop."

Bass stepped aside and turned, eyes searching the room around him for anything they could use. He needed something strong and solid. Any kind of fabric would be too weak and hang limply across the roof peak. The fire department was on their way with the bucket truck, but every second that passed was taking Jamie closer to a deadly misstep.

Bass muttered absently to himself. *Think, think, think. God, help me. Help me-*

The painting tarps!

"Jimmie, you hang tight. I'll be right back."

He took off for the stairs and pounded down all the way to the main floor, using the railings as a slide to skip the last five steps. He remembered seeing the paint cans and brushes set off to the side amidst the painting tarps just outside

the chapel doors. He dove to them now and started pulling and
lifting the tarps, looking for what he prayed was there.

Something plastic clanked on the floor and he tossed
aside a black trash bag, simultaneously wrapping his hand
around something circular and thin. He picked it up and held it
out into the pale moonlight, seeing the long paint roller
attached to the end of the extension stick. He gave it a try and
stretched the pole out further, and discovered the extender was
more than adequate for what he needed it for.

Satisfied, he turned on his heel and raced back up the
stairs with the roller in hand. As he returned into the tower, he
skipped a step as he made a wide birth around those intrusive
pews.

"Here!" he breathed. Jimmie turned quickly, eyes going
down to the pole.

"What is it?"

"It's a long extension rod. We can feed it out to Jamie
and try to get her to take hold of it."

"Oh! Good work, partner. But, this roller is hard as a
rock. There's no way she can hold on to it with a sure grip."

"Way ahead of you." Bass said, handing Jimmie the
pole. He quickly unhooked his gun-belt, then undid his actual
leather belt and whipped it out of the belt loops. Jimmie tried
but was was only able to pull the dried paint roll off about half
way, but it was enough to weave Bass's belt through the wires
of the brace and make a large loop that hung like a contraption
used to catch stray dogs.

The belt was cinched tight, and looking like something
MacGyver would be very pleased with, Jimmie helped Bass
feed the invention out and across the roof towards Jamie.

"Jamie, grab this!" Jimmie called out quietly. "You
don't have to come back, just grab hold of that loop and hang

on."

They were able to keep the rod level with Jamie's head as they held the rounded end of the rod. All she had to do was reach up and grab the hanging loop of the belt. Bass kept it to himself that it was more than likely his contraption wouldn't be able to hold Jamie's weight very long if she did indeed fall. But her chances went up considerably, and now they could wait for the firetruck to arrive with a little less anxiety.

"Leave me alone!" Jamie suddenly shrieked back at them.

"I can't do that, Aimes. You've got four little babies waiting for their mom to come home, and I'm going to do my best to make sure that happens."

Jamie Reeves-Kurtz scoffed in a rather angelic, floating tone of voice. "Nice! They teach you that line in the Marines?"

"Nope, came up with it on my own. Now, would you just grab on to the belt?!"

She gave the contraption next to her a glance, but wasn't interested. She stretched her arms out a little farther for balance and took two more tightrope steps forward towards the end of the building.

"Jamie!" Jimmie roared.

They tried to extend the rod out further but she was out of reach and they were out of length. The extender was starting to bow in the middle with the uneven weight.

"Take a breath, Jimmie." Bass whispered, knowing his friend was seconds away from completely losing his mind. They could hear the sirens coming down the road behind them, and it brought only a little comfort.

"Keep talking to her. I'm going down to help the others."

two bullets

"I'll be here."

Bass let go of the extender rod and Jimmie moved over to take his place and get a better grip. Bass grabbed his gun belt on the way out and wrapped it around his waist, taking off back down the stairs and up the aisle to the back of the church. He sprinted out the back door and around the corner.

He slowed his jog and looked up, catching sight of Jamie up through the various levels of the roof. She stood on the end of the main sanctuary. If she fell forward, she would hit the next roof down, which would slow her down, then it would be a tumble off into the overgrown shrubbery.

Bass ran the rest of the way out to the parking lot, waving his hands over his head at Gunther standing at the front of his squad car.

"Get around to the back and keep an eye on things and you let me know the second anything changes."

Gunther had heard the call come over the radio and quickly nodded, hurrying away.

Bass stepped out into the parking lot and waved to the driver of the firetruck. They came around the outer edge of the parking area, then pulled up to a stop in front of the church. Bass ran and climbed up onto the side of the truck as the passenger windows was being rolled down.

"We got a young woman on the roof," he said to the chief. "I need you to get in as close as you can and get your ladder up there."

"Suicidal?"

Bass gave an unclear shrug and nodded. "Treat it as such."

"What about the bucket? Will it reach?" The gruff man asked from inside the dark interior, his face illuminated by all the buttons and screens on the dash

"You guys can decide that one. But you need to get up in there and get in position either way."

"What about an air bag? Is there time to set one up?"

"Probably not. She's right on a double sided plunge. There's no way to know which side to set up on. We need to just get up there and grab her. Just drive up on the sidewalk and through the fence. We'll deal with the historical society later..."

The man inside saluted with a grin. "You got it. Hang on tight."

The engine lurched forward and Bass stuck his hand through the window and held on tight. He peered out ahead through the headlights as the engine drove up over the curb and through the white picket fence and bushes thereafter, crushing them flat. He leaned back and looked over the engine's roof, squinting to see past the blinding red lights that flashed. He could see the thin shadow of the extender he'd made still hanging out of the window. Jamie was now seated on the farthest end of the roof, her legs hanging down over the side.

The fire engine came to a stop and Bass hopped down out of the way of those getting out. He walked around to the front of the truck, moving to where he could see into the tower windows, then reached for his radio. "Jimmie. You there, buddy?"

"She sat down. Why'd she sit down?"

"I don't know, brother. She's got about a four foot drop to the next roof, then it's straight down to the ground."

"Are they going to climb up to her?"

"That's the plan. You have any suggestions?"

"Just get her down."

Bass noticed then that one of the firemen was carrying

a type of body harness.

"They've got a harness, Jimmie. They'll take care of her."

"Sorry your little invention here didn't work."

Bass chuckled, eyes up on the window where he knew Jimmie was standing. "Don't worry about it. Hang tight."

He put the radio away and grabbed the fire chief, pointing him to the area just under the lower roof. "If she goes off forward, that's where she'll land."

"Follow me." The chief quickly took him to the side of the engine and opened a small compartment door and pulled out something like a tarp. "Get four men, one on each corner and get under that overhang. Just don't pull it too tight or she'll bounce right off."

Bass unfolded the tarp as he ran, calling for Gunther to help him. Two firemen stepped in and offered their help, the tarp unfolding to its full size. The men wiggled their way into the bushes and figured out the best place to stand, then waited.

"Jamie, if you're going to fall, fall forward." Bass said out loud as he stared up into the dark.

two bullets

Chapter Twenty-Three

Soon the parking lot of the Heart of Mary's Catholic Church was filled with vehicles. An ambulance had arrived, three more police cars, and a psychologist from the mental health ward was also there, watching from behind the police tape. There were also newspaper reporters, and members from the Historical Society who were less than happy about the broken fence and tire marks in the flower beds.

The angle of the building and roof had thrown some kinks into the rescue effort, making it difficult for the cherry picker on the fire engine to get in close to Jamie.

For all of the happenings going on around her and the attention her act was garnering, Jamie seemed content and unaware. She just sat there on the edge of the roof, humming to herself as she stared out over the grounds of the church towards a small pond. Jimmie had become impatient with being stuck behind the walls in the tower and had come down to join the others on the ground.

Sly arrived not long after the fire engine, and now stood with the fire chief. Sly wanted to go up in the bucket so he could talk to Jamie.

"I swear it's like trying to get a cat out of a tree." Jack Stone said, looking up from where he stood near the front of the fire truck. He still wore his security uniform from the hospital, having come directly from work when he got the news.

No one chided him for the remark.

Bass stood next to him, head tilted back in what

two bullets

seemed to be the normal position for those on the ground. Jimmie was on the other side of Jack, the trio forming a short line down the pathway next to the fire engine, parked along the side of the sanctuary.

"I almost feel bad making her come down," Jimmie said wistfully. "She looks so happy. Who am I to say she's wrong?"

Jack broke out of formation to turn and face Jimmie. "Because she is sitting on the roof of an abandoned church at eleven o'clock at night with no shoes on!"

Jimmie dropped his head to look at Jack. "She's out of her mind, Jack. Happy doesn't have to look normal."

"Yeah, well playing with fire makes me happy, but you don't see me going down to the quilt store and starting a bonfire," Jack retorted, retaking his place in formation, feet planted and his arms crossed.

Jimmie smirked at this. Of course he wanted his sister down off the roof. But there was a strange sense of relief seeing her now sitting down, content to hum while staring off into what ever delusion was playing through her head. She would be coming down from the roof eventually, but after the last half hour of his gut riding in his throat, this was the easy part of the night.

"Looks like Sly's on his way up," Bass announced. All heads turned toward the bucket sitting on a mechanical arm on top of the engine. Sly was inside with a fireman next to him, who now gave a signal to a buddy at the control panel. There came the sound of a loud rumble and the arm began to extend upwards. It slowly climbed and came abreast with the peak of the roof, a good eight feet away from Jamie's back.

The whirring of the machine quieted as the bucket came to a stop and was locked in place, and now everyone on the ground became quiet, straining to hear.

To everyone's surprise, Sly didn't stay in the bucket. He climbed up onto the narrow edge of the bucket wall and leaned out, grabbing the top edge of the roof and pulled himself up. With some fancy foot work and a lot of guts, he balanced his way over to Jamie.

It was then Bass felt the presence of someone next to him and he looked to his left to see Lock stepping up, eyes following everyone elses gaze up to the roof.

"Hey," he said, reaching out his arm. He wrapped it around her and pulled her in close to his side, their eyes moving back to the roof.

Jimmie and Jack were leaning forward, looking at Bass and Lock with intrigue. Then they straightened back up, giving each other a knowing look.

On the roof, Sly was now sitting with Jamie, their legs hanging over the edge. Chief Handson and three firemen were still standing with the tarp at the base of the building, the tension having reduced some and the tarp having gone slack in their hands.

"What do you think he's saying to her?" Jack asked curiously.

The men knew Sly was an unconventional, but result getting chaplain. The fact that he had put himself in danger just to get on Jamie's level spoke volumes of his character. But no one had an answer for Jack's question. That was when Lock said simply, "He's telling her that Jesus loves her. And that she's got a lot of life left to live."

Her profound statement hung in the air, encircling the others who stood down the line. There was a soft, clear innocence in the way she spoke the words, as if she herself had once been on the other end of Sly's counseling. She'd

two bullets

reminded them that there was more going on than just trying to get Jimmie's sister down from her psychotic break. Her heart and soul were also at stake.

Bass glanced down at Lock ever so carefully. Man, did he love this woman.

Jamie was strung out, and lost in a psychotic break that had her shivering uncontrollably and constantly fidgeting in her seat. It took Sly a little while to get on her level, asking her some basic questions, but he was less concerned with her answers and more about *how* she answered them. He was watching everything. He had known the Reeves family for awhile now, having been there on multiple occasions when Jamie was off her meds, walking around town in a haze. He knew what she was like sober and clear headed. But as of now, he was having to start from scratch. Jamie was so far out of it that he wasn't even sure she knew who he was, or where she was.

She wanted to talk about heaven, so Sly talked to her about heaven. Then she wanted to talk about baseball, so they talked about baseball. Eventually, he got around to asking her where she had been the last week. He asked it in such a nonchalant way that it seemed like he was just asking how she'd been since he'd last seen her.

Her answer was choppy and full of dead space where it seemed like her mind had caught a train and she'd disappeared for awhile, her eyes going blank.

two bullets

"You are very stubborn tonight." Sly observed.

"I am always stubborn," Jamie said, licking her lips as she moved to push her greasy bangs back out of her face.

"Have you seen your brother today?"

"No."

"Why not?"

"He thinks I'm crazy. He doesn't come around much anymore."

"Oh, I don't think that's true. I know Jimmie personally, and he adores you."

"Well, you just tell Craig that. Craig never liked my twin brother. Said we were too much alike."

Sly snapped to attention at her mention of her deceased husband, and looked over at the shadowy figure next to him. He squinted through the dark to see her face. "You've never talked about him before."

"Jimmie?"

"No...Craig."

"Well why wouldn't I?" Jamie asked incredulously. "He's my husband."

Sly's heart sank. Jamie was in a world where her first husband was still alive. He would have to walk carefully now, or be prepared for a total break down.

"Jamie, you'll have to remind me. How long have you and Craig been married?"

"Almost a year!" She answered, her voice instantly brightening.

"Any kids?"

Jamie giggled, shrugging back. Then she flipped her hair out of her face and looked at Sly straight on. "Can you keep a secret?"

He held up three fingers. "Scout's honor."

two bullets

Convinced, she nodded and looked back out over the garden below. "I'm pregnant as we speak."

"You are?!" He asked with surprise, playing along.

Jamie giggled. "But don't tell anyone. I haven't even told Craig yet. I'm going to tell him tomorrow."

"Tomorrow huh? How are you going to be able to sleep with such exciting news?"

"Craig is always out in the garage into all hours of the night working on his four-wheeler. I will tell him in the morning over breakfast."

Sly knew the details of Jamie's first husband's death, but he had never heard it from Jamie's mouth. She had never wanted to talk about that day.

"Well, then don't you think we better get down from here so you can get a good night's sleep?"

"No!" Jamie exclaimed, moving so quickly that Sly reached out, concerned she'd fall.

"Okay, okay," he said, nodding, trying to calm her back down. "But why?"

"Because if I go to sleep, when I wake up, everything will be different. I have to stay awake."

"What do you think will happen if you go to sleep?"

"Bad things." she whispered.

Sly didn't reply as he watched Jamie become uneasy, rubbing her palms together compulsively.
He slowly reached over and cupped his hand over hers and she immediately stopped shaking. Her chin dipped to her chest, and when she spoke Sly knew she was crying.

"My husband's dead, Pastor."

He nodded, whispering, "I know."

Jamie began to sob. It had taken some time, but the real Jamie was back again with him. But for how long?

two bullets

Sly spoke again, "But you know who isn't dead? Your four children. And Dane, he's alive, wishing you'd come home to share your home with him. And Jimmie. Jimmie is alive and waiting on the ground to love you and hold you. Craig is gone. But you're not alone."

Jamie took in a deep breath and blew it out, tears falling from her chin down onto Sly's hand.

"I miss him so much." she said when she could speak again. "I miss my husband. I want him here with me."

"Jamie, you have blamed yourself for Craig's death for ten years. It's time that you understand that he made his choice. And there was absolutely nothing you could do."

"But I'm his wife!" She exclaimed, voice cracking with pain. "I should have been able to help him! If I hadn't gone to sleep that night, if I had just told him about...." she couldn't even say the words, only pointing to her belly.

"There's no way you can know that," Sly assured her gently. "And all these years you spend wishing you could change the past, you are missing out on your present. You're letting something you had no control of ruin your entire life. Think about what you're doing is effecting Dane. You lost one husband, and now Dane feels like he's lost his wife. And your children feel like they've lost their mommy. But you're here, and you can be with them."

"But Craig..."

"Craig's gone," Sly said firmly, knowing that despite Jamie's struggle, she needed someone to speak the truth. "He's a body in a grave, but his memory is alive and well in your heart. And in your twin's faces. You just have to take the time to notice and not be so caught up in the past. I'm not going to sugar coat it for you, Jamie. You think that you are the only one in pain, and that you're the only one who knows what it's like to lose someone. But you're not. And you won't be the last. You're life isn't over. It's not ruined. It's a little messed up, but who's life isn't?"

Jamie scoffed, rolling her eyes. "You don't understand what I've been through."

"Oh no, you don't get to say that. I've lost people close to me. I've spent years watching people slowly kill themselves in front of me. Now I may have never lost a spouse, but I do know very well what you're going through. And despite what the doctor's tell you, you are not crazy. Your mind has become jumbled, but you're not crazy. You can get better. And you will. But it's not something you can do alone."

"But no one knows..."

"I'm not talking about other people. I'm talking about a Heavenly Father who knows exactly what you're going through. And He knows it hurts. You've got to stop punishing yourself. You've carried the burden long enough. It's time to let someone much Greater than yourself do the carrying."

Irritated now, Jamie groaned, waving him off. "Oh please. I have no use for religion."

"Good, because that's not what I'm offering. The Creator of the universe wants a personal relationship with you, Jamie. But it's entirely up to you. Do you want to live broken and eventually die, living in an eternity complete separated from Him and your family?"

Despite her fighting him, Jamie shook her head.

"Jesus Christ loved you so much that he came to earth, leaving Heaven to die a brutal death on the cross, taking every single one of your pains and sins onto himself. He died, but he rose again so that you could live forever with him in Heaven."

"Really?" Jamie turned to look at him now. Sly could see his words had connected.

"Really."

Jamie gushed in befuddlement. "No one has ever told me that before."

"The gift of Salvation is completely free, Jamie. All you have to do is say Yes."

two bullets

Chapter Twenty-Four

After forty-five minutes of anxiously waiting on the ground, there was finally movement on the roof. Everyone on the ground snapped to attention. Cameras were lifted by the news crews and there were flashes as multiple people took pictures.

A ladder was extended from the cherry-picker on the firetruck over to the flat area of the roof for Sly and Jamie to climb down. As Jamie began to climb down, Jimmie ran from his friends to the firetruck and climbed up to the top to wait.

Someone handed him a blanket and he held it in expectation as Jamie finally made it into the bucket. The motor engaged, slowly refolding the arm as the bucket slowly lowered back down. There was a resounding round of applause as the bucket finally landed. The fireman opened up the small door on the side of the bucket and helped Jamie out. She instantly ran into the waiting embrace of her brother. He held her close, then wrapped the blanket around her shoulders and the two were helped down from the engine.

Lock stayed back as Bass and Jack moved forward to be there when Jamie and Jimmie got down. Sly was then brought down off the roof and Lock moved forward to be there when he finally climbed down to solid ground.

"Good job," she said smiling.

"You saw that, huh?" Sly said, looking a little embarrassed.

Lock nodded. "I did. I guess we know now where I get my unnatural ability to climb things."

"Yeah." he sighed, rubbing his thighs. "I'm getting too old for this stuff."

"How did you finally get her to come down?"

"She's agreed to meeting with me three times a week for counseling. And I agreed to tell her more about Jesus." Sly's eyes were sparkling, even in the dark. It was obvious he was spiritually drained, but his love for hurting people shone through. "She's going to have to go into psychological therapy and may not get to go home for awhile."

"Do you think she'll get better?"

"She's taken the first big step," Sly said with a nod, looking over to the young woman surrounded by loving people.

"What step would that be?" Lock asked.

"Well, she decided to stop trying to do everything on her own." Sly turned to her. "Lock, she accepted Jesus as her Lord and Savior tonight. She still has a tough road ahead, all the trauma and pain has really messed with her head. It'll take time but with friends like that, I think she'll be just fine."

Sly smiled wide, then they both turned, watching as Jamie, with a radiant smile on her face, told Jimmie that she wasn't the same girl she had been who had climbed out on the roof.

Mentally and spiritually exhausted, Sly fell asleep in the time it took for Lock to drive the pickup out of old town

two bullets

onto Main street. This gave her fifteen minutes of a silent cab to do a lot of thinking as she headed for home. More retrospection than anything, her thoughts settled on Bass. She'd made the decision practically on the spot to agree to stay in Barrier Ridge. She hadn't even had the chance to talk to Sly about it all. But there was a peace in her soul, and she believed that it was God telling her that she'd made the right choice. The details would have to work themselves out eventually.

She'd never had good experiences with men in the past. Not from a romantic stand point. As it went, she would get overly invested in the simple idea of there being something more, while the guy was merely friendly and had no desire to pursue a relationship. It was tiresome.

She'd found, because of her personality and standing at work, that she would become the pursuer of more than just friendship, which in turn just scared the guys off. And yet somehow, in an unconventional way, and in only a couple of weeks, she seemed to have found her perfect match. The more she prayed about it, the better she felt. Sly had always told her to wait for a relationship that didn't involve drama. It was easy with Bass. They had a strong bond forged quickly through rather intense circumstances, then finalized in spending time together. He treated her exactly how she'd always hoped a man would.

For the first time in a long time, Lock actually felt like she was where she was supposed to be. Danson no longer had control over her or her decisions. Cincinnati and the grief and fear that came with it were quickly becoming a distant memory. Barrier Ridge and all that it entailed living there were her new life. She had new friends, a church, and a possible job. What more could she ask for now?

Sly was fast asleep, worn out from his night of talking

someone literally off the edge of a cliff. As Lock neared home, she didn't want to wake him up and bother him. Maybe a nice little drive on some back roads would be nice. She was awake and no where near ready to go back to the house and have nothing to do.

Knowing Sly had some sermons on CD in the visor overhead, she kept an eye on the road as she felt around above her and grabbed the first one she caught the edge of. She pulled it down and slipped it into the CD player. The soothing sound of country music cut off and was replaced by the soft, southern accent of a middle aged man getting ready to start a service. Lock immediately smiled, recognizing the voice as one she'd grown up listening to and watching on TV.

The topic of the sermon was on worry. Every word speaking into Lock's heart and washing away the stress and tension that had built up in her mind. She rolled down the window and let the fresh air fill the cab, the sweet smell of green grass and hay fields causing her to take deeper and deeper breaths, basking in the cold air caressing her face.

When the first part of the four part series ended, Lock reached forward and snapped the radio off, the dark cab filling with silence. Next to her, Sly's coat rustled as he moved, then his sleepy, groggy voice mumbled, "Put on the next one."

Lock startled a little, glancing over through the dark to the passenger side. "I'm sorry. I thought you were asleep."

"It's okay. I feel like a baby being soothed to sleep." he said in a sleepy voice.

Lock smiled. "Mind if I keep driving around?"

"I'd mind if you didn't. Are we lost yet?"

Lock looked out at the remote road out in the middle of nowhere. "Yep."

Sly sighed, tucking his chin into his shoulder as he

slipped further down in his seat. "Good."

"What would you think if I said I wanted to stay here? Permanently?"

"It's about time."

Well that was easy.

She pressed play on the next sermon and settled back into her seat. She continued to navigate into the dark landscape, seeing nothing past the reach of the bright head-beams, a crescent moon hanging over the dark edges of a mountain peak.

two bullets

Chapter Twenty-Five

Friday

Born Trapper Steven Jensen, T.J. had grown up into a grizzly bearded old man who lived true to his given name. He lived high up in the Crimson mountains, away from chaos and the nonsense of civilization. He kept to himself deep in the woods living off the land, and whatever he caught in his traps went either into his belly, or to use around his log cabin. Sometimes dinner was fish, sometimes it was fresh meat from the traps he had set up for miles in every direction of his humble log home.

He sold the furs he collected and tanned himself to a local trading post that proudly sold authentic skin hats, fur coats and rugs for tourists that came through. Every six months he would make his way down the mountain to the trading post and meet Skip. After shooting the breeze, they would make the trade.

Today was the day to make the meet, so T.J. piled the new furs and some canned jam he had made himself into the back of his rusty old GMC, and set out to drive the eighty miles down to civilization. A wad of chew in his bottom lip, he listened to the scanner as he maneuvered his pickup along the rutted road.

He'd taken a bath and brushed out his beard, but the calluses on his hands and the worn out clothes he wore were anything but spiffy. He liked it that way. His mama had raised him to have manners, but having lived so long among the wild with no human contact, it was easy to over look his personal hygiene from day to day.

On the way he decided to pull in and say hi to Alonzo Two Feet, the old Indian he'd known since he was a young pup. Alonzo wasn't as much of a hermit as T.J. was, but he didn't get out much, having a small farm he ran with his wife Stella outside of Petersville.

T.J. turned in at the gate for Two Feet Herds and drove up the long road to the ranch house, his mouth already watering for some of that store bought coffee Stella kept on hand. He hadn't had a good cup of coffee in months, having run out of grounds during a long camping trip that hadn't brought in many furs.

As he pulled up into the barnyard, T.J. immediately knew something was wrong. There was a strong odor coming through his open window. It was a smell that the old trapper was all too familiar with; that of decomposing flesh. With a closer look into the corrals on his right across from the house, he didn't see a single animal. All he could see were brown heaps of fur through the slats in the fence, at least a dozen of them all across the ground inside the fences.

"What in tarnation....?"

He pulled up into the carport next to the house, not seeing Alonzo's feeder truck or Stella's black van with the broken back window. Nothing. The place was deserted, the front door of the single story house hanging open.

Climbing out, T.J. called for the one eyed hound dog that always made a racket when he pulled up to the house. No dog, no Stella. Nothing. Not a sound except for a horrible buzzing of blow flies making a terrible noise in his ear.

That awful smell was overwhelming now and T.J. spun around, giving the barnyard a long, sweeping look with his eyes. The outbuildings laced through the maze of corral fences that usually were bustling with cattle were eerily silent. And it sent a chill down the mountain man's spine.

He hurried into the house, calling for Stella and Alonzo as he went room to room, but he found what he had feared. Empty. Not a single stick of furniture remained. Even the wood burning stove in the living room was gone, leaving just a piece of pipe hanging out of the ceiling.

Going back outside, he walked across the gravel to the first line of wood corral and peered through the slats, then climbed up for a better view. Before him Alonzo's entire herd, little as it may be, littered the muddy ground in decomposing heaps of bone and fur, at least two days old.

T.J. pulled a handkerchief out of his back pocket and held it to his nose as flies buzzed his head. Horror crashed through him. Fear sent a chill down his spine. What once had been a loud and obnoxious herd, was now just a sea of carcasses under the hot sun.

What in the world had happened here?!

He would understand if Alonzo had sold the place and moved on without a word, but there was no way the old Indian would just kill his entire herd; there was too much money out there.

It wasn't until T.J. found his friend's body floating in the water tank near the barn that the old trapper finally showed any emotion.

Something horrible had happened out here, and poor Alonzo had lost his life because of it.

Crossing himself and saying a prayer for his deceased friend, T.J. headed for the barn to grab a shovel.

two bullets

Lock sat at the kitchen island painting her fingernails a dark purple color. She had her parents on the phone at the moment, and they were discussing the idea, which was becoming more and more like a plan, of Lock officially staying in Washington. She had prepared herself to have to defend her desire to her parents, and was surprised when they gave their blessing. They discussed her apartment in Cincinnati that she was still paying rent on, and tried figuring out what she should do about it. Her mom told her to just go ahead and cancel her lease, then she offered to take care of getting Lock's belongings packed up.

"We'll get a U-haul and drive it up to you. I can drive your car and dad can drive the U-Haul. Right Honey? Is that okay?"

"Sure. I'm okay with that."

Excitement rippled through Lock. This was happening! This was really happening!

She was finishing up talking with them when Sly emerged from his office/ garage for lunch.

"It's all settled," she announced. "I'm just going to pay the fine and cancel my lease. And dad and mom are going to get my stuff and bring it up here for me!

"Congrats!" Sly grinned and reached over the island to give her a high-five.

"And like I said, I'll pay you rent."

He waved his hand. "Don't even worry about. I'm just excited that you're sticking around."

He went to the fridge, only to discover that in all the craziness from the last few days, he hadn't bought groceries.

"Do you mind running an errand for me?"

Lock screwed the lid back on to the polish and began blowing on her nails. "What's that?" she asked in between

two bullets

breaths.

"There's a guy who sells fresh eggs and milk up the mountain. I have a standing account with him, so you just need to show up and say you're there to pick it up."

"Sounds easy enough. Where is it?"

Sly quickly jotted down the directions, informing her it was a good jaunt up back roads through the mountains due north. Lock liked a challenge, and assured him she was good to go for him.

"Since you're headed into bear country, take your gun with you. Just to be safe." He added.

She nodded. "I'd have it with me anyway."

Sly had been less than forthcoming about the condition of said back roads. Lock soon discovered they were narrow and poorly paved, and she had to keep both hands on the wheel for fear of running off the road and taking a plunge straight down the mountain onto oblivion. Her stomach did a few flip-flops as she crossed over high bridges and followed the narrow switchbacks up and around the mountains.

She was finally able to take a breath when she came to solid, wide ground, passing through a small town that boasted having the last available gas for the next fifty miles. According to Sly's directions, she needed to pass through the town and follow more back roads for fifteen minutes. Soon enough, she finally saw the sign for fresh eggs painted in blood red, an arrow below pointing her down a long driveway to the Two Feet ranch.

Passing under a thick canopy of leafy trees, the view cleared and she saw the ranch house and barnyard up ahead. She quickly double checked that the money in her pocket was still there and hadn't slipped out from the poorly graded road she'd been bouncing on for the last thirty miles.

two bullets

There was a rusted out old pickup parked under the cover of the carport to the left of the house, and she pulled in to park behind it, seeing the bed of the pickup was piled up high with furs and wooden crates.

The second she opened her door and moved to step out, the smell hit her like a brick in the face. Her arm immediately went to cover her mouth and nose to ease the assaulting stench. It was the smell of heat baked death, and she could almost taste it, it was so pungent. She reached around to the small of her back and gave her gun a reassuring pat, looking around as she kicked the door closed behind her with a solid thud. It struck her odd at how quiet the barnyard around her was, given its size.

She turned around and headed up to the house, painfully aware of the swarm of flies that seemed to have descended upon her, buzzing her face and hair. Something was definitely off with this place. There wasn't even a dog on a leash waiting around the corner of the house for her when she stepped up to knock on the front door. She let the hollow sound hang in the air, turning at the waist to look around the yard a second time. That's when she caught sight of the door to the barn hanging open, and a man walking out with a shovel in his hand. She stepped off the stoop and crossed the yard, getting out onto the gravel before calling out, "Hello!"

The man pulled up short to look her way. He was a wild looking mountain man with worn out clothes and jewelery she assumed was home made hanging from his neck. A tattered cowboy hat sat low on his head.

Walking up closer, she called, "Mr. Two Feet?"

"Who wants to know?" The man moved his hand up to his face, covering his nose and mouth with a black handkerchief.

two bullets

Lock swatted at the flies buzzing her head. "I was hoping to buy some eggs and milk." *Though I'm seriously reconsidering it now.* She came to a stop, seeing the man more clearly now in front of her. His beard was gray and bushy, hanging just above the collar of his leather jacket. The skin around his eyes was wrinkled and weathered from a lot of time in the sun. He was eying her suspiciously as if he thought she was there to cause trouble, and she did her best to appear unassuming, slipping her hands into her back pockets as she shifted her weight to her left leg. The awful smell had only intensified in her approach and she breathed through her mouth. She tried to keep her face blank of expression to keep from being rude.

"You're out of luck, lady," the man said gruffly, his lips smacking a few times. "Alonzo's dead."

"Is that what smells so bad?"

"Look lady, I don't mean to be rude but I've got a lot of work to do. And I don't know you. So you better just head on down the road." He turned to walk away, heading for a corner of the corral fence. She let him go, looking around her feeling rather befuddled. Then she saw it. At least fifty lumps dotting the corral floor. Dead cows everywhere. The revelation brought about an eerie, frightening feeling.

"What happened here?" She breathed, forgetting to breathe through her nose and coughed.

"Couldn't tell you. Just got here myself."

"Well, have you called the police?" Lock asked, following the man to the fence, unable to take her eyes away from the carcases on the other side.

"No need for brown bears up in these parts. We bury our own." The older man was working to keep his balance as he climbed the wooden slats to the top of the corral. She

two bullets

climbed up onto the fence as the man jumped down on the other side, landing on a blue tarp laid out next to the water trough. Shock struck through her then suddenly at the sight of the body floating in the water.

"That's a body!" She exclaimed.

"They teach you good down in those city schools, don't they?"

Lock balked. "What makes you think I'm from the city?"

He motioned to her feet. "Well those boots you're wearing ain't made for walking in mud now are they?"

She looked down, then quickly shook her head. They were getting off point. She waved her hand, "Never mind. Sir, do you mind telling me why there is a body floating in that tank?"

The man had rolled up his sleeves and was leaning over the cloudy water, reaching for the jacket on the body to pull it closer.

"What in tarnation?" He mumbled, seeing something on the head of the corpse.

Lock was leaning over from the fence, trying to get a better look, when the puttering of a small engine suddenly broke the quiet of the barnyard. She snapped to attention, spinning around as she clung to the fence.

Coming up the dirt trail between the house and the barn, three four-wheelers broke out into the open. At the sight of Lock, the kid in the lead jerked the four-wheeler to the side and skidded to a stop. With the engine still muttering, he stood up in his seat and pulled around a rifle that had been hanging down his back.

Lock's eyes widened and she managed to jump down out of the way just as a shot exploded, whizzing overhead at where she had just been. The bullet sparked and pinged as it hit the light post inside the corral, just over the mountain man's head. He dropped the shovel and flew backward.

"Confound it, woman!" He cried, "Don't shoot!"

two bullets

Chapter Twenty-Six

"Get down!" Lock yelled. The mountain man dropped to the ground and scrambled to get behind the water tank.

She scrambled up from the ground, gravel biting into the palms of her hands. She ran towards the back end of the barn in front of her, bullets chasing her into hiding. Bracing against the wall, she pulled her gun from its holster.

"Hold your fire!" She shouted around the corner.

She was answered with a rain of bullets, wood splintering overhead and she ducked back further out of the way. Looking behind her, she saw the mountain man lifting his head to peer over the water tank back towards the shooters. She shouted for him to stay down. He obeyed and dropped back to his seat, quickly reaching to snatch his hat off his head.

"Hold your fire!" She yelled again, daring to look around the corner at the riders.

"Hey, look Allen!" One of them called to the other, "More target practice!"

The boys stood next to each other in the side yard, each with a rifle to their shoulder as they swung the muzzles back and forth between the barn and the water tank. They were teenage boys, probably nearing eighteen, and cocky as one would assume for immature boys with no sense of morality.

Laughing, they opened fire and chunks of wood sprayed from the wall next to Lock, and she dove away to the ground, covering her head.

She was no longer afraid; now she was just downright mad. Jaw clenched, she crawled back up to her feet, and instead

two bullets

of going back to the corner of the barn, she ran ahead to the back side of the barn. She slipped around the corner, following the wall along as she ran quietly through the tall grass, leaping over rotted out timbers melting into the dirt.

She slowed when she came to the final corner, creeping up onto it as she kept herself flat against the wall. Then she slid down onto one knee, and ever so slowly leaned forward so as to sneak a peek around the corner. The boys were still laughing, attention on the barnyard in front of them and the hiding mountain man who gave them a good challenge.

From where Lock hid, she was just out of their peripheral vision at their eight o'clock. Carefully and quietly, she lifted her weapon, setting her sights on the wrist of the boy nearest her, took in a steadying breath, closed her left eye and held her breath.

Only she was never able to take the shot; out of the break in the trees along the trail, two more four-wheelers came streaking out, apparently having fallen behind on the trail. They were whooping and hollering as one by one they crashed into the yard.

Spotting Lock, they shouted and began shooting. She turned and fired a few blind shots behind her before taking off at a dead sprint back the way she had come and around the end of the barn, slipping on the wet grass before finally doing a somersault to get into cover.

"I see you're back," the mountain man called from the corral rather grimly.

Breathless, Lock nodded as she crawled back up to the corner. The teenagers were laughing and having a gay ol' time at their living target practice. She hastily pulled her phone out of her back pocket and dialed 911.

two bullets

"Richard County Dispatch."

"I am taking fire. I repeat, I am taking fire at the Two Feet Herd Ranch."

"Say again? You're breaking up."

Lock placed her lips against the phone and said loudly, "I. Am. Being. Shot. At. I need help!"

"You are being fired upon?"

"Yes!"

The phone crackled from the poor phone service as the woman replied, "Okay, calm down. Where are you?"

"I told you; the Two Feet Herd Ranch!"

"Whe........Ok.......ju....he.... please hold."

Lock jerked the phone from her ear, "Seriously?"

"I told you, cops ain't good for nothing 'round here," Grizzly Adams called as she slipped her phone back into her pocket. She shot the man a look.

"What's your name?"

"Trapper Jensen. T.J. if you like."

"Alright T.J., I'm gonna shoot, and I want you to take off running and get over here with me. You follow?"

"You want me to come out?" The man cried in dismay.

She nodded. "Yes. Stay low. I'll cover you."

"Lady, I don't think that's a good-" More shots suddenly exploded through the air.

Lock folded herself over away from the corner, shouting over her shoulder, "Never mind. Stay there!"

"Well thank you! I think I'll do just that!"

It was time to put her two years running as second best Marksmen in the division to good use. Dropping to her belly, she crawled up to the corner of the barn. She was amazed to see all five of the teens, standing out there in the open shoulder to shoulder like a firing squad, laughing and firing randomly as if it was just another day at the range.

She fired twice, once at the ground in front of them, and once into the trunk of the cottonwood tree behind them. This got their attention and startled, they broke ranks and started running, calling out in surprise as they ran for cover.

"T.J.! Now!" Lock cried and adjusted her aim, firing at the feet of one of the boys running towards the house. Her other shots were a little less organized and flew through the air above the runners. One had made it to the four-wheelers and deserted his friends, flying back up the trail. Three were hiding behind the house, and the final kid was terrified and frozen behind the wide trunk of the cotton wood.

T.J. was making his move, huffing and puffing as he dropped to his knees and clawed his way under the lowest slat in the wooden corral. Then he scrambled up to his feet and streaked across the open space, leaping over Lock's prone body to safety.

Her final two shots were only clicks. She reached around to her back and pulled out the extra clip, releasing the empty magazine with her thumb and it fell to the ground. She quickly rammed the second clip up into the gun and released the spring.

Seeing that for now, things were quiet, she rolled over onto her left side, facing T.J. as he sat clutching his hat, gasping for air.

"Those blasted punks!" the man puffed angrily, his large belly rising and falling with each gasp for air, straining against the brass buttons of his home made shirt.

"You know them?"

"They belong to the neighbor to the south," he said with a jerk of his head back behind him, "they've been bothering Alonzo for years, doing anything and everything to

two bullets

pester and torment him and Stella."

"But why? That's awful!"

T.J. shrugged. "They're white and Alonzo isn't. They
fell into the wrong crowd, getting recruited by a white
supremacist group around here. They've got nothing better to
do than torment a kind old man and his wife."

"You think they were the ones who killed him?" Lock
asked with wide eyes.

The man shook his head unsure, wiping his wet eyes on
the sleeve of his jacket.

Moved with compassion for the poor man, Lock
reached up to touch his arm. "I'm sorry about your friend. I
sincerely am. But we can't jump to conclusions. The two might
not be connected."

T.J. just nodded, clearing his throat. Lock pursed her
lips, trying to give a reassuring smile. Inwardly, what she really
wanted to do was storm out to the house and go all Rambo on
those boys and teach them a lesson.

Hate is a strong motivator, and it wasn't a long leap to
think boys who have been brainwashed into hating a person for
their skin could get a little too big for their britches and shoot
someone just to see what it felt like. Lock had seen that a lot
with the gangs back in Cincinnati; boys trying to prove their
worth by doing horrible things. But in the end, they weren't
always bad people, some were just lost.

She got back to her feet and returned to the corner,
calling out as loud as she could, "Put your guns on the ground
and lay down with your hands on your head. I have back-up on
the way. It's over."

There was no reply. The kid hiding behind the tree had
run to join his friends behind the house, and now the yard sat
silent.

two bullets

"There's a rifle in my pickup," T.J. said quietly.

Lock looked back over her shoulder at him. "Let's go say hello."

They made a quick plan, then Lock slipped out into the open first, walking up the side of the barn as if one wrong move would cause those teenagers to come charging out at her. Her gun shifted directions as she shifted her line of sight from side to side, from the corner of the barn ahead all the way around to the entrance of the driveway. So far the windows of the house were empty, and no one was peeking around the corner of the house. They were in the clear.

Lock turned and nodded at T.J., then together they started running across the gravel driveway. She stopped off at the front right corner of the house while T.J. hurried on to the carport.

Lock crept along the right side of the house with purposeful steps, quietly moving towards the back of the house. When she got to the corner, she stepped out and swung wide, only to find the area was abandoned, and the screen door hanging open.

T.J. appeared in front of her at the other end of the house, and she lifted her hand and motioned him to go back around to the front. He nodded and disappeared. She waited there alone, giving the man enough time to get into position. Then taking a deep breath, she moved up to the backdoor and kicked it open, intending to shock whoever was inside.

Through the galley kitchen and across the living room, T.J. did the same, bursting in with his rifle pulled up into his shoulder as the door bounced off the wall. He moved to his left and out of sight as Lock ran through the kitchen to join him.

In the back of the house, they found the suddenly very

repentant and terrified teens in the first floor bedroom. The three boys were working on trying to climb out the window into the back yard, but when Lock and T.J. came in shouting and ordering them to stop moving, the first boy with his foot up in the windowsill stepped back and threw his hands up over his head.

It surprised Lock to see the fear in all of their eyes, and the change from self-assurance to self-preservation. They weren't so tough now that they weren't in control.

T.J. and Lock moved the boys over to the other corner of the room, away from the windows, and told them to lay down on their bellies.

"Now which one of you shot my friend?" T.J. demanded, playing the part of the wild mountain man very well as he stood over the boys, shifting the aim of his rifle over each one.

"Mitch!" one of the boys with sandy blond hair said, gesturing off in the direction the lone four-wheeler had fled. "Mitch shot that old man!"

"And you just stood by and let him?!" T.J. roared, stepping in to shove the muzzle of the rifle into the back of the boy's shoulder.

"T.J...." Lock cautioned.

"He had to!" Another boy cried out, shaking like a leaf next to his friends. "They'd kill him if he didn't."

"Who?" Lock asked, her interest piqued. She was standing in the doorway, blocking the exit, hands crossed in front of her over her belt. The pale faced boy looked up at her, and she instantly felt sorry for him.

"Jerry. He told us we had to prove we had what it takes to be a Ferry-man, and if Mitch didn't shoot Alonzo, then it'd be us that were buried."

two bullets

This was the easiest interrogation Lock had ever conducted. In the face of targets that could shoot back, the boys had lost their cockiness and courage and returned to the little boys they really were. Seeing them up close, Lock realized they weren't as old as she had guessed.

"How old are you?" She asked.

"F-f-fourteen." The pale boy answered, eyes shifting from Lock down to the floor.

"Will your friend come back?" she asked, taking a step forward, her shoes landing with just enough weight to sound intimidating.

"I don't know," the boy said frantically, shaking his head. Then he scoffed nervously, "Look, man, we're sorry for shooting at you. We were just having fun."

"Did Jerry tell you to kill all those cows too?" Lock asked, ignoring the apology.

The boy glanced sideways at his friends, and one by one they nodded.

"Why?"

"To scare Alonzo. They were supposed to be moved out by now, and Jerry said they needed some encouragement."

"Alonzo wasn't going anywhere," T.J. snapped. The boys flinched.

"He agreed to sell the farm," the first boy assured him, then licked his lips. "But I guess he changed his mind- something about not wanting to lose the herd- and that really ticked Jerry off. He wanted to teach the Indian a lesson."

"Does this Jerry have a last name?" Lock asked. The four boys looked at each other, none of them knowing. They all shrugged, shaking their heads.

Lock stepped out of the room into the hallway and pulled out her phone to call 911 again. When she returned to

two bullets

the bedroom, T.J. was in the middle of giving the boys a lesson on respect and moral integrity, and they were hanging on his every word, though their eyes seemed drawn to the rifle he had laid across his knee.

Lock relaxed and leaned against the door jam as she listened. These boys must have already had some sense of hatred rooted in their hearts to make it so easy to be swayed and brainwashed by intimidation. This Jerry guy was able to strike the right nerve and demand loyalty. What was it with racism out here in the middle of nowhere?

Whether they had been promised money, respect, or honor from some higher being, each one of these boys had allowed themselves to be pressured, and lied to. Lock found herself having pity on them, but had to make herself not get emotionally involved. They had crossed a line and would have to answer for it.

T.J. on the other hand, wasn't so easily moved, and continued to put the fear of God in those boys until the law showed up.

Chapter Twenty-Seven

Bass shut off the shower and stepped out onto the bathroom rug, grabbing the towel from the hook on the wall. Light streamed in through the window at the end of the room, casting yellow hues across the blue bathroom. His phone beeped from the corner of the sink, then started buzzing with a new notification.

"Alright, alright, I hear ya," he said, stepping up to the sink and caught the phone before it buzzed its self off on to the floor. He hit play on the voice-mail as he got dressed, the voice of the county clerk asking him about some paperwork he'd filed. He grunted and pushed end.

He started out of the room, eyes down at the phone as he opened the door and shut off the light, stepping out into the shallow hallway. He was about to press the call button when the feeling of wind tousling his wet hair distracted him, his bare shoulders shivering from the cold as he looked around for the source. Looking to his right, at the front of the cabin, he saw the front door of the cabin hanging open, swinging gently in the wind.

Well, that's weird. He must have not shut it all the way when he came in. He set his phone down on top of the refrigerator as he passed through the kitchen and headed for the door. The whole living area of the front of the cabin was an open floor plan, from the kitchen to the area left of the front door where a dining table sat. The living room took up the other side of the room, but it was around the corner from the hallway, and subsequently, made a blind spot for anyone coming down the hallway through the kitchen.

This is why Bass didn't notice the man pressed up against the living-room wall, just out of sight of Bass whose attention was on the swinging front door. The pasty-white, bald headed man with cloudy blue eyes stepped out of his hiding spot as Bass passed by unknowingly, his left hand pulled back holding a large rock, then let it drop with a *thwack* on the back of Bass's skull.

Everything went black as the throbbing in the back of Bass's head continued to throb, growing slower and slower and more distant. For a moment, Bass thought that he was in a different world, at a different time, with a different name. It was all a dream that he wouldn't remember when he woke up, but it was so real that he didn't even know about the whole being hit on the head thing.

Suddenly he was hit in the face with the ice cold water of an ocean wave, just like the ones he used to go swimming in back in Queensland. But then cold hard reality set in, and Bass found himself sitting in the middle of his living room, tied to a chair with water dripping from his face and soaking his pants.

A man stood in front of him holding a plastic cup, having just splashed its contents on Bass. The bald man seemed rather pleased at his accomplishment. Bass winced at the throbbing in his head and started to bring his hand up to touch it, but discovered his hands were tied behind him.

"Oh that's real nice," he mumbled, shooting a chiding look up at the middle aged bald guy with a crooked nose.

Someone started dragging another chair from the table, the legs scraping across the hardwood floor, gouging marks into the stained wood, and it seemed to Bass that the trail was also being gouged into his brain. He grimaced, shaking his head, willing the pain to go away. This was worse than any hangover.

The dragged chair was set down in front of Bass backwards and the bald man stepped out of the way. The wavering lines that made up the object in Bass's poor eyesight soon produced a second man taking a seat. He lowered himself down, filling Bass's squinty, fuzzy vision, arms coming up to lay across the top of the chair.

This was surprisingly not Bass's first time being tied to a chair, but it was his first time being held against his will. The time his brothers had tied him to a chair had been more about not falling out when the rolling desk chair went shooting up the ramp and flew through the air. He had been ten, but in that one experience he had learned a lot about chairs. Like, they go with you wherever you go due to the whole being tied up thing.

Bass kept this in mind as he mentally made a note of the placement of his hands behind his back, duct-taped to each side of the spindles on the back. His legs, though also bound, were free from the chair itself, his ankles were duct-taped to each other but swinging free under him.

He realized that the man sitting in front of him was staring, presenting himself as a threat, and Bass realized he was supposed to be scared.

But he wasn't.

He was annoyed.

"You know who I am, Deputy?" The man asked, cocking his head to the side, a leer pursing his lips and squinting his eyes. He was trying to look tough, but to Bass he just looked like a man trying too hard.

"I know who you are," Bass said, addressing the man absently as if he was less than important as he dipped his head and looked down in his lap.

Archer Banks didn't appreciate Bass's lackadaisical attitude. He bit his tongue, reaching up to slowly remove the black felt cowboy hat from his head, moving it down to hook over and hang from his knee. His short, silver and black hair was cut so as to accommodate his receding hair line, cowlicks in the front gently lifting the hair up into a natural spike. His skin was brown from the sun, laugh lines around his eyes gave him a sense of humanity, though his present smile was less friendly and more belittling.

"The problem with thinking you know a man is that you then think you understand him." Archer brushed at some unseen wrinkle on his black shirt as he spoke, drawing Bass's line of sight to the cross necklace hanging from a silver chain around the man's neck.

Archer Banks was considerably different than his little brother. While Lee was a poster boy for the White Society with his bald head, combat boots and beliefs, Archer was a little more put together. Slick and purposeful with his image. He wore black like it was an extension of his personality; black hat, black button down shirt with a loose black tie, black pants with belt, and black, square toed western boots.

He was tall and slender, but next to Bass, who had well developed muscles, he looked like a man who had never quite achieved manhood. Which could be why he had chosen to meet Bass on level ground by sitting down.

Archer's teeth were normal, clean and white, but his breath was terrible after having spent the whole morning smoking cigarettes and drinking whiskey. The man attempted an appearance of cool, but Bass wasn't buying it.

"That could go both ways," Bass said, "you think you understand me, but you have no idea."

Archer was impressed. "You make a good point. But I

two bullets

think I do understand you." He then reached around behind his back. When he pulled his hand out, he held an automatic hand gun. Bass looked at it for a second, then nodded. "It matches your whole outfit. Did you plan that?"

A warning punch came from Baldy standing next to Bass. His head whipped to the right, his jaw popping from the hit. He spit out blood onto his floor.

Archer eyed Bass as he straightened himself back up. "Don't get smart. We have a long way to go and I think you would like to hold off on the pain as much as possible."

"Well, Archer," Bass sighed, working his jaw back and forth, "that's where we differ." He leaned as far forward as his restraints would let him towards Archer. "You'd rather fend off the pain. Where as my opinion is, bring on your worst."

Archer's cold eyes danced from Bass's left eye, then to his right. This deputy had a lot of spirit left in him, and that just wouldn't work for Archer. He needed an attitude adjustment before Archer could go on.

He picked his hat up from his knee and settled it back down on his head, then patted the chair back as he stood. He nodded to his man standing next to Bass and then turned to walk away as the first of what would be many blows landed on Bass's body.

Jimmie Reeves heard the footsteps approach the garage. From the amount of time Archer had been gone, he guessed that Bass had been as useful as he himself had been—which meant Bass was getting the same type of talking to.

Jimmie had already fought off his attackers twice, which was why he was hanging like a bug caught in a spider web, ropes tied to his wrists strung up to opposite sides of the garage interior. His feet were chained and secured to three cylinder blocks to keep him from doing any more kicking.

But, at least he had a view as he hung there; the garage door was open, revealing the crystal clear waters of Gibson Lake straight out across Bass's drive way. He could see the ridge of mountains around town, bold and towering straight across the lake, trees and rocks painting a beautiful pallete on the mountain sides, blue sky mixed with rain clouds in the background. His left eye was beginning to swell shut, so he was only getting about half the view now, but it kept his spirits high.

"Your friend's got about as much fight in him as you do," Archer said as he stepped into the open garage.

Jimmie spit. "Yeah." He ran his tongue slowly over his lips, feeling the tender splits and coppery taste of blood. "Sucks for you."

Archer's eyes widened at this, his hand going to his chest. "Me? I'm not the one being used as a human punching bag right now."

Jimmie grinned smugly, despite his black eye and the blood of his abusers mingled with his own running down his cheeks. "Not yet, anyway."

"Careful, deputy; I don't think Jesus would be pleased with threats of violence."

Jimmie was unable to repress a scoff. "You really want to spend your time discussing religion?"

Archer's arms went out in a full shrug. "Why not?"

two bullets

Jimmie scowled. "Don't tell me I'm going through all of this for nothing. I thought you had a plan. Or are you just beating us up because you have nothing better to do?"

Archer looked down at his hand, opening and closing his fist slowly. "You're right; I have a bigger bone to pick with you than our beliefs."

"*Your* beliefs," Jimmie corrected. "Our faith is not the same."

Archer looked up, snapped his fingers and pointed, "Now that is one thing we can agree on."

Jimmie was learning there was a fine line that kept him out of the dog house and not slapped or punched. Archer had spent the last hour doing everything he could to break Jimmie down and make him compliant, but Jimmie was a veteran at mind games and physical abuse. He could do this all day. But it seemed that maybe in the process, he had been able to sand down some of Archer's sharp edges, making him less uptight and touchy. Now they were able to toss insults back and forth, like a playful tug-o-war between adversaries, and Jimmie was able to keep what was left of his teeth.

Archer pulled a soft pack of cigarettes from the pocket of his coat that hung over a workbench in the front corner of the garage.

"So," Jimmie said, watching Archer pat out a cigarette while he leaned against the inside track of the garage door. "Are you going to tell me what you want from us? Or are we supposed to guess?"

The end of the cigarette glowed red as Archer held the flame of the lighter up to it, then white smoke streamed from his lips. "I thought it would be pretty obvious."

The only time Jimmie had ever met Archer Banks was at the raid on the White Society compound. And "met" was a strong word- he had seen the man, learned his name and had read his file online when they ran the names of everyone at the compound. That was it.

Reading between the lines, Jimmie and the others had figured out that Archer was a promoter for the White Society cult, meaning he traveled around, shaking hands, gathering support, raising money and recruiting angry people who were searching for answers. He also moonlighted as a drug dealer, traveling all over the Midwest to make meets and acquire "funding," which he then was able to use to provide for the group back in Washington.

And yet, Jimmie still had no idea why the man had it out for Bass and himself.

"You're gonna have to help me, I think," Jimmie said. "I'm a little scatter brained right now."

Archer looked at him incredulously, holding his arms out in front of him, "Seriously? Something about praying for my niece doesn't ring a bell?"

Rochelle. Lee Bank's daughter, the one he and Bass had prayed for in the shop at the compound.

"Yeah. So?"

Archer pushed off the door, walking in closer to Jimmie. "You really don't know what you did, do you? When you prayed for Rochelle, you broke the third rule of our Standards. And Lee, Creator have mercy on his soul, allowed it."

Jimmie was not following. "And the 'third standard' is what exactly?"

"'Thou shall not pray for one who has broken the first standard.'"

Jimmie rolled his eyes. He thought it was going to be something really spooky and spiritual. "Oh, is that all."

two bullets

"Don't disrespect the Law Giver or his talents," Archer warned, still enjoying his cigarette. "The first rule is the most important rule."

Dumbfounded, Jimmie shook his head as if he'd just gone through a bout of dizziness. "Wow, that's gotta get confusing. Are you saying Rochelle broke Law one?"

Archer sighed impatiently. "She broke the first rule of the standards. 'Thou shalt obey your parents, for the lord will deal according to the individual as he sees fit.'"

That was such a convoluted, diluted version of scripture that Jimmie wasn't even sure it could be considered scripture. "Hold on, let me get this straight. So Rochelle had disobeyed her parents, and her broken leg was her punishment? So in contrast, no one could pray for her, because that would be breaking the Third standard? Am I getting it?"

Archer seemed relieved to finally have it all straight. He grinned and nodded. "Yes!"

Jimmie frowned. "That's the stupidest thing I've ever heard, man. You're coming after me and Bass, who aren't members of your group, because we prayed for your dying niece? Are you kidding me?"

Archer's face fell as Jimmie continued laughing at the man's reasoning. Archer's hands balled into fists as anger and rage overtook him until finally it poured out of him.

"I had to kill my own brother because of you!!!" He roared, stomping forward.

Jimmie's laugh subsided and he stared curiously at the no longer couth and reserved drug dealer. Lee was dead?

The good news was that if Jimmie and Bass survived, Archer had just hung himself for murder.

two bullets

Chapter Twenty-Eight

A chubby faced deputy with too-short pant legs debriefed Lock near his car. The Petersville sheriff and another officer walked out the four teenagers from the house to the waiting cars. The air was much colder up this high, and with the shadows from the trees, Lock fought off shivers as she talked. She hadn't thought to bring a sweatshirt or jacket, seeing as how it had been warm when she left Sly's. She rubbed her hands up and down her bare arms and continued to explain how it had been random for her to have arrived at the ranch, to meet T.J., and then get shot at. The officer said something about bad luck, to which Lock just grinned and said, "Better me, who has training, than someone else. I'm just glad I was here to help T.J."

The smell of decay was still ever present in the air, and everyone coughed and held their hands over their nose and mouths whenever possible.

Lock learned from the deputy that Alonzo's wife had been located and was safe with family, which T.J. was very pleased to hear. The parents of the boys had been called. Lock made sure to reaffirm with the officer that the boys who had been left behind were very helpful and compliant, throwing in her own opinion that they had probably been peer-pressured into the whole thing. She asked that she be kept in the loop about what was going to happen to them, and though surprised at the request, the deputy agreed and took down her number.

It was interesting to note that Mitch, the older boy who had allegedly killed Alonzo, turned out to be the son of the

Petersville's sheriff. After meeting the man, Lock understood what must have made the teen such an easy target for the man named Jerry; Sheriff Hopslow was a domineering, cocky man with a rather callous view of life and made sure to correct every little thing Lock said. As angry as it made her, she could only imagine what it must be like for Mitch to live with that every day, all the time. Mitch had probably jumped at the chance to prove himself to his old man and strike out on his own. But he'd gotten too far down the rabbit hole in the end, looking for respect from some loser named Jerry.

It had been hours since Lock had left home. She was hungry, and ready for a long hot shower. She found the time to call Sly to let him know what had happened. He laughed at Lock's propensity to find trouble so easily. Before they hung up, he mentioned he was going to Canyon City with Cassidy for the afternoon. His phone was dying and he didn't have a charger, so not to worry if she couldn't get a hold of him.

As a thank-you gift for her keeping him alive, T.J. gave Lock a crate full of homemade jams, and a necklace made out of tiny beads and a feather pendant that he kept hanging from his rear view mirror. It was a generous gift, and Lock graciously accepted it, admiring the craftsmanship of the strands hanging over her hand.

T.J. also remembered why Lock was there in the first place, and he hurried into the barn and grabbed a couple of glass jugs filled with milk from a fridge and gave them to her. She paid him, T.J. promising to get the money to Stella. Then they hugged good-bye and T.J. closed the door of her vehicle.

With the necklace hanging from the rear view mirror, and the crate of jams and milk sitting in the seat next to her, Lock started the long trek back to paved roads. She found herself humming, despite the sight of the murder and hatred in

two bullets

the rear view mirror.

It was for days like today that she had become a cop in the first place. She wanted the danger, to be in the middle of a life threatening instance and be fighting for survival with adrenaline crashing through her. She liked it. She liked the unknown, the strange cases, that feeling of your hair standing up on the back of your neck. The feeling of answering a burning question and giving a family some peace.

Not too many people can say they feel happy and alive after just being through a shoot-out, but today, Lock could. Everyone in her family, on the side that she didn't speak to, were either professionals or white collar CEO's, with the exception of a second cousin. He had taken to growing pot in his bedroom and now lived in a three story mansion in Denver. No one really talked to him.

The point was, the people in Lock's family, the ones who didn't understand her, wouldn't know excitement and adventure if it took an ad out in the paper. They'd find something to ridicule and make fun of, like they did about most things they didn't understand, and then return to their quiet, boring lives in suburbia without so much as a second thought to the world outside their bubble. But Lock wasn't wired that way, and had spent her whole life wondering why she was so different.

Today she felt like her old self again. The cheerful, ambitious girl who thought chasing bad guys down dark alleys was fun. It seemed as if the dark clouds she'd been under had cleared and the heavy veil of depression and sadness were all gone. She was so thankful for finally getting out of that rut.

*　　*　　*　　*

two bullets

Lock returned home to find a plate of dinner that had been saved for her. She was ravenous by now, and immediately heated up the lasagna and green-beans, scarfing it all down while standing up.

Her phone beeped, showing a text from Bass that hadn't been able to come through until she had come down out of the land of poor service. He asked her to come out to his house to hangout. Then he promised a surprise, so of course Lock had to say yes. She hurried to take a quick shower, hoping to get the smell of death out of her hair, repeating the wash and rinse cycle three times, and used half a bottle of body wash.

Feeling a little bit more human, primped and scrubbed, she started out the house, excited to see Bass. Judy whined from behind her, sitting in the kitchen patiently with her tail wagging, eyes begging.
Lock took pity on the animal and invited her along, putting her in the backseat of the pickup. Then they headed into town.

All her running around had made the fuel gauge drop, so before heading up to the lake, she stopped at the last gas station on the west side of town. Barrier Ridge was quiet as she put the nozzle into the tank and set the handle to lock, letting it continue on its own.

From the road came a loud rumbling of a motorcycle. It slowed and turned, coming down into the pump area. The loud roar of the bike grew obnoxiously louder as it neared and pulled in on the other side of the pump Lock was using.

She noticed the bike and rider, but she was in the middle of wondering if Sly had a skull cap in the pickup. She searched under the back seat and around the fast food wrappers. She finally found a hunter orange knitted cap stuffed into the back pocket of the driver's seat. It didn't match her outfit at all, but it'd work.

The gas pump thunked to a stop while Lock was busy fixing her hair in the side mirror, pushing her curls back and out of her eyes. She liked what she saw, then straightened and turned around to finish with the gas. But it was then she saw she wasn't alone and she drew a sharp breath.

A man stood facing her on the other side of the gas hose. His blonde hair was full and wavy, falling down to his collar in a cut the world hadn't seen since the eighties. It was then she found her self looking into familiar blue- gray eyes belonging to the mysterious stranger who had brought Ezra Crane to the ER not so many weeks ago.

At her startled reaction, the man held up his hands and said quickly, "I'm sorry, I didn't mean to scare you."

She dropped her hand from her weapon still in the small of her back, bringing the other up to her heart, "You could have cleared your throat or something."

"You're right," he nodded apologetically, "that's my bad."

Recovered from the initial shock, she walked forward, reaching for the nozzle and pulled it out, eyeing the man curiously out of the corner of her eye as she returned the pump into its holder.

"Something I can help you with? I don't have a cigarette for you this time."

A grin cracked the man's face and he relaxed. "Me either. But as I recall, it was a lighter you offered."

He lifted a booted foot up to rest on the bumper of her truck, leaning forward to rest his forearm across his thigh as he observed her.

Lock smiled politely. "You're right." Then she turned and pressed the button for her receipt, then stole another look

two bullets

at the man using her pickup as a footrest. "I haven't seen you since the hospital. Did you hear about Ezra?"

The stranger with glorious patience and rough hands pulled a toothpick out of the breast pocket of his jacket and popped it into his mouth.

"I did," he nodded. "He's a good kid with a bright future."

Her receipt printed and she ripped it from its slot, folding it up and slipping it into her jeans without even looking at it. She was intrigued by this man who seemed to know he was mysterious and owned it. She moved towards him, coming to lean against the side of the pickup bed.

"You sure do seem to know a lot about people," she said, looking him directly in the eye as she tried to get a read on him, "but they don't seem to know a lot about you."

The man, who didn't seem to be aware, or care, that the eighties had been over for quite a few years, shrugged, eyes sparkling.

"I'm always around," he said, "It's up to people if they notice me or not."

"How long have you been in town?"

The man returned to leaning over his leg. This question wasn't expected, and she noticed that though he covered up well, he had to go looking for the right answer.

"I come and go," he said.

There was something about the man that made Lock trust every word he said. It wasn't explainable, it was just a fact she found herself accepting. Maybe it was those eyes that seemed to hold every secret of the universe. Or maybe that way his face lit up with careless joy. He could tell her the sky was green and she'd second guess every thing she'd ever learned.

two bullets

He pulled the toothpick out of his mouth and held it between his thumb and pointer finger, looking at it curiously. He was suddenly very serious now with a furrowed brow as he said, "Lock, I'm going to be honest. I came here to find you."

She crossed her arms. "Find me? Why?"

He angled himself towards her, their eyes meeting. "Do you remember when I told you evil would come?"

She nodded slowly.

"It's time. You got a text from Deputy Jones, am I right?"

Something went thunk in Lock's brain, like someone dropping a wrench off the work bench. Goosebumps rolled up and down her body. How could he possibly know that?

"You need to trust me when I tell you that that text didn't come from Bass," the man said, gesturing to her as if the phone was in her back pocket. Which it was.

She shook her head incredulously. "Of course it was from him. And how could you possibly know that?"

He smiled sympathetically. "No, it wasn't him. Someone has Bass's phone and is trying to lure you into a trap. It's a long story, but the bottom line is they have Bass. And Jimmie. A man named Archer Banks. Your friends need your help."

"And you know this how?"

"Lock, this is where faith comes in. I'm here to help you," he said firmly, as if warning her she was out of questions.

On the outside, it appeared that she was sizing him up with her eyes, looking at him, trying to read his face and see if he was pulling her leg. But inside, in her mind, she was praying. Asking God for wisdom. Could she trust this man? Were Bass and Jimmie really in trouble? What was she supposed to do?

two bullets

The man waited patiently, watching her with eyes that seemed to see into the deepest part of her. She found herself caught up in his gaze as she continued to pray in words only her spirit knew. Then something clicked inside of her and she had her answer. The sweetest feeling of peace passed over her and she released a pent up breath of air, soft and relaxed.

"Where are they?"

The man smiled, eyes flashing brightly. "I was hoping you'd say that."

He straightened, coming to stand on both of his feet as he rose to his full height. Then he stuck out his hand. "The name is Slade, by the way."

Chapter Twenty-Nine

Bass woke up on the floor, laying on his side. His new friend had exhausted himself and had left the room, washing the blood from his hands probably. Baldy had wasted no time jumping right into the fun once he got the okay from his boss, then when Bass ended up falling over, the henchman had turned to kicking. Bass had passed out halfway through and had missed the worst. But no worries; there was plenty left over to feel afterwords

He had thought he knew pain, but he was learning that there were all different kinds and multiple levels to physical affliction; there was a stabbing pain in his mouth; a constant stinging coming from his nose; a throbbing in his head and in his chest. With each pulse of his heartbeat, the muscles in his chest, arms, and shoulders just hobbled along with the beat. His stomach, face, and ribs ached and throbbed, lacerations and sections of raw skin stung as his sweat mingled with the blood.

He wasn't sure if he was in shock, numb, or if his whole face had been ripped off, but he wasn't feeling anything above his neck. Head resting on the floor, he counted his teeth with his tongue, moving his jaw as little possible. He tasted blood, felt the spots where he'd bit himself, and discovered a loose tooth on the left side, but there were no gaping holes.

His whole body jerked with a muscle spasm, and again came a fresh new wave of pain. Blinding pain took him by surprise, but he clenched his jaw and fought back the scream crawling up through him.

Across the room, he heard the side door near the

two bullets

kitchen open with a squeak, then boots stepped onto the hardwood floor and thudded to where he lay in front of the living-room couch.

Archer Banks stood over him for a minute, looking at the results of his best henchman.

"Most men give up by now." He snapped his fingers at the two men who had come in with him and they picked Bass up and sat him back down in the chair.

Moving his hands, Bass discovered that his left arm, the one he had fallen onto, was loose. If there was a positive thing to being covered in sweat and blood, it was that it had gotten under the tape wrapped around his wrists and had ruined the stickiness. He kept this revelation to himself.

Forgoing the chair this time, Archer lowered himself down into a crouch in front of Bass. "How ya feeling?"

Bass lifted his head, his hair wet with sweat hanging limp over his forehead. He glared at Archer through half-open eyes, then his lips parted into a large, cheesy smile.

"Ready to ask me for your call?"

Bass spit to the side. "No reason to."

Archer looked up sharply at his men and snapped, motioning with a loose wrist as he said, "Cut him free."

Bass was surprised he didn't get another fist to the stomach, but he wasn't about to complain. Thing 1 and Thing 2 pulled out pocketknives and made short work of the twisted gray tape around Bass's hands, then freed his feet.

As he gratefully pulled his hands into his lap and massaged life back into his arms, Bass looked up at Archer. "How rude of me. Can I get you gentlemen something to drink?"

Archer didn't reply. He just continued staring at Bass with a wry smile, as if he was deciding what to do next. He

two bullets

picked at his thumb with the fingers of his other hand, resting his elbow on his knee. He smiled. "You want to know why I'm doing this?"

"Sure. Wouldn't you?"

This genuinely tickled Archer and he chuckled, dropping his head to his chest as his head bobbed. "Yeah, I guess I would. I already went off script and told the other one, so I guess I can tell you."

Archer was looking for a reaction and got it. He loved seeing the confusion in the pretty boy's face, the surprise mixed with doubt. He stood up as Bass asked, "Who else do you have?"

Archer shrugged. "Just a friend of yours."

"Who?" Bass asked, voice low, almost warning the man to be careful with his answer.

"Lieutenant Reeves," Archer replied with an absent shrug. He walked back into the dining area and ran his finger over the table top, then stopped. With his back to Bass, he looked out through the window that faced north towards the garage. He was daring Bass to make a move on him, but Bass was too smart for that. Also too tired.

"Why us?"

Archer spun around, speaking in a rather loud voice as he answered, "Because you boys need to learn to not stick your nose in other family business."

Bass shook his head, not following, then it clicked. Somewhere in his brain foggy with pain, the dots connected.

"Rochelle," he breathed.

Archer was pacing now, knuckles deep in his jeans pockets. "Rochelle, yes. You interfered with God's plan for her life, and in turn got my brother all spun around and confused. And so it falls on me to be the one who brings everything back into balance. Standard ten."

"I really don't care about your standards."

"Oh, but you should, Deputy. They're the rules that keep everything flowing the way it's supposed to."

Bass sniffed and shook his head as he looked anywhere but up at Archer. "I'm new to the whole faith thing. I don't know how to win souls in five easy steps. I don't know how to argue with someone who believes differently and still come out of it as friends. But this one thing I know; Satan is a liar. He's the enemy, and he'll do what ever he can to drag souls down into hell. That's all you are, Archer. That's all your faith is. It's a tool to make people side with the devil while saying they love God. I feel sorry for you, mate. I really do."

In three long strides, Archer was in front of Bass, grabbing him by the jaw. Seething, Archer stared him in the eye. "And what makes your faith so great?"

Unintimidated, and with his cheeks squished in, making his lips bunch together, he simply replied. "We don't keep anyone out."

"Ha!" Archer mocked, releasing Bass and stood back up. "Right. Okay. Ha-ha- don't make me laugh."

"Some people do, I agree with you, but that is man's flaw, not an order from God. After Jesus came and died, He made a way for everyone to come to God the Father and receive forgiveness. Not based on works or color of skin-"

Archer had a reply that obviously came from twisted interpretation of scripture and a lifetime of White Society brainwashing. Not a word of it made sense to Bass, and so for a brief moment while Archer went on his rant, Bass got lost in his own thoughts.

It wasn't just him anymore. Jimmie was here too. Having to consider another person made his ideas of escape

two bullets

much more difficult. Why couldn't it just be him? Not that he had come up with an escape plan, but if he did, it would now have to accommodate two men who may or may not have all of their physical strength. On the other hand, Jimmie had been a Marine, so he probably felt right at home with all of this.

Bass waited for the right time, then he said, "I want to see Jimmie."

Archer had to think about it, but when he couldn't come up with a reason to say no, he motioned for Bass to follow him and led him out the side door. Bass walked between Thing 1 and Thing 2, and it would be a lie to say the thought of taking off running hadn't crossed his mind.

But then he saw the flat tires on his pickup, and no other vehicle in sight. He'd have to either jump in the lake and swim, or run for the woods. On any other day this would be just fine, but his ribs were bruised, if not broken, and he was having enough trouble just walking.

Archer led the way to the open garage door and showed Bass in. At the sight of his friend hanging with his arms out like Christ on the cross, he swallowed hard.

"Jim?"

Jimmie's head lifted from where it hung to his chest, revealing a bruised jaw and a nasty cut on his cheek under a swollen eye. He smiled, "You look terrible."

"Speak for yourself, buddy." Bass said, shuffling to him. He turned back to the men standing in the garage door. "Cut him down now."

"You're not giving the orders, Jones." Archer said with a shake of his head.

"Come on," Bass pleaded, showing his cards a little sooner than he had planned, "you've made your point. Cut him down."

two bullets

Archer shook his head. "Nope."

Bass felt helpless, feeling it all the way to his very core. He turned back to Jimmie and offered him an apologetic smile.

"It's alright," Jimmie said, reassuring him with half a smile.

Bass staggered in closer. "I didn't know you were here until he told me a few minutes ago."

Jimmie bobbed his head. His swollen eyes were glaring over his friend's shoulder at the figures blocking his view of the lake. "Yeah, I guess I'm losing my edge. They got the drop on me when I came to meet you."

Through swollen eyes, Bass's eyes narrowed. "Meet me? Today?"

"Yeah, I got a text from you to come over."

Bass shook his head. "I didn't send you a text." He turned around and looked at Archer, who smiled and nodded.

"You really should have had a pass code on your phone."

Rage boiled up in Bass. "I'll remember that," he spat, fighting to keep his cool.

Archer pulled the phone out of his pocket as he took a few steps forward. "A person can find out a lot of things about someone by looking at their phones. Especially the texts."

He turned on the phone and looked at it, then said in a mock tone, "Aww, look at that. You and Lock really are sickeningly sweet together."

Bass went for Archer then, but was pushed back by Thing 1 and 2, and Archer merely turned his back on him and walked away.

"Try to stay alive long enough for you three to say good-bye to each other."

two bullets

*   *   *   *

Lock and Slade found Jack Stone at his day job at the hospital, sitting with his feet propped up on the table in the break room. He was flipping through a magazine as he waited for the last five minutes of his break to end. He was dressed in the security uniform black polo shirt and cargo pants, his hair pulled back tightly into a braid, a yellow feather tied to the end.

"Jack," Lock said as she swept into the room, "we got a problem."

Still holding the magazine up in front of him, Jack tilted his head back to look up at her, obviously not bothered by the urgency in her voice.

"Hey, Cincinnati, how's it going? Want some coffee?"

"Bass and Jimmie are in trouble."

Jack nodded thoughtfully, head still tilted back. His eyes dropped from hers to look around her to where Slade stood in the doorway. Jack motioned to him with his chin. "Were they taken by Detective Riggs back there?"

Lock rolled her eyes, "Jack, I'm serious. Some guy named Archer Banks took them."

"Banks? Like Lee Banks' brother?"

She nodded. "The Order of the Pure guy."

"What does he want with Jimmie and Bass?"

Lock looked back at Slade as she shook her head, answering, "We don't know. We just know they have them. He has Bass's phone and texted me pretending to be Bass. I'm supposed to be out there in twenty minutes, and I don't want him to find out that I knew what's going on."

Jack bit the inside of his cheek as he nodded slowly.

two bullets

Then his eyes went back to Slade. "And what does he have to do with this?"

"He knows where Jimmie and Bass are. He's good people, Jack. We can trust him."

Jack seemed to be coming around. Albeit too slowly for Lock's liking.

"Did you call Cassidy?" Jack asked with an arched brow.

"He's with Sly in Canyon City. But there's no time to involve anyone else." She motioned back at Slade, "We're going to get Bass and Jimmie back. Are you in?"

Jack dropped the magazine on the table top, then picked up his coffee mug as he stood. "Of course I'm in."

He walked past her to the door, but instead of walking through, he stood in front of Slade, chest puffed out, eyeing the man as he took a drink of his coffee. "Why do you know all of this? You a part of it?"

Lock rolled her eyes from behind him, "Jack, we don't have time for you to vet him."

But he just briskly hushed her and waved her off. To Slade, "You're supposed to get Lock and I to trust you, is that it? So you can deliver us to your boss on a silver platter?"

Slade returned Jack's icy glare with a soft, knowing smile. "I know that that's your sixth cup of coffee today. I also know that without Bass and Jimmie, you'd be an alcoholic. What is it now, three years sober?"

Lock had never seen anyone successfully get under Jack's skin like this. He was absolutely flabbergasted. Shocked to his core at his secret coming out of a stranger's mouth. He instantly took an angry step forward, daggers shooting from his eyes, and Lock just knew he was going to kill Slade. She winced and was about to jump in between the two, but then

two bullets

Slade, calm and patient as always, held up his hand. "God's not asking for you to be perfect, Jack. I know you've been hurt, but you're gonna have to let that all go if you want the peace you've been looking for."

Jack didn't kill the man. He never even raised his hand. He was struck dumb by Slade's words. He stood there, looking the man in the eye. It was like looking up into the sky in the middle of night with millions of tiny stars staring right back. It pulled at Jack's soul, finding himself wanting to ask a hundred questions, knowing this man had the answers.

Jack suddenly blinked and just stared at Slade as if the stranger had just landed in a spaceship. Jack himself felt like he had just traveled thousands of miles through time and space, and had returned to find that no time had passed, and yet everything was different.

He shot a look back at Lock. She nodded, "I know. He's good."

Without saying a word, Jack continued to glare at Slade as he pushed his way past and out the door. Lock came up to Slade, pausing to put her hand on his shoulder. "Go easy on him. I don't think he's used to all of this."

Slade looked at her with a twinkle in his eye. Then he shrugged. "Used to all of what?"

Then he walked away after Jack, and Lock was left to just shake her head. She was going after Bass and Jimmie with a mysterious drifter and an angry Indian.

"Lord Jesus, I hope you know what you're doing. Because I sure don't."

two bullets

Chapter Thirty

"She should be here by now!" Archer roared, kicking over a potted plant. The clay pot bumped and rolled, flinging dirt out like a fan. When it came to a stop, the flowers inside were still clinging to dirt and life, but they were a little less buoyant.

"Actually, Sir, she said three-thirty. It's only three-fifteen." The man in hunter camouflage with a orange hat said, cradling a rifle in his arms.

"Maybe I should text her again," Archer said, pulling the phone out of his pocket.

"I don't know, Sir, you don't want to give yourself away. She was a cop after all. She'll be able to tell if something's off. She's on her way, I'm sure of it."

Archer cussed and in a fit of anger, threw Bass's phone out over the bank into the lake water below. His man next to him clamped his mouth shut and said nothing, afraid that with his boss's temper, it could be him going into the water next. Archer was a loose cannon like that, and rather psychotic when things didn't go his way.

"This is all Lee's fault." Archer announced. Then he turned away from the lake to face his man. "All of this could have been avoided if he would have just stood his ground like a man and not let those cops onto the compound." He looked at the cabin and garage, set back from the lake a good fifty feet on a nice plot of green grass. "Now I have to come in and clean up his mess like I always do."

He could see everything from where he stood on the bank; the road snaking around from behind the cabin on the

two bullets

left, and the field of weeds to the right of the garage where tracks led up to the edge of the woods and then disappeared.

It was a beautiful spot, and Archer had started entertaining the idea of staking his claim on it once all of this was over. But of course, that was just a pipe dream. He had to get out of town as soon as possible, never to return. He had a fake passport and a plane ticket to Iceland all ready for him in the car they'd hidden. All he needed now was for Elizabeth Locksley to show up.

He'd play with her like a cat plays with a mouse before killing it, then he'd put a bullet in all three of their heads and he'd leave. Of course, his leaving would put all of Lee's people out to pasture with no leader, but that wasn't really his fault. He was a promoter, a recruiter; not a pastor. He just brought in the numbers and the money and made sure the cops were taken care of.

The Washington Chapter of the Pure Alliance, a subgroup of the nation wide White Society, would do like most failed chapters did; it would fade and dry up, eventually disappearing and becoming a passing story. But where one chapter died, ten more would pop up in other places and the legacy of a pure race and family values would live on. It wasn't ideal, but it was the circle of life for their alliance, and it wouldn't stop now.

He would take Les with him, the fresh faced man standing next to him, when he left. And he might take Frank, the man in the garage with the black haired deputy. He would definitely take Harris, the man in the house who knew how to inflict pain. That guy had a gift, and Archer would need someone on his security staff that would be able to do what was required. The other one he could do without. He was here for the money and dumb as a box of hair. There was also Paul, a former follower of Lee's who was now waiting at the airport to fly them to Denver when all of this was over. Archer was still on the fence about Paul; he had been loyal to Lee, but he also had a family, and Archer had no interest in dragging women and children along to his hide-out.

But that was later. Right now, he needed to worry about Bass's girlfriend, and keeping the two deputies alive long enough to watch her die.

Bringing Lock into the mix had been a whim, Archer only coming up with the idea last minute after learning who she was. She still didn't know the two of them had a past; she'd been a little distracted at their first meeting.

The deputies were strong and full of convictions and defiance. They would end up dying without learning any lesson, dying just to spite him. But by adding Ms. Locksley into the mix meant taking something that meant a lot to the pompous deputies and crushing it in front of them, inflicting emotional pain that would satisfy his black soul. Men don't do well when a female is in danger.

They would feel pain like they never knew, and he would be satisfied when they understood just a little of what it was like for him to pull the trigger on his little brother.

Creator be blessed, it was going to be a long day.

Lock was pacing back and forth in front of Jack, who sat on the tailgate of her pickup. They were parked in a isolated pull-off on Gibson Road, which was the twisted two lane road that ran south out of town up into the mountains,

two bullets

snaking up and around the perimeter of Gibson Lake. It was quiet here, sheltered on all sides by tall, leafy trees, and was eerily quiet so far away from the traffic of town.

Lock continued to pace anxiously, hands on her hips. With every turn back to the south, she stared at the spot where Slade had pranced off, going on foot through the woods to do recon on Bass's cabin. On foot it was a twenty minute walk, ten if you run. It had already been thirty minutes, and Lock wasn't sure she could wait much longer.

Jack watched her pace. It was obvious she was distraught, although she wore it well, mostly in the way she held her mouth. She constantly bit the inside of her cheek, pursing and unpursing her lips, sighing through her nose as each agonizing moment with no word passed. She looked lost in her head, but very angry, and he thought how bad he felt for anyone who got on her bad side.

Finally he couldn't stand it any longer. "Would you sit down? You're making me nervous. And I don't get nervous."

She shook out her arms, hands balled into fists. She sighed as she turned to him. "Sorry. I just really want to get this show on the road."

Jack nodded. Then he patted the spot next to him. Lock broke her stance and walked to him, turning around as she pushed herself up. Jack held out a bag of sunflower seeds to her and she reached in for a handful.

"So this Slade guy," Jack started, looking down as he brushed shells from his pants, "is he for real?"

"Yeah, I think so. I've been praying ever since he gave me the news, and I just keep getting this feeling like Slade is the key to saving the guys."

Jack scoffed. "Right. I still think he's involved."

Lock wasn't quick to dismiss the idea. She shrugged,

two bullets

biting down on the shell between her teeth until it cracked open. "Maybe. But to what end? I mean, he warned me that the text wasn't real. Why would he do that? Why would they set up two ruses?"

"Hey, I don't have all the answers. I just know he gives me the creeps."

Lock smiled, staring out into the shadows of the trees. When she spoke, she spoke as if the trees were listening, "He knows things. I don't know how, but he does, and right now we need that."

Jack leaned in closer, whispering back, "But don't you think it's odd that he knew who was keeping the guys and where? I mean come on, one might make sense, but both? That's like cheating."

She couldn't argue with that, but something deep down in her gut told her she needed to trust Slade. She didn't know if he was an angel, or just really in tune with God, but there was just something angelic about him, something that put you at peace around him. Jack had felt it to, that's why he hadn't hauled off and hit him like he would have any other time he felt disrespected. Not to mention, Slade seemed to show up at just the right time and tell you something that helped.

"If it weren't for Slade, I would have walked right into a trap. I could be dead right now. And Bass and Jimmie too. We can trust Slade. We have to."

"That's exactly what he's counting on." Jack retorted, still not buying it. They would have to leave it at that; a soft warbling whistle sounded through the air, and Jack quickly whistled back. A little ahead of them and too the right, Slade emerged from the woods. He wore the hood up on his sweatshirt, having covered his blonde hair from obvious viewing as he snuck through the woods.

two bullets

Lock and Jack hopped down from their seat.

"Well?" Lock said, "How'd it go?"

Slade pushed back his hood, wincing as he caught his breath. "They definitely have your friends, they're both tied up in the house."

"How are they?" Jack asked.

Slade sucked on his teeth and he shook his head. "They need out of there as soon as possible."

Lock clicked her tongue, then breathed out a heavy sigh that puffed up her cheeks. Then she asked, "How many goons?"

"Five, including Archer."

Lock shot a look up at Jack, "That sounds too easy."

"Maybe," Slade said, "but they're no sissies. They're gonna give us a challenge. We can do this."

Lock could tell Slade's wheels were spinning. She smirked as she nodded her head. "You got a plan."

He smiled back at her. "Yep. But we're going to need some weapons."

Jack piped up then. "I know a guy."

Both Lock and Slade looked at him curiously. His eyes widened. "Me, guys. It's me."

Smiles split the tension on the three faces.

"Alright," Lock said, "let's go get our boys back."

two bullets

Chapter Thirty-One

Lock thought her heart was going to burst out of her chest. Her hands were sweaty, and she dropped them from gripping the steering wheel to quickly brush down her jeans. But she was calm. Her mind was quiet. She was worried, sure, but she had to keep her cool otherwise she'd lose focus and it could kill a lot of people. The thought of Bass in trouble, and more than likely hurt, made her sick, but she had to just pray and cast the worry over onto God.

"I love him, God," she said as she neared the turn. "I want to marry him. I'm not ready to say good-bye."

Lock's part of the plan was simple. She was going to wait until Slade gave the signal, then she was going to hit the cabin. While the bad guys were distracted with the fireworks near the wood's edge, Lock was going to find Bass and Jimmie and get them to the truck. It wasn't a complicated plan, but hopefully it would be effective. Without knowing exactly what they were up against, they had decided the best attack was shock and awe. Going through the front door.

She pulled off on to the final turn and stopped, grabbing her radio and pushed the talk button, "Slade, how we looking?"

"Thirty seconds."

"Jack, you ready?"

"Ready when you are."

✳ ✳ ✳ ✳

two bullets

She ran from where she'd parked the pickup, hidden behind some trees just up the driveway from the cabin. Judy stayed close, jogging behind Lock until she was told what to do next. Lock slowed when she got to the side of the cabin, then crept her way up to the concrete patio. The nerves in her fingers tingled, her stomach rolling over and over as she tried to stay low, creeping past the front windows of the cabin to the front door, stealing a quick peak as she went.

The man with silver hair and glasses stood with his back to her, getting himself a drink from the kitchen sink. No sign of Bass or Jimmie.

She slipped around to the front door and crouched down. Placing her radio to her mouth, she whispered ever so quietly, "Lock, in position. Slade, do your thing."

*   *   *   *

The sudden sound of popping and snapping explosions like gunshots broke the quiet, echoing off the still waters of the lake, and sent birds resting in the branches of trees squawking and flying.

Archer stood in front of the kitchen sink, filling a glass from the faucet. At the noise, he jumped, eyes going out the window. He saw his men who had been laying in wait inside the garage appear, their attention away from the cabin, out into the field on the north side of the garage.

Archer cursed and slammed his cup down on the counter, then picked up his gun. He hurried around the counter separating the kitchen from the dining room. Passing the table, he stopped in front of the window and watched his men run in search for the source of the noise.

Outside the door, Lock slipped her hand around the doorknob, then she looked at Judy with wide eyes. "You ready? Don't get shot, okay?"

Judy's pink tongue quickly tasting the air, her body wiggling with anticipation.

"Okay," Lock said, fixing her feet as she moved up into a crouch, turned the knob and threw the door open. "Judy, attack!!!"

Judy flew over her, swinging out wide around the dining table. Archer turned just as Judy leaped at him. He cried out, a shot exploding from his gun. The bullet just barely missed the wolf, then Archer fell to the ground with Judy on top of him.

Lock ran in then and hurried to snatch Archer's fallen gun from the floor. Archer was now a scared little boy with Judy sitting on top of him. Her bared teeth inches from his face.

"Get it off of me!" Archer cried, arms covering his face.

"Better stay still," Lock said, unable to a hide a smile. Then, as she looked into the man's face, she was hit with a flashback.

Cincinnati.

The warehouse.

The man in the suit.

two bullets

She was looking down into the face of the man who had given Danson the gun and told him to shoot her.

Lock's world spun for a moment as revelation cascaded over her. It couldn't be! How? Why?

Then she remembered Bass and she had to force herself to concentrate. She wiped a sweaty palm down the side of her leg as she stepped back. Any movement Archer made was met with a growl and warning snap from Judy. Leaving Archer in Judy's capable paws, Lock moved on through the house, advancing with sure steps as she cleared the bathroom. Then from behind the closed door at the end of the hall, she heard thumping.

"Bass! Jimmie!" She called, "You guys in here?"

She slowly inched her way closer to the door, eyes down on the thin crack between the bottom of the door and the floor.

There was no clean way of doing this. Opening the door could either prove someone was on the other side waiting to shoot her dead, or it could prove Bass and Jimmie were in there.

She dropped to her stomach and peered under the door. Two people sat on the floor near the bed, but there was no one else. She hopped back up onto her knees, readjusting her grip on the gun as her eyes followed her hand to the door knob. Her heart was going crazy now. She was so close!

Gun muzzle pointed at the doorjamb, she turned the knob and pushed the door in.

No one shot her.

She refused to drop her guard and stayed in cop mode until she was sure the room was empty, checking behind the door and on the other side of the bed, but the room was empty of bad guys.

Only then could she let her heart break at the sight of Bass and Jimmie. They were sitting on the floor with their backs to each other, hands tied together. Neither wore a shirt, their bodies covered in bruises, lacerations, and blood. There was a lot of blood.

"I've got Bass and Jimmie. They're alive," she said into her radio.

She dropped to her knees in front of Bass, seeing him smiling at her around the gag in his mouth despite his battered face. She quickly untied the gag and pulled it out of the way.

"That's my girl," he said. "Have I ever told you you're beautiful?! You're wonderful."

She quickly cut the chord tying the men together with her knife, then helped Jimmie take off his gag.

"How'd you find us?" he asked as Lock gave him a quick hug.

"An angel," she told them breathlessly. "Come on."

They followed her back through the house and entered the main living area where Archer still lay under Judy.

"Judy, come." Lock commanded, patting her thigh. Judy turned and hopped down off of the man's chest. She padded over to Lock's side where she spun and took a seat.

"Archer, roll over onto your belly and put your hands behind your head," Lock said, her gun leveled on the man's head. He obeyed.

Bass went to a drawer and grabbed a pair of handcuffs and tossed them underhand to Lock.

"You keep extra handcuffs in the kitchen?" Lock asked.

"You never know when your house is going to get broken into."

"Ask him where he hides his extra handguns," Jimmie

two bullets

said, having taken a slow seat onto the couch.

Lock went and took the handcuffs to where Archer lay on the hardwood floor. Crouching down, she reached for his hand and wrapped the cuff around his wrist.

"Do you know who I am?"

"Of course I do," Archer grunted.

"You couldn't kill me in Cincinnati, so you came all this way to finish the job?" She was having a hard time keeping her emotions in check, her voice cracking as she bit off the words.

The man gave no reply.

Irritated, Lock got to her feet and started for the door. "I'll be back."

She marched her way across the side yard towards the garage, aiming for the field where Slade had set up the distraction with some firecrackers. Her mind was spinning, trying to wrap her head around the fact that Mr. Suit was here, in Washington.

In front of the open garage door, she stopped. Near the line of trees, a few black heaps lay on the ground, hands on their heads with Slade walking around them.

"Slade, you good?" Lock said into the radio.

Rocks suddenly scattered from behind her and her pulse shot up. She turned her head to her left and saw the two-by-four swinging at her head just in time. She ducked, dropping and scurried backwards as the board *whiffed* through the air overhead.

Slade, you missed one.

She scrambled to get back on her feet, turning to face her attacker. He came at her again with the two-by-four, but this time her reaction was more controlled. When he went at her, she used his momentum against him, grabbing his wrist and pulled him forward. His upper body leaned forward and she lifted her right leg to kick, then dropped her elbow into his back. The man dropped down to all fours with a roar of pain, the two-by-four clattering to the ground.

"Stay down!" Lock yelled, only to realize her gun had been knocked out of her hands and lay a couple feet behind her. She turned around and started for the gun, but the bald man reached out and grabbed her ankle, yanking her leg out from under her. She hit the ground with her head leading the way. her hands unable to break her fall in time.

The fall knocked the wind out of her lungs and she gasped. Spots formed in front of her eyes and for a moment she thought she was going to pass out. Her gun laid just above her head but she didn't have time to notice before Mr. Friendly had stepped around her and snatched it up. Then he crouched down next to her and grabbed her by her hair, lifting her face up to him. She immediately spat in his face.

Enraged, the man dropped her head and stood, wiping at his cheek, throwing a kick in to Lock's side for good measure. She absorbed the hit and rolled over, still gasping for air, eyes closed to the world around her. Her mind screamed at her to get up, and she knew she needed to, but her body was slow in responding.

A shadow crossed over her as a form blocked the sunlight. She opened her eyes up at the man, her gun in his hand now pointed at her face. Her vision filled with the barrel of the gun, the man's finger on the trigger. The irony was too much for her and she started laughing.

"What are you laughing at?" The man growled. She shook her head, hand going to her chest. She was laughing at the fact that once again, she had a gun in her face. Laughing at the fact that once again she was laying on her back, a bullet away from seeing her Savior.

"Laugh all you want. You're dead, hussy."

Suddenly the man's chest burst open as a high caliber bullet ripped through his chest from behind. He was dead before he hit the ground. Her gun fell with him and landed next to her head.

"Thank you, Jack," Lock breathed, closing her eyes. Then she lifted her head to look towards the hill that rose above the woods in front of her. A blurred figure rose on the ridge. The radio crackled from where it lay. "You good, Cincinnati?"

She lifted her hand and gave a limp wave.

From the cabin Jimmie and Bass ran to Lock. Bass got to her first and helped her to sit up.

"What are we gonna do with you," Jimmie asked as he approached. "Wrap you in bubble wrap?"

Lock smiled as Bass held her tightly. He kissed the top of her head, his bloody hand brushing back her hair. "I've never had a woman nearly take a bullet for me, Elizabeth Locksley. You're the only one for me."

"I'll always come for you, Deputy," she smiled.

Who needed danger and adventure in the city when you had this?

two bullets

Chapter Thirty-Two
Three Weeks Later

Lock stooped to reach into the fridge for the pitcher of freshly made lemonade and set it on the counter. The front door of the cabin hung open behind her, a gentle wind sweeping off the lake rustled the table cloth on the kitchen table. Golden sunlight, pure and angelic, filtered down through the budding branches and brightened the humble interior of the lake side cabin.

She scooped ice from the plastic bag in the sink, pausing for a moment to look out into the yard where all of her favorite people sat, gathered around a burning bonfire in the middle of the day, their laughter and teasing voices flying on the breeze through the open window. A smile parted Lock's lips as the sound of joy and happiness washed over her.

"You are going to make a man very happy someday," a male voice said from the doorway.

Lock smiled. She turned her head to the side door leading in from the yard. "And what would that day look like?"

Bass, noticeably flinching as he pushed himself off the door-jam, started to walk towards her, a grin now draping across his face. "It would be perfect. Perfect weather. Perfect friends."

He stopped in front of her, hands on her hips as he glanced over at the pitcher of lemonade and nodded towards it. "Perfect lemonade."

Lock giggled, inexplicably happy as she gazed up into the blue eyes that were surrounded by fading hues of green

two bullets

326

and purple as the bruising continued to go down. She smiled, moving a stray piece of hair from his forehead. She would spend the rest of her life staring in to those eyes, hopefully minus the bruises someday.

Bass adjusted his unsteady stance, reaching to take her extended hand and pulled it down for a better look. "It looks good on you," he said, dropping a kiss on the gold band she wore on her left ring finger.

"It's perfect." She nodded. They kissed, but it had to be short and sweet for the stitches in his lower lip.

She gingerly rubbed his shoulders, careful not to press to hard. "You shouldn't be up. I can get the lemonade."

"Nah," he said, waving her off. He reached down into the bag in the sink and pulled out a piece of ice, touching it to his lip. Lock scooped out ice into the pitcher of lemonade, then gave it a spin with a wooden spoon.

"Now dear," she said playfully, "Dr. Martin said you weren't to move any more than necessary until your ribs are healed and those dressings on your back are taken off."

"I seem to recall a certain rebel who by this time in her recovery was running around a hospital shooting bad guys." Bass replied. "I think I can steal a couple kisses from my new bride in private."

Carrying the pitcher in her hand as she passed him, she stopped, saying lovingly, "You're so cute when you're all manly and pretending you didn't get tortured." Then she stood on her tip toes to plant a kiss on his nose.

"There's more where that came from, Mrs. Jones," he teased.

They returned outside to their guests sitting in the shade next to the house. There was Jack, still dressed in his silk vest and dress pants, the purple tie having matched perfectly with the flowers in Lock's bouquet that now acted as a center piece on the picnic table. Jimmie was dressed to match, with bruises equal in color and stage of healing as Bass's littering his smiling face. Dr. Martin was also there. As was Sly, having ditched his tie, but still wore the purple shirt and black pants he had worn as he officiated the ceremony. Lock's mom and dad were also there, having brought the U-haul loaded with Lock's personal belongings, now parked out in the driveway.

Sheriff Cassidy also sat at the fire, in the middle of one of his famous animated and detailed stories, the reason for all the happy laughter. Also in attendance was the one and only Trapper Jensen, wearing his very best fringed leather jacket and purple boutonniere pinned at the collar. His wild hair had been combed and pulled back into a short pony-tail. He had made quick friends with Judy, the wolf now laying under his feet. Sly's friend Aria had made it to the wedding ceremony, but had to leave soon after to go on a call.

Bass returned to his seat with the others around the fire pit while Lock finished organizing the collection of desserts and treats on the picnic table. Lock's mom Kerri rose from the group and came over to help, her dark purple dress highlighting her tanned skin and dark eyes, her hair down over her shoulders in soft, natural waves. "Everything is perfect, Lizzy. I'm so glad we could be here."

"Oh mama, me too! It's done my heart good seeing you and daddy, and introducing you to everyone."

"Are you doing okay?"

"Of course!" Lock said, setting down the pitcher. "Why wouldn't I be?"

Kerri just shrugged, moving a plate of brownies from off the edge of the table. "Well, I just want to make sure. So much has happened! Between getting hurt, coming out here, and now being married...and Archer of all people showing up!"

Lock smiled as her mom popped a strawberry in her mouth.

"Well when you put it that way..." but she shook her head, "No, honestly, I feel so good about all of this. I'm really, really happy."

She looked over at the people she had come to cherish so deeply all together in one place. Her heart burst with happiness at the sight. Now that Jimmie and Bass were doing better, it finally felt like life was back on track and the gang was back together. She belonged here. God had told her as much the same day as Bass's marriage proposal. She would spend the summer getting used to her new job as wife and homemaker, and then in the fall, she would start her next adventure as a Barrier Ridge deputy sheriff. She would have to return to Cincinnati soon to testify in court at Danson's hearing. Archer had spilled everything to the police, and Danson was finally paying for what he had done.

Thanks to God and His amazing way of working things out for the better, Lock's life was once again whole and complete. There were still days when she was tempted to be pulled back into the dark world of bad memories, but she didn't feel so helpless. She was stronger now, though it wasn't her strength; it was the strength of God in her that let her receive love, find joy in the little things, and see just how good life was.

She wasn't alone, and she never would be; God was her constant companion, and He had brought her a loving family and supportive friends who she could never repay for the sacrifices they had made. For the love they constantly displayed.

As Lock and her mom continued to stand at the table

two bullets

talking, her dad came over, and then Sly joined them as if they were all drawn together by an invisible string that bonded them. Lock was grateful for this simple moment that was all their own as they sat at the dessert table talking. The four of them, a family once again, in their own little world laughing at inside jokes and teasing in passing conversation. Lock savored this moment, her heart praying a prayer of thankfulness to have been blessed with such wonderful people. She knew her life wouldn't be the same with out them, and she would never again take what they had for granted.

The future was bright.

God's love for Lock was more tangible than ever when she looked around at the men who would forever have her back. There had been a time when she thought trust and friendships would never be. But the day had come, in exceedingly and abundant ways. Where one man had betrayed her and broken her, five men had come along and picked up the pieces.

All of them had stories yet to be written, and this was only the beginning.

The end...

. . . . .

...for now

two bullets

two bullets

About The Author

Sheshanah Smith is an author, a muscian, and lover of all things cryptic. She has been writing in one form or another all of her life, and enjoys creating something that makes the reader or listener feel what she's feeling, see what she's seeing, and experience what she's learned. "Two Bullets" is her first completed novel, and the first installment in the"Barrier Ridge Series."

You can connect with her on facebook, instagram, twitter, and youtube.

She currently resides in Kansas City, Missouri.

CPSIA information can be obtained
at www.ICGtesting.com
Printed in the USA
FFOW04n2102140916
27623FF